Pretty Little Liars

WICKED

SARA SHEPARD

www.atombooks.net

ATOM

First published in the United States in 2009 by HarperTeen,
an imprint of HarperCollins Publishers
This paperback edition published in 2011 by Atom
Reprinted 2011

alloy**entertainment**

A CIP catalogue record for this book
is available from the British Library.

ISBN 978-1-907410-83-3

Typeset in Sabon by M Rules
Printed and bound in Great Britain by
Clays Ltd, St Ives plc

Atom
An imprint of
Little, Brown Book Group
100 Victoria Embankment
London EC4Y 0DY

An Hachette UK Company
www.hachette.co.uk

www.atombooks.net

To Colleen, Kristen, Greg, Ryan, and Brian

The sun also shines on the wicked.
    – Lucius Annaeus Seneca

Inquiring Minds Want To Know . . .

Wouldn't it be nice to know exactly what people are thinking? If everyone's heads were like those clear Marc Jacobs totes, their opinions as visible as a set of car keys or a tube of Hard Candy lip gloss? You'd know what the student casting director *really* meant when she said, 'Good job,' after your *South Pacific* audition. Or that your cute mixed doubles partner thinks your butt looks hot in your Lacoste tennis skirt. And, best of all, you wouldn't have to guess whether your best friend was mad that you ditched her for the hot senior with the crinkly-eyed smile at the New Year's Eve party. You'd just peek into her head and know.

Unfortunately, everyone's heads are locked tighter than the Pentagon. Sometimes people give away clues to what's going on inside – like the casting director's grimace when you missed that high A-sharp, or how your best friend frostily ignored all your texts on January 1. But more often than not, the most telling signs go unnoticed. In fact, four years ago, a certain Rosewood golden boy dropped a huge hint about something horrible going on inside his nasty little head. But people barely raised an eyebrow.

Maybe if someone had, a certain beautiful girl would still be alive.

The bike racks outside Rosewood Day overflowed with colorful twenty-one-speeds, a limited edition Trek that Noel Kahn's father had gotten directly from Lance Armstrong's publicist, and a candy pink Razor scooter, shined to a sparkle. Seconds after the last bell of the day sounded and the sixth-grade class began to pour into the commons, a frizzy-haired girl skipped clumsily to the rack, gave the scooter an affectionate pat, and began to undo the bright yellow Kryptonite U-lock around its handlebars.

A flyer flapping against the stone wall caught her eye. 'Guys,' she called to her three friends by the water fountains. 'C'mere.'

'What is it, Mona?' Phi Templeton was busy untangling the string of her new butterfly-shaped Duncan yo-yo.

Mona Vanderwaal pointed at the piece of paper. 'Look!'

Chassey Bledsoe shoved her purple cat-eye glasses up the bridge of her nose. 'Whoa.'

Jenna Cavanaugh bit a baby pink fingernail. 'This is huge,' she said in her sweet, high-pitched voice.

A gust of wind kicked up a few stray leaves from a carefully raked pile. It was mid-September, a few weeks into the new school year, and autumn was officially here. Every year, tourists from up and down the East Coast drove to Rosewood, Pennsylvania, to see the brilliant red, orange, yellow, and purple fall foliage. It was like something in the air made the leaves there extra gorgeous. Whatever it was made everything else in Rosewood extra gorgeous, too. Shiny-coated golden retrievers that loped around the town's well-kept dog parks. Pink-cheeked babies carefully nestled in their Burberry-by-Maclaren

strollers. And buff, glowing soccer players running up and down the practice fields of Rosewood Day, the town's most venerable private school.

Aria Montgomery watched Mona and the others from her favorite spot on the school's low stone wall, her Moleskine journal open on her lap. Art was Aria's last class of the day, and her teacher, Mrs. Cross, let her roam the Rosewood Day grounds and sketch whatever she liked. Mrs. Cross insisted it was because Aria was such a superior artist, but Aria suspected it was actually because she made her teacher uncomfortable. After all, Aria was the only girl in the class who didn't chatter with friends during Art Slide Day or flirt with boys when they were working on pastel still lifes. Aria wished she had friends, too, but that didn't mean Mrs. Cross had to banish her from the classroom.

Scott Chin, another sixth-grader, saw the flyer next. 'Sweet.' He turned to his friend Hanna Marin, who was fiddling with the brand-new sterling-silver cuff bracelet her father had just bought her as an *I'm sorry Mom and I are fighting again* present. 'Han, look!' He nudged Hanna's ribs.

'Don't *do* that,' Hanna snapped, recoiling. Even though she was almost positive Scott was gay – he liked looking through Hanna's *Teen Vogue*s almost more than she did – she hated when he touched her doughy, yucky stomach. She glanced at the flyer, raising her eyebrows in surprise. 'Huh.'

Spencer Hastings was walking with Kirsten Cullen, chattering about Youth League field hockey. They almost bumped into dorky Mona Vanderwaal, whose Razor scooter was blocking the path. Then Spencer noticed the flyer. Her mouth dropped open. 'Tomorrow?'

Emily Fields nearly missed the flyer, too, but her closest swimming friend, Gemma Curran, looked over. 'Em!' she cried, pointing at the sign.

Emily's eyes danced over the headline. She shivered with excitement.

By now, practically every Rosewood Day sixth-grader was gathered around the bike rack, gawking at the piece of paper. Aria slid off the wall and squinted at the flyer's big block letters.

Time Capsule Starts Tomorrow, it announced. *Get ready! This is your chance to be immortalized!*

The nub of charcoal slipped from Aria's fingers. The Time Capsule game had been a school tradition since 1899, the year Rosewood Day was founded. The school forbade anyone younger than sixth grade to play, so finally getting to participate was as big a rite of passage as a girl buying her first Victoria's Secret bra ... or a guy, well, getting excited over his first Victoria's Secret catalogue.

Everyone knew the game's rules – they'd been passed down by older brothers and sisters, outlined on MySpace blogs, and scribbled on the title pages of library books. Each year, the Rosewood Day administration cut up pieces of a Rosewood Day flag and had specially selected older students hide them in places around Rosewood. Cryptic clues leading to each piece were posted in the school lobby. Whoever found a piece was honored in an all-school assembly and got to decorate it however they wanted, and all the reunited pieces were sewn back together and buried in a time capsule behind the soccer fields. Needless to say, finding a piece of the Time Capsule flag was a *huge* deal.

'Are you going to play?' Gemma asked Emily, zipping up her Upper Main Line YMCA swimming parka to her chin.

'I guess so.' Emily giggled nervously. 'But do you think we have a shot? I hear they always hide the clues in the high school. I've only been in there twice.'

Hanna was thinking the same thing. She hadn't even been in the high school *once*. Everything about high school

4

intimidated her – especially the beautiful girls who went there. Whenever Hanna went to Saks at the King James Mall with her mom, there would inevitably be a group of Rosewood Day high school cheerleaders gathered at the makeup counter. Hanna always covertly watched them from behind a rack of clothes, admiring how their low-slung jeans fit perfectly around their hips, how their hair hung straight and shiny down their backs, and how their smooth, peachy skin was blemish-free even without foundation. Before she went to sleep every night, Hanna prayed that she would wake up a beautiful Rosewood Day cheerleader, too, but every morning it was the same old Hanna in her heart-shaped makeup mirror, her hair poop brown, her skin blotchy, and her arms like chunky sausages.

'At least you know Melissa,' Kirsten murmured to Spencer, also overhearing what Emily said. 'Maybe she was one of the people who hid a piece of the flag.'

Spencer shook her head. 'I would've heard about it already.' It was as much an honor to be selected to hide a piece of the Time Capsule flag as it was to find one, and Spencer's sister, Melissa, never failed to brag about her Rosewood Day responsibilities – especially when her family played Star Power, the game where they went around the table describing their most ambitious accomplishment of the day.

The school's heavy double doors opened, and the remaining sixth-graders spilled out, including a group of kids that seemed to have walked right out of a page of a J. Crew catalogue. Aria returned to the stone wall and pretended to be busy sketching. She didn't want to make eye contact with any of them again – a few days ago, Naomi Zeigler had caught her staring and cawed, 'What, are you in *love* with us?' These were the sixth-grade elite, after all – or, as Aria called them, the Typical Rosewoods.

Every single one of the Typical Rosewoods lived in gated mansions, multi-acre-spanning compounds, or luxurious converted barns with horse stables and ten-car garages. They were such cookie cutters: the boys played soccer and had ultra-short haircuts; the girls had the exact same laughs, wore matching shades of Laura Mercier lip plumper, and carried Dooney & Bourke logo bags. If Aria squinted, she couldn't tell one Typical Rosewood from another.

Except for Alison DiLaurentis. No one mistook Alison for anyone else, ever.

And it was Alison leading the crowd down the school's stone path, her blond hair streaming behind her, her sapphire blue eyes sparkling, her ankles steady in her three-inch platforms. Naomi Zeigler and Riley Wolfe, her two closest confidantes, followed her, hanging on her every move. People had been bowing down to Ali ever since she'd moved to Rosewood in third grade.

Ali approached Emily and the other swimmers and stopped short. Emily was afraid Ali was going to tease them all about their dry, greenish-tinted, chlorine-damaged hair – *again* – but Ali's attention was elsewhere. A sneaky smile crept over her face as she read the flyer. With a quick flip of her wrist, she tore the paper off the wall and spun around to face her friends.

'My brother's hiding one of the pieces of the flag tonight,' she said, loud enough for everyone else in the commons to hear. 'He already promised to tell me where it is.'

Everyone began to murmur. Hanna nodded with awe – she admired Ali even more than the older cheerleaders. Spencer, on the other hand, seethed. Ali's brother wasn't supposed to *tell* her where he was hiding his Time Capsule piece. That was cheating! Aria's charcoal crayon flew furiously over her sketchbook, her eyes fixed on Ali's heart-shaped face. And Emily's nose tickled with the lingering vanilla scent of Ali's perfume – it was as heavenly as standing in the doorway of a bakery.

The older students began to descend the high school's majestic stone steps across the commons, interrupting Ali's big announcement. Tall, aloof girls and preppy, handsome guys ambled past the sixth-graders, heading for their cars in the auxiliary lot. Ali watched them coolly, fanning her face with the Time Capsule flyer. A couple of puny sophomores, white iPod headphones dangling from their ears, looked downright intimidated by Ali as they unlocked their ten-speeds from the rack. Naomi and Riley snorted at them.

Then a tall blond junior noticed Ali and stopped. 'What up, Al?'

'Nothing.' Ali pursed her lips and stood up straighter. 'What's up with you, *Eee*?'

Scott Chin elbowed Hanna, and Hanna blushed. With his tanned, gorgeous face, curly blond hair, and stunning, soulful hazel eyes, Ian Thomas – *Eee* – was second on Hanna's All-Time Hottie list, just under Sean Ackard, the boy she'd crushed on since they were on the same kickball team in third grade. It was unclear how Ian and Ali knew one another, but the gossip said upperclassmen invited Ali to their A-list parties, despite the fact that she was a lot younger.

Ian leaned against the bike racks. 'Did I hear you saying you know where a piece of the Time Capsule flag is?'

Ali's cheeks pinkened. 'Why, is someone jealous?' She shot him a saucy grin.

Ian shook his head. 'I'd keep it down, if I were you. Someone might try and steal your piece from you. It's part of the game, you know.'

Ali laughed, as if the idea was incomprehensible, but a wrinkle formed between her eyes. Ian was right – stealing someone's piece of the flag was perfectly legal, etched in the

Time Capsule Official Rule Book that Principal Appleton kept in a locked drawer of his desk. Last year, a ninth-grade goth boy had stolen a piece that was dangling out of a senior crew member's gear bag. Two years ago, an eighth-grade band girl had snuck into the school's dance studio and stolen *two* pieces from two beautiful, thin ballerinas. The Stealing Clause, as it was known, leveled the playing field even more – if you weren't smart enough to figure out the clues that would allow you to find the pieces, then maybe you were cunning enough to snag one from someone's locker.

Spencer gazed at Ali's perturbed expression, a thought slowly forming in her mind. *I should steal Ali's piece of the flag.* More than likely, everyone else in sixth grade would simply let Ali find the piece *completely unfairly,* and no one would dare to take it away from her. Spencer was tired of Ali getting everything handed to her so easily.

The same idea formed in Emily's mind. *Imagine if I stole it from Ali*, she thought, shuddering with an unidentifiable emotion. What would she say to Ali if she trapped her alone?

Could I *steal it from Ali?* Hanna bit an already nubby fingernail. Only ... she'd never stolen anything in her life. If she did, would Ali invite Hanna into her circle?

How awesome would it be to steal it from Ali? Aria thought too, her hand still moving over her sketchbook. Imagine, a Typical Rosewood dethroned ... by someone like Aria. Poor Ali would have to go searching for another piece by actually reading the clues and using her brain for once.

'I'm not worried,' Ali broke the silence. 'No one would dare steal it from me. Once I get the piece, it's going to be on me at all times.' She gave Ian a suggestive wink, and with a flip of her skirt, she added, 'The only way someone is going to get it from me is if they kill me first.'

Ian leaned forward. 'Well, if that's what it takes.'

A muscle under Ali's eye twitched, and her skin paled. Naomi Zeigler's smile wilted. There was a chilly grimace on Ian's face, but then he flashed an irresistible *I'm just kidding* smile.

Someone coughed, making Ian and Ali look over. Ali's brother, Jason, was walking straight up to Ian from the high school steps. His mouth tight and his shoulders hunched, Jason looked like he had overheard.

'What did you just say?' Jason stopped less than a few feet from Ian's face. A crisp wind blew a few stray golden hairs up off his forehead.

Ian rocked back and forth in his black Vans. 'Nothing. We were just fooling around.'

Jason's eyes darkened. 'You sure about that?'

'Jason!' Ali hissed, indignant. She stepped between them. 'What's up your butt?'

Jason glared at Ali, then at the Time Capsule flyer in her hand, then back at Ian. The rest of the crowd exchanged confused glances, not sure whether this was a fake fight or something more serious. Ian and Jason were the same age, and both played varsity soccer. Maybe this was a pissing contest because Ian had stolen Jason's opportunity for a goal in yesterday's game against Pritchard Prep.

When Ian didn't answer, Jason smacked his arms to his sides. 'Fine. Whatever.' He wheeled around, stomped to a black, late-sixties sedan that had pulled into the bus lane, and slumped in the passenger seat. 'Just go,' he said to the driver as he slammed the car door. The car sputtered to life, coughed up a cloud of noxious-smelling exhaust, and squealed away from the curb. Ian shrugged and sauntered away, grinning victoriously.

Ali ran her hands through her hair. For a split second, her expression seemed a little off, like something had slipped out of her control. But it quickly passed. 'Hot tub at my house?' she chirped to her posse, looping her elbow around Naomi's. Her friends followed her to the woods behind the school, a shortcut back to her house. A now-familiar piece of paper peeked out of the side pocket of Ali's yellow satchel. *Time Capsule Starts Tomorrow*, it said. *Get ready.*

Get ready, indeed.

A few short weeks later, after most of the Time Capsule pieces were found and buried, the members of Ali's inner circle changed. All of a sudden, the regulars were ousted, and others took their places. Ali had found four new BFFs – Spencer, Hanna, Emily, and Aria.

None of Ali's new friends questioned why she'd chosen *them* out of the entire sixth grade class – they didn't want to jinx things. Now and then, they thought about pre-Ali moments – how miserable they'd been, how lost they'd felt, how certain that they'd never mean anything at Rosewood Day. They thought about specific moments, too, including that day Time Capsule was announced. Once or twice they recalled what Ian had said to Ali, and how uncharacteristically worried Ali had seemed. Very little fazed her, after all.

For the most part, they shrugged off thoughts like that – it was more fun to think about their future than dwell on the past. They were now *the* girls of Rosewood Day, and with that came a lot of thrilling responsibility. They had a lot of good times to look forward to.

But maybe they shouldn't have forgotten that day so quickly. And maybe Jason should've tried a bit harder to keep Ali safe. Because, well, we all know what happened. Just a short year and a half later, Ian made good on his promise.

He killed Ali for real.

1
Dead And Buried

Emily Fields leaned back on the chestnut brown leather couch, picking at the chlorine-dried skin around her thumb. Her old best friends, Aria Montgomery, Spencer Hastings, and Hanna Marin, sat next to her, sipping Godiva hot chocolate from striped ceramic mugs. They were all in Spencer's family's media room, which was filled with state-of-the-art electronics, a seven-foot movie screen, and surround-sound speakers. A large basket of Baked Tostitos sat on the coffee table, but none of them had touched it.

A woman named Marion Graves was perched on the checkered love seat across from them, a flattened, folded-up trash bag on her lap. While the girls were in ratty jeans, cashmere sweats, or, in Aria's case, a beat-up denim miniskirt over a pair of tomato red long johns, Marion was in an expensive-looking deep blue wool blazer and matching pleated skirt. Her dark brown hair shone, and her skin smelled of lavender moisturizer.

'Okay.' Marion smiled at Emily and the others. 'Last time we met, I asked you guys to bring in certain items. Let's put them all on the coffee table.'

Emily offered a pink patent leather change purse with a swirly *E* monogram on the pocket. Aria reached into her yak-fur tote and pulled out a creased, yellowed drawing. Hanna tossed out a folded-up piece of paper that looked like a note. And Spencer carefully laid down a black-and-white photograph along with a frayed blue rope bracelet. Emily's eyes filled with tears – she recognized the bracelet instantly. Ali had made one for each of them the summer after The Jenna Thing happened. It was supposed to bind them together in friendship, to remind them never to tell that they'd been the ones who'd accidentally blinded Jenna Cavanaugh. Little did they know that the *real* Jenna Thing was a secret Ali was keeping from *them*, not something they all were keeping from the rest of the world. It turned out that Jenna had asked Ali to set off the firework and blame it on her stepbrother, Toby. This fact was one of the many heart-breaking things they'd discovered about Ali after she'd died.

Emily swallowed hard. The leaden ball that had been lodged in the middle of her chest since September began to throb.

It was the day after New Year's. School started again tomorrow, and Emily prayed this semester would be a little less action-packed than the last. Practically the minute she and her old friends stepped through Rosewood Day's stone archway to start eleventh grade, each had received mysterious notes from someone known simply as A. At first, they all thought – in Emily's case, *hoped* – that A might be Alison, their long-lost best friend, but then workers found Ali's body in a cemented-over hole in Ali's old backyard. The notes continued, prying deeper and deeper into their darkest secrets, and two dizzying months later, they found out that A was Mona Vanderwaal. In middle school, Mona had been a *Fear Factor*-obsessed dork who spied on Emily, Ali, and the others during their regular Friday-night sleepovers, but once Ali disappeared, Mona transformed into a queen bee – *and* became Hanna's best friend. This fall, Mona had stolen Alison's diary, read all the secrets Ali had written about her friends, and set out to destroy their lives just as she believed Emily, Ali, and the others had ruined hers. Not only had they teased her, but sparks from the firework that blinded Jenna had burned Mona, too. The night Mona plunged to her death down Falling Man Gorge – almost bringing Spencer with her – the police also arrested Ian Thomas, Ali's super-secret older boyfriend, for Ali's murder. Ian's trial was set to start at the end of that week. Emily and the others would have to testify against him, and while getting up on the witness stand was going to be a million times scarier than when Emily had had to sing a solo part at the Rosewood Day Holiday Concert, at least it would mean the ordeal would really, truly be over.

Because all of that was *way* too much for four teenage girls to handle, their parents had decided to call in professional help. Enter Marion, the very best grief counselor in the Philadelphia area. This was the third Sunday Emily and her friends had met with her. This particular session was dedicated to the girls letting go of the many horrible things that had happened.

Marion smoothed her skirt over her knees as she looked at the objects they'd laid on the table. 'All of these things remind you of Alison, right?'

Everyone nodded. Marion shook open a black garbage bag. 'Let's put everything in here. After I leave, I want you girls to bury it in Spencer's backyard. This ritual will symbolize laying Alison to rest. And with her, you'll be burying all the harmful negativity that surrounded your friendship with her.'

13

Marion always peppered her speech with New Age phrases like *harmful negativity* and *the spiritual need for closure* and *confronting the grieving process*. Last session, they'd had to chant, *Ali's death is not my fault*, again and again, and drink stinky green tea that was supposed to 'cleanse' their guilt chakras. Marion urged them to chant things into the mirror, too, stuff like, *A is dead and never coming back*, and, *No one else wants to hurt me*. Emily longed for the mantras to work – what she wanted more than anything in the entire world was for her life to be normal again.

'Okay, everyone up,' Marion said, holding out the trash bag. 'Let's do this.'

They all stood. Emily's bottom lip quivered as she eyed the pink change purse, a gift from Ali when they'd become friends in sixth grade. Maybe she should've brought something else to this purging session, like one of Ali's old school pictures – she had a million copies of those. Marion fixed her eyes on Emily and nudged her chin toward the bag. With a sob, Emily dropped the change purse in.

Aria picked up the pencil drawing she'd brought, a sketch of Ali standing outside Rosewood Day. 'I drew this before we were even friends.'

Spencer gingerly held the edges of the Jenna Thing bracelet between her index finger and thumb as if it were covered in snot. 'Good-*bye*,' she whispered firmly. Hanna rolled her eyes as she tossed in her folded-up piece of paper. She didn't bother explaining what it was.

Emily watched as Spencer picked up the black-and-white photo. It was a candid of Ali standing next to a much younger-looking Noel Kahn. Both were laughing. There was something familiar about it. Emily grabbed Spencer's arm before she could drop it in the bag as well.

'Where'd you get that?'

'Yearbook, before they tossed me out,' Spencer admitted sheepishly. 'Remember how they did that whole spread of Ali pictures? This was on the cutting-room floor.'

'Don't throw that in,' Emily said, ignoring Marion's stern look. 'It's a really good picture of her.'

Spencer raised an eyebrow but wordlessly put the photo on the mahogany credenza next to a large, wrought-iron statue of the Eiffel Tower. Out of all Ali's old friends, Emily was definitely having the toughest time handling Ali's death. It was just that she'd never had a best friend like Ali, before or since. It didn't help, either, that Ali had also been Emily's first love, the very first girl she'd ever kissed. If it were up to Emily, she wouldn't be burying Ali at all. She was perfectly fine with keeping her Ali memorabilia on her nightstand for-ever and ever.

'We good?' Marion pursed her merlot-colored lips. She cinched the bag tight and handed it to Spencer. 'Promise me you'll bury this. It will help. Honest. And I think you girls should meet Tuesday afternoon, okay? It's your first week back at school, and I want you to stay connected and check up on one another. Can you all do that for me?'

Everyone nodded glumly. They followed Marion out of the media room, down the Hastingses' grand marble hall, and into the foyer. Marion said good-bye and climbed into her navy Range Rover, turning on the wipers to knock the excess snow off her windshield.

The big grandfather clock in the foyer began to strike the hour. Spencer shut the door and turned around to face Emily and the others. The trash bag's red plastic ties dangled from her wrist. 'Well?' Spencer said. 'Should we bury this?'

'Where?' Emily asked quietly.

'What about by the barn?' Aria suggested, picking at a

15

hole in her red leggings. 'It's appropriate, right? It's the last place we ... saw her.'

Emily nodded, a huge lump in her throat. 'What do you think, Hanna?'

'Whatever,' Hanna mumbled in a monotone, as if she'd rather have been anywhere else.

Everyone pulled on their coats and boots and tromped through the Hastingses' snowy yard to the back of the property. They were silent the whole way. Although they'd grown close again during A's awful notes, Emily hadn't seen much of her old friends since Ian's arraignment. Emily had tried to arrange outings at the King James Mall, and even between-classes meetings at Steam, Rosewood Day's coffee bar, but the others hadn't seem interested. She suspected they were avoiding one another for the same reasons they'd drifted apart after Ali went missing – it was just too weird to be together.

The old DiLaurentis house was on their right. The trees and shrubs that divided the yards were bare, and there was a crusty layer of ice on Ali's back porch. The Ali Shrine, which consisted of candles, stuffed animals, flowers, and curling photos, was still on the front curb, but the news vans and camera crews that had camped out for a month after Ali's body had been found had thankfully vanished. These days, the media were hanging around the Rosewood courthouse and the Chester County prison, hoping to get more news about Ian Thomas's upcoming trial.

The house was also the new home of Maya St. Germain, Emily's ex. The St. Germains' Acura SUV was in the driveway, which meant they'd moved back in – the family had steered clear of the house during the height of the media circus. Emily felt a pang as she looked at the cheerful wreath on the front door and the overflowing garbage bags of

16

Christmas wrapping paper at the curb. When they were together, she and Maya had discussed what they'd get each other for Christmas – Maya wanted tripped-out, DJ-style headphones, and Emily wanted an iPod shuffle. Breaking up with Maya had been for the best, but it felt strange to be completely disconnected from Maya's life.

The others were ahead of her, approaching the back of the two yards. Emily jogged to catch up, her big toe dipping in a muddy slush puddle. To the left was Spencer's barn, the site of their very last sleepover. It bordered the thick woods that stretched for more than a mile. To the right of the barn was the partially dug hole in the DiLaurentises' old yard where Ali's body had been found. Some of the yellow police tape had fallen down and was now half-buried in the snow, but there were a lot of fresh footprints, probably belonging to curious gawkers.

Emily's heart pounded as she dared to look at the hole. It was so *dark*. Her eyes filled with tears as she imagined Ian savagely shoving Ali down there, leaving her to die.

'It's crazy, isn't it?' Aria remarked quietly, looking into the hole, too. 'Ali was here all along.'

'It's a good thing you remembered, Spence,' Hanna said, shivering in the frigid, late-afternoon air. 'Otherwise, Ian would still be out there.'

Aria paled, looking worried. Emily bit her fingernail. The night of Ian's arrest, they'd told the cops that everything they needed to know about what happened that night was in Ali's diary – her very last entry was about how she was planning to meet up with Ian, her secret boyfriend, the night of their seventh-grade sleepover. Ali had given Ian an ultimatum – either he break up with Spencer's sister, Melissa, or Ali was going to tell the world they were in love.

But what really convinced the cops was the repressed

memory Spencer had recalled from that night. After Spencer and Ali had fought outside the Hastingses' barn, Ali had run to someone – Ian. It was the last anyone saw of Ali, ever, and everyone assumed exactly what happened next. Emily would never forget how Ian had stumbled into the courtroom the day of his arraignment and dared to plead innocent to Ali's murder. After the judge ordered Ian to prison without bail and the bailiffs walked him back down the aisle, she caught Ian shooting them a searing, bitter glare. *You girls picked the wrong person to mess with*, his look seemed to say, loud and clear. It was obvious that he blamed them for his arrest.

Emily let out a little whimper and Spencer looked at her sternly. '*Stop.* We're not supposed to dwell on Ian … or any of this.' She stopped at the back of the property, pulling her blue and white Fair Isle earflap hat farther down her forehead. 'Is this a good spot?'

Emily blew on her fingers as the others nodded numbly. Spencer began to dig up mounds of half-frozen dirt with the shovel she'd grabbed from the garage. After the hole was sufficiently deep, Spencer dropped the trash bag inside. It made a heavy plop in the snow. They all kicked the dirt and snow back on top of it.

'Well?' Spencer leaned against the shovel. 'Should we say something?'

They all looked at one another. 'Bye, Ali,' Emily said finally, her eyes filling with tears for about the millionth time that month.

Aria glanced at her, and then smiled. 'Bye, Ali,' she echoed. She looked at Hanna next. Hanna shrugged, but then said, 'Bye, Ali.'

As Aria took her hand, Emily felt … better. Her stomach unknotted and her neck relaxed. Suddenly it smelled so good back here, like fresh flowers. She felt that Ali – the sweet, wonderful Ali from her memories – was here, telling them that everything would be okay.

She glanced at the others. They all had placid smiles on their faces, as if they sensed something too. Maybe Marion was right. Maybe there was something to this ritual. It was time to put the whole dreadful fall to rest – Ali's killer had been caught, and the whole A nightmare was behind them. The only thing left to do was look toward a calmer, happier future.

The sun was sinking through the trees fast, turning the sky and snowdrifts a milky lavender. The Hastingses' windmill slowly rotated in the breeze, and a group of squirrels began fighting near a large pine. *If one of the squirrels climbs the tree, things have settled down for good*, Emily said to herself, playing the superstitious game she'd relied on for years. And just like that, a squirrel scampered up the pine, all the way to the top.

2

We Are Family

A half hour later, Hanna Marin burst through the front door of her house, nuzzled her mini Doberman, Dot, and flung her embossed-snakeskin satchel on the living room couch. 'Sorry I'm late,' she called.

The kitchen smelled like tomato sauce and garlic bread, and Hanna's father; his fiancée, Isabel; and Isabel's daughter, Kate, were already seated in the dining room. There were big ceramic bowls of pasta and salad in the center of the table, and a scallop-edged plate, napkin, and tall flute of Perrier waited at Hanna's empty seat. On her arrival Christmas Day – practically seconds after Hanna's mother had boarded a jumbo jet to her new job in Singapore – Isabel had decided that every Sunday dinner would be in the dining room, to make things feel more special and 'family-esque.'

Hanna slumped in her seat, trying to ignore everyone's looks. Her father was shooting her a hopeful smile, and Isabel was making a face that indicated that she was either trying to contain a fart or was disappointed that Hanna was tardy to Family Time. Kate, on the other hand, tilted her head pityingly. And Hanna just *knew* which of them would speak first.

Kate smoothed her irritatingly straight chestnut-colored hair, her blue eyes round. 'Were you with your grief counselor?'

Ding ding ding!

'Uh-huh.' Hanna took a giant gulp of Perrier.

'How did it go?' Kate asked in her best Oprah voice. 'Is it helping?'

Hanna sniffed haughtily. Honestly, she thought the meetings with Marion were bullshit. Maybe the rest of her old best friends could get on with their lives post-Ali and A, but Hanna was struggling with not one best friend's death, but two. Hanna was reminded of Mona practically every moment of her day: when she let out Dot to run around the frozen backyard in the Burberry plaid doggy coat Mona had gotten him as a birthday gift last year. When she opened her walk-in closet and saw the silver Jill Stuart skirt she'd borrowed from Mona but never returned. When she looked in the mirror, attempting to say Marion's lame-ass chants, and saw the teardrop earrings she and Mona had stolen from Banana Republic last spring. She saw something else, too: the faded, Z-shaped scar on her chin from when Mona had hit Hanna with her SUV, after Hanna realized that Mona was A.

She hated that her future stepsister knew every detail of what happened to her this fall – especially that her best friend had tried to kill her. Then again, all of Rosewood knew; the local media had talked of little else since. Even weirder, the country had been infected with A mania. Kids across the country had reported receiving texts from someone called A, all of which ended up being from jilted ex-boyfriends or jealous classmates. Hanna had even received a few faux-A texts of her own, but they were obviously spam – *I know all your dirty secrets! And hey, wanna purchase three ringtones for a dollar? So* lame.

Kate's gaze remained fixed on Hanna, perhaps waiting for her to spill her guts. Hanna quickly grabbed a piece of garlic bread and took a giant bite so she wouldn't have to speak. Ever since Kate and Isabel set foot in this house, Hanna had been spending all her time either locked in her bedroom, retail-therapying at the King James Mall, or hiding at her boyfriend Lucas's place. Even though things had been shaky between them before Mona died, Lucas had been unbelievably supportive in the aftermath. Now they were inseparable.

Hanna preferred to be out because whenever she *was* in plain view in her house, her dad kept assigning little chores for Hanna and Kate to do together: clearing out Hanna's extra clothes from Kate's brand-new bedroom closet, taking out the garbage, or shoveling snow off the front walk. But hello? Wasn't that what housekeepers and snow removal services were for? If only the snow removal people could remove *Kate*, too.

'Are you girls excited to start school again tomorrow?' Isabel wound pasta around her fork.

Hanna shrugged one shoulder and felt a familiar pain radiate down her right arm. She'd broken it when Mona slammed into her with her SUV, yet *another* lovely reminder that her friendship with Mona had been a sham.

'*I'm* excited,' Kate filled the silence. 'I looked through the Rosewood Day catalogue again today. The school has really amazing activities. They put on four plays a year!'

Mr. Marin and Isabel beamed. Hanna ground her molars together so furiously, her jaw started to go numb. All Kate had talked about since arriving in Rosewood was how thrilled she was to be going to Rosewood Day. But

22

whatever – the school was huge. Hanna planned on never seeing her.

'The place seems so confusing, though.' Kate daintily wiped her mouth with a napkin. 'They have separate buildings for different subjects, like a journalism barn and a science library and a greenhouse. I'm going to get *so* lost.' She twirled a piece of chestnut hair around her index finger. 'I would love it if you showed me around, Hanna.'

Hanna almost burst out laughing. Kate's voice was faker than a ninety-nine-cent pair of Chanel sunglasses on eBay. She'd pulled this *let's be friends* act at Le Bec-Fin, too, and Hanna would never forget how *that* had turned out. When Hanna fled into the restaurant's bathroom during the appetizers, Kate followed behind, acting all sweet and concerned. Hanna broke down and explained to Kate that she'd just received a note – from A ... er, Mona – that Sean Ackard, whom she'd *thought* she was still dating, was at the Foxy benefit with another girl. Kate immediately sympathized and urged Hanna to ditch their dinner, go back to Rosewood, and kick Sean's ass. She even said she'd cover for her. That's what almost-stepsisters were for, right?

Wrong. When Hanna returned to Philadelphia, surprise! Kate had tattled instead *and* told Mr. Marin that Hanna was carrying around a bunch of Percocet in her purse. Mr. Marin had been so angry, he'd cut the trip short ... and hadn't spoken to Hanna for weeks.

'Of course Hanna will show you around,' Mr. Marin piped up.

Hanna clenched her fists under the table and tried for a dismayed tone. 'Oh, wow, I'd love to, but my school day is *so* jam-packed!'

Her father cocked an eyebrow. 'What about before school or at lunch?'

Hanna sucked her teeth. *Way to sell me out, Dad.* Had her father forgotten that Kate had stabbed Hanna in the back at their disastrous dinner at Le Bec-Fin in Philadelphia this fall – the dinner that was supposed to be for Hanna and her dad *only*? But then, her dad hadn't seen it that way. In his mind, Kate wasn't a backstabber. She was *perfect.* Hanna looked back and forth from her father to Isabel to Kate, feeling more and more helpless. All at once, she felt a familiar tickle rising in the back of her throat. Pushing back her chair, she stood up, let out a grunt, and stumbled to the downstairs bathroom.

She hung over the sink and dry-heaved. *Don't do this*, she told herself. She'd been so good about the purging thing the past few months, but it was like Kate was a trigger. The very first time Hanna had puked on command was the one and only time Hanna had visited her father, Isabel, and Kate in Annapolis. She'd brought Ali along, and Ali and Kate had gotten along instantly – that pretty-girl bond or something – while Hanna shoveled handful after handful of popcorn into her mouth, feeling fat and hideous. Her dad calling her a little piggy had been the last straw. She'd run into the bathroom, snatched Kate's toothbrush from a cup by the sink, and forced herself to vomit.

Ali had walked in as Hanna was in the middle of her second heave. She'd promised Hanna her secret was safe with her, but Hanna had learned a lot about Ali between then and now. Ali kept a lot of secrets from a lot of people – and had played people against each other. Like how she'd told Hanna and the others that they'd caused The Jenna Thing when really, Jenna and Ali had orchestrated it all along. Hanna wouldn't have been surprised to learn that Ali had marched back out to the patio that day and told Kate everything.

After a few minutes the sick feeling passed. Hanna took a deep breath, stood back up, and reached into her pocket for her BlackBerry. She opened up a new text message. *You won't believe this*, she typed. *My dad wants me to be the Rosewood Day Welcome Wagon for Psycho Kate. Can we do emergency mani-pedis tomorrow a.m. to discuss?*

She was halfway through scrolling down her Contacts list when she realized she had no one to send the text to. Mona had been the only person she'd gotten mani-pedis with.

'Hanna?'

Hanna whirled around. Her father had cracked the bathroom door open a couple inches. His eyebrows were crinkled in concern. 'Are you okay?' he asked, using a gentle tone of voice Hanna hadn't heard in so long.

Mr. Marin stepped closer and put his hand on Hanna's shoulder. Hanna swallowed hard, ducking her head. Back when she was in seventh grade, before her parents divorced, she and her dad had been really close. It had broken her heart when he'd left Rosewood after the divorce, and when he'd moved in with Isabel and Kate, Hanna had worried that he'd traded ugly, chubby, poop-brown-haired Hanna for pretty, skinny, perfect Kate. A few months ago, when Hanna was in the hospital after Mona hit her with her SUV, her dad had promised to be a bigger part of Hanna's life. But in the week her dad had been here, he'd been too busy helping redecorate the house according to Isabel's tastes – lots of velvet and tassels – to make much time for her.

But maybe he was going to apologize for all that. Maybe he was going to apologize for dropping her cold this past fall without getting her side of the story ... and for dropping Hanna for Isabel and Kate for three whole *years*.

Mr. Marin patted her arm awkwardly. 'Listen. This fall has been terrible for you. And I know testifying at Ian's trial on Friday must be creating stress for you. And I realize that Kate and Isabel moving here was a little ... abrupt. But Hanna, this is a huge life change for Kate. She abandoned her friends in Annapolis to move here, and you've barely spoken to her. You need to start treating her like family.'

Hanna's smile drooped. It felt like her father had conked her over the head with the mint green soap holder on the porcelain sink. Kate certainly did *not* need Hanna's help, not one bit. Kate was like Ali: graceful, beautiful, the object of everyone's attention ... and incredibly manipulative.

But as her dad lowered his chin, waiting for her to agree with him, Hanna realized there were two little words he'd left off of his last statement. Two words that were very indicative of how things were going to be around here from now on.

Hanna needed to start treating Kate like family ... *or else.*

3
Aria's Art Scene Debut

'Oh, ew.' Aria Montgomery wrinkled her nose as her brother, Mike, dipped a piece of bread into a ceramic cauldron of molten Swiss cheese. He swirled the bread around the bowl, pulled it out, and licked up a long, gooey string of cheese that hung off the fork. 'Do you have to turn everything into a sexual act?'

Mike smirked at her and kept making out with the bread. Aria shuddered.

Aria couldn't believe that it was the very last day of a very weird winter break. Aria and Mike's mother, Ella, had decided to treat them to homemade cheese fondue with the fondue set she'd found in the basement under some boxes of glass Christmas ornaments and Mike's Hot Wheels race-track. Aria was almost positive the set had been a wedding present for Ella and Aria's father, Byron, but she didn't dare ask. She'd tried to avoid all references to her father – such as the weird hours she and Mike had spent with him and his girlfriend, Meredith, at the Bear Claw ski slope on Christmas Eve. Meredith had sat in the lodge the whole time, doing yoga stretches, nursing her small-but-obviously-pregnant stomach, and begging Aria to teach her how to knit a pair of baby booties. Aria's parents had only officially separated a few months ago, at least partly because Mona-as-A had sent Ella a letter telling her that Byron was cheating on her with Meredith, and Aria was pretty sure Ella hadn't gotten over Byron yet.

Mike eyed Ella's bottle of Heineken. 'You sure I can't have one little sip?'

'No,' Ella answered. 'For the third time.'

Mike frowned. 'I've had beer before, you know.'

'Not in this house.' Ella glared at him.

'Why do you want beer so badly?' Aria asked curiously. 'Is Mikey nervous about his first date?'

'It's not a date.' Mike pulled his Burton snowboard beanie lower down on his forehead. 'She's just a friend.'

Aria smiled knowingly. Amazingly, a girl had fallen for Mike. Her name was Savannah, and she was a sophomore at the public school. They'd met in a Facebook group about – big surprise – lacrosse. Apparently Savannah was as obsessed with the game as Mike was.

'Mikey's going on a date at the mall,' Aria singsonged. 'So are you going to get a second dinner at the food court? Mr. Wong's Great Wall of Chicken?'

'Shut up,' Mike snapped. 'We're going to Rive Gauche for dessert. But dude, it's *not* a date. I mean, she goes to public school.' He said *public school* like others would say *sewage-filled pit of leeches*. 'I only date girls with money.'

Aria narrowed her eyes. 'You're disgusting.'

'Watch it, Shakespeare-lover.' Mike smirked.

Aria paled. *Shakespeare* was Mike's nickname for Ezra Fitz, Aria's quasi – ex-boyfriend – *and* ex-AP English teacher. It was the other secret Mona-as-A had tormented her about. The media had tactfully kept all their A secrets private, but

28

Aria suspected Mike had found out about Ezra from Noel Kahn, his lacrosse teammate and Rosewood Day's biggest gossip. Aria had made Mike swear never to tell Ella, but he couldn't resist dropping a few hints.

Ella speared a piece of bread. 'I might have a date coming up, too,' she suddenly blurted.

Aria lowered her long fondue fork. She couldn't have been more stunned if Ella just told her she was moving back to Reykjavik, Iceland, where her family had spent the past three years. 'What? When?'

Ella fiddled with her chunky turquoise necklace. 'Tuesday.'

'With who?'

Ella ducked her head, revealing a thin strip of gray roots at her scalp. 'Just someone I've been talking to on Match.com. He sounds nice ... but who knows? It's not like I know that much about him. We've talked mostly about music. We both like the Rolling Stones.'

Aria shrugged. As seventies rock went, she was more of a Velvet Underground girl – Mick Jagger was thinner than she was, and Keith Richards was downright terrifying. 'So what does he do?'

Ella smiled sheepishly. 'I actually have no idea. All I know is that his name is Wolfgang.'

'*Wolfgang?*' Aria, almost spit out a bite of bread. 'As in Wolfgang Amadeus Mozart?'

Ella's face was getting more and more flushed. 'Maybe I won't go.'

'No, no, you should!' Aria cried. 'I think it's great!' And she *was* happy for Ella. Why should her father have all the fun?

'*I* think it's gross,' Mike piped up. 'It should be illegal for people over forty to date.'

Aria ignored him. 'What are you going to wear?'

29

Ella stared down at her favorite eggplant-colored tunic. It had floral embroidery around the neck and what looked like a scrambled egg stain near the hem. 'What's wrong with this?'

Aria widened her eyes and shook her head.

'I got it in that sweet little fishing village in Denmark last year,' Ella protested. 'You were with me! That old woman with no teeth sold it to us.'

'We have to get you something else,' Aria demanded. 'And re-dye your hair. And let *me* do your makeup.' She squinted, envisioning her mother's bathroom counter. Usually it was cluttered with watercolor paints, tins of turpentine, and half-finished jewelry projects. 'Do you even *own* makeup?'

Ella took another long sip of her beer. 'Shouldn't he like me for who I am without all that ... embellishment?'

'It'll still be you. Just better,' Aria encouraged.

Mike swiveled back and forth between them, then brightened. 'You know what *I* think makes women look better? Implants!'

Ella gathered their plates and carried them to the sink. 'Fine,' she said to Aria. 'I'll let you give me a makeover for my date, okay? But now I have to drive Mike to *his* date.'

'It's not a *date*!' Mike whined, stomping out of the room and up the stairs.

Aria and Ella snickered. Once he was gone, they regarded each other shyly, something warm and unspoken passing between them. The last few months hadn't been particularly easy. Mona-as-A had also told Ella that Aria had kept her father's secret for three long years, and for a while, Ella had been too disgusted to even let her daughter in the house. Eventually, she'd forgiven Aria, and they were working hard on getting their relationship back to normal. They weren't quite there yet. There were a lot of things Aria still couldn't mention; they still hardly spent any time alone; and Ella hadn't confided in Aria once, which she used to do all the time. But it was getting better every day.

Ella raised an eyebrow and reached into her tunic's kangaroo pocket. 'I just remembered.' She pulled out a rectangular card with three intersecting blue lines on the front. 'I was supposed to go to this art opening tonight, but I don't have time. You want to go instead?'

'I don't know.' Aria shrugged. 'I'm tired.'

'Go,' Ella urged. 'You've been too cooped up lately. No more being miserable.'

Aria opened her mouth to protest, but Ella had a point. She'd spent the whole winter break in her bedroom, knitting scarves and absently flicking the Shakespeare bobblehead Ezra had given her before he left Rosewood in November. Every day she thought she'd hear something from him – an e-mail, a text, *anything* – especially since so much about Rosewood, Ali, and even Aria herself had been on the news. The months slid by ... and nothing.

She pressed the corner of the invitation into the pit of her palm. If Ella was brave enough to get back into the world, then so was she. And there was no better time to start than right now.

On her way to the art opening, Aria had to pass Ali's old street. There was her house, same as it had been earlier that day. Spencer's house was next door, and the Cavanaughs' was across the street. Aria wondered if Jenna was inside, getting ready for her first day back at Rosewood Day. She'd heard that Jenna would be having private, all-day tutoring sessions.

A day didn't go by when Aria didn't think about the last – and only – time she and Jenna had spoken. It had been at the Hollis art studio, when Aria had had a panic attack during a thunderstorm. Aria had tried to apologize once and for all for what they'd done to her that horrible night when Jenna was blinded, but Jenna explained that she and Ali had conspired together to launch the firework to get rid of Jenna's stepbrother, Toby, for good. Ali had agreed to the plan because, apparently, she had sibling problems too.

For a while, Aria obsessed over what *sibling problems* meant. Toby used to touch Jenna inappropriately – could Ali's brother, Jason, have been doing the same thing to Ali? But Aria hated to think that way. She'd never sensed anything weird between Ali and Jason. He'd always seemed so protective.

And then it hit Aria. *Of course.* Ali didn't have problems with Jason; she'd simply made that up as a way to earn Jenna's trust and get her to spill what was going on. She'd done the same thing with Aria, acting all empathetic and devastated when she and Aria had caught Byron and Meredith making out in the Hollis parking lot. Once she knew Aria's secret, Ali had held it over Aria's head for months. And she'd done the same thing to her other friends. Only, why had Ali cared about something dorky Jenna Cavanaugh was hiding?

Fifteen minutes later, Aria reached the gallery. The art opening was being held in an old, lofty farmhouse in the woods. As she parked Ella's Subaru on the gravel embankment and got out, she heard rustling. The sky was so black out here.

Something made a strange squawking noise off in the woods. And then ... more rustling. Aria took a step back. 'Hello?' she called quietly.

A pair of curious eyes stared back at her from behind a dilapidated wooden fence. For a moment, Aria's heart stopped. But then she realized the eyes were surrounded by white fur. It was only an alpaca. As several more trotted to the edge of the fence, batting their enviably long eyelashes, Aria smiled and exhaled, figuring the farm must have a whole herd of them. After months of being stalked, it was hard to shake the paranoid feeling that someone was watching.

The inside of the farmhouse smelled like freshly baked bread, and a Billie Holliday song was playing softly over the stereo. A waitress carrying a large tray of Bellinis swept past. Aria eagerly grabbed a glass. After she downed the whole thing, she looked around the room. There were at least fifty paintings on the walls, with small plaques bearing the title, artist's name, and price. Thin women with angularly cut dark hair loitered in clusters near the appetizers. A guy in dark-framed glasses talked anxiously to a buxom woman with a beet-red beehive. A wild-eyed man with frizzy gray hair sipped what looked like a glass of bourbon, whispering something to his Sienna-Miller-look-alike wife.

Aria's heart thumped. These weren't the normal, local collectors who came to Rosewood art openings – people like Spencer's parents, who dressed in business suits and carried thousand-dollar Chanel purses. Aria was pretty sure this was the authentic art world, maybe even from New York City.

The exhibit featured three different artists, but the majority of the onlookers were gathered around abstract paintings by someone named Xavier Reeves. Aria walked up to one of his only pieces that didn't have an enormous crowd of people around it and assumed her best art critic pose – hand on chin and frowning like she was deep in thought. The painting was of a large purple circle with a small, darker purple circle in the middle.

Interesting, Aria thought to herself. But honestly … it looked like a giant nipple.

'What do you think of the brushstrokes?' someone murmured behind her.

Aria turned around and found herself looking into the soft brown eyes of a tall guy in a ribbed black sweater and dark blue jeans. An excited jolt shot through her body, leaving her toes tingling in her scuffed satin flats. With his prominent cheekbones and super-short hair that stood up in a tuft at the front, he reminded Aria of Sondre, the hot musician she'd met in Norway last year. She and Sondre had spent hours in a fisherman's pub in Bergen, drinking homemade whiskey and making up stories about the mounted trophy fish that hung on the pub's wood-paneled walls.

Aria assessed the painting again. 'The brushstrokes are very ... powerful.'

'True,' the guy agreed. 'And emotional.'

'Definitely.' Aria was thrilled to be having an authentic art critic conversation, especially with someone so cute. It was also nice to not be around Rosewood people and have to listen to the constant gossip about Ian's upcoming trial. She scrambled for something else to say. 'It makes me think of ...'

The guy leaned closer, smirking. 'Suckling, maybe?'

Aria's eyes widened in surprise. So she *wasn't* the only one who saw the resemblance. 'It does look a little bit like that, doesn't it?' she giggled. 'But I think we're supposed to take this seriously. The painting's called *The Impossibility of the Space Between*. Xavier Reeves probably painted it to represent solitude. Or the proletarian struggle.'

'Shit.' The guy was so close to Aria, she could smell his cinnamon-gum-and-Bellini-scented breath. 'I guess that means the one over there called *Time Moves Handily* isn't a penis, huh?'

An older woman in multicolored cat-eye glasses looked

over, startled. Aria covered her mouth to keep from laughing, noticing how there was a crescent moon-shaped freckle right by her new friend's left ear. If only she hadn't worn the same pilled green cowl-necked sweater she'd lived in the entire winter break. She should've wiped the fondue stain off the collar, too.

He polished off the rest of his drink. 'So what's your name?'

'Aria.' She chewed coyly on the swizzle stick that had come with her Bellini.

'It's nice to meet you, Aria.' A group of people swept by, pushing Aria and her new friend closer together. As his hand bumped against her waist, heat rose to Aria's cheeks. Had he touched her by accident ... or on purpose?

He grabbed two more drinks and handed one to her. 'So do you work around here, or are you still in school?'

Aria opened her mouth, contemplating. She wondered how old this guy was. He looked young enough to be a college student, and she could picture him living in one of the shabby-chic Victorian houses near Hollis College. But she'd made that same assumption about Ezra, too.

Before Aria could say a word, a woman in a fitted houndstooth suit inserted herself between them. With her spiky black hair, she bore more than a passing resemblance to Cruella De Vil from *101 Dalmatians*. 'Mind if I borrow him?' Cruella looped her arm around his elbow. He gave Cruella's arm a little squeeze.

'Oh. Sure.' Aria stepped away, disappointed.

'Sorry.' Cruella smiled apologetically at Aria. Her lipstick was so dark it was almost black. 'But Xavier's quite in demand, as you know.'

Xavier? Aria's stomach dropped. She grabbed his arm. '*You're* ... the artist?'

Her new friend stopped. There was a naughty little sparkle in his eye. 'Busted,' he said, leaning in to her. 'And by the way, the painting really *is* a boob.'

With that, Cruella pulled Xavier forward. He fell into step with Cruella and flirtatiously whispered something in her ear. They both giggled before marching into the throng of the art elite, where everyone gushed over how brilliant and inspirational Xavier's paintings were. As Xavier grinned and shook his admirers' hands, Aria wished there was a trapdoor in the wood floor she could disappear through. She'd broken the cardinal rule of art openings – don't talk about the work to strangers, since you never know who's who. And for God's sake, don't insult an up-and-coming hotshot's masterpiece.

But judging by the sneaky little smile Xavier had just shot in Aria's direction, maybe he didn't mind her interpretation much at all. And that made Aria very, very happy, indeed.

4

Bottom Of The Class

Monday morning, Spencer Hastings hunched over her desk in AP English, scribbling a few sentences on her timed *The Sun Also Rises* essay quiz. She wanted to add a few quotes from one of the Hemingway critical essays in the back of the book in an attempt to earn some extra brownie points with her teacher, Mrs. Stafford. These days, she had to scramble for every little crumb of brownie she could get.

The PA speaker at the front of the room crackled. 'Mrs. Stafford?' called Mrs. Wagner, the school secretary. 'Can you please send Spencer Hastings to the office?'

All thirteen students looked up from their papers, staring at Spencer as if she'd come to school in the lacy blue Eberjay bra and panties set she'd bought at the Saks after-Christmas sale. Mrs. Stafford, who looked nearly identical to Martha Stewart, but who had almost certainly never cracked an egg or embroidered an apron in her life, laid down her wrinkled copy of *Ulysses*. 'Fine, go.' She shot Spencer a *what have you done* this *time?* look. Spencer couldn't help but ask herself the same question.

Spencer stood up, did a few covert yoga fire breaths, and

placed her quiz facedown on Mrs. Stafford's desk. She couldn't really blame her teacher for treating her like this. Spencer had been the very first Rosewood Day student to be nominated for a Golden Orchid essay award. It had been a *huge* deal, big enough to land her on the front page of the *Philadelphia Sentinel*. In the very last round, when the judge had called Spencer to tell her that she'd won, she'd finally blurted out the truth – that she'd stolen the AP Economics paper from her sister, Melissa. Now, all of her other teachers wondered if she'd cheated in *their* classes, too. She was no longer in the running for valedictorian, and the school had asked her to step down as student council vice president, bow out of her role in the school play, and resign as the yearbook editor in chief. They had even threatened to expel her, but Spencer's parents had cut some sort of deal that most likely involved a hefty donation to the school.

Spencer understood why Rosewood Day couldn't just let this blow over. But after all the tests she'd aced, committees she'd commandeered, and clubs she'd created, couldn't they cut her just a teensy bit of slack? Didn't they care that Ali's body had been found a few feet from her own backyard, or that she'd received horrific messages from crazy Mona Vanderwaal, who was trying to *impersonate* her old, *dead* best friend? Or that Mona had almost pushed Spencer over the precipice of Falling Man Gorge because Spencer hadn't wanted to be A along with her, or that it was because of Spencer that *Ali's, murderer was now in jail?* Nope. The only thing that mattered was that Spencer had made Rosewood Day look foolish.

She shut the door of the English room and started toward the office. The hall smelled as it always did, like pine-scented floor wax and a confused tangle of perfume and cologne.

Hundreds of glitter-covered paper snowflakes hung overhead. Every December, Rosewood Day Elementary held a schoolwide snowflake-making contest, and the winning designs were displayed in the elementary and high schools all winter. Spencer used to feel so devastated when her classroom lost – the judges announced the winner right before winter break, so it kind of ruined Christmas. Then again, Spencer found every defeat crushing. She still seethed at how Andrew Campbell had been elected class president instead of her, that Ali had taken Spencer's rightful spot on the JV field hockey team in seventh grade, and that she hadn't gotten to decorate a piece of the Time Capsule flag in sixth grade. Even though the school had continued to hold the contest every year after that, it had never mattered as much as it had that first year she'd been able to play. Then again, Ali hadn't gotten to decorate a piece in the end, either, which had softened the blow.

'Spencer?' Someone crept around the corner. *Speak of the devil*, Spencer thought grumpily. It was Andrew Campbell, Mr. Class President himself.

Andrew walked up to her, pushing his longish blond hair behind his ears. 'What are you doing roaming the halls?'

Typical nosy Andrew. He was undoubtedly thrilled that Spencer was no longer in the running for valedictorian – the Spencer voodoo doll she was convinced he had stashed under his bed had finally worked its magic. He probably thought it was comeuppance, too, for how Spencer had invited him to the Foxy benefit last fall, only to ditch him once they got there.

'They want me in the office,' Spencer said icily, hoping against hope that it wasn't bad news. She picked up the pace, her chunky-heeled boots ringing out on the polished wooden floor.

39

'I'm going that way, too,' Andrew chirped, walking alongside her. 'Mr. Rosen wants to talk to me about the trip I took to Greece over the break.' Mr. Rosen was the Model UN advisor. 'I went with the Philadelphia Young Leaders Club. Actually, I thought you were coming too.'

Spencer wanted to slap Andrew's ruddy cheeks. After the whole Golden Orchid debacle, PhYLC – which always reminded Spencer of the noise one made when hocking up phlegm – had immediately revoked her membership. She was positive Andrew knew. 'I had a conflict of interest,' she said frostily. Which was actually true: She'd had to house-sit while her parents went to their ski chalet in Beaver Creek, Colorado. They hadn't bothered to invite Spencer along.

'Oh.' Andrew peered at her curiously. 'Is something ... wrong?'

Spencer stopped dead, astonished. She threw up her hands. 'Of course something's wrong. *Everything's* wrong. Happy now?'

Andrew stepped back, blinking rapidly. Realization washed slowly over his face. '*Ohhh*. The Golden Orchid ... stuff. I forgot about all that.' He squeezed his eyes shut. 'I'm an idiot.'

'Whatever.' Spencer gritted her teeth. Could Andrew seriously have *forgotten* what had happened to her? That was almost worse than him gloating about it all winter break. She glared at a neatly cut-out snowflake over the handicapped water fountain. Andrew used to be good at cutting out snowflakes, too. Even back then, it was a private battle between the two of them to see who could be the best at everything.

'I guess I put it out of my head,' Andrew blurted out, his voice rising higher and higher. 'Which was why I was so surprised when I didn't see you in Greece. It's too bad you

40

weren't there. No one on the trip was really very … I don't know. Smart. Or cool.'

Spencer fidgeted with the leather tassels on her Coach bucket bag. It was the nicest thing anyone had said to her in quite a while, but it was too much for her to bear, especially coming from Andrew. 'I have to go,' she said, and hurried down the hall to the headmaster's office.

'He's expecting you,' the head secretary said when Spencer burst through the office's double glass doors. Spencer walked toward Appleton's office, passing the large papier-mâché shark that had been left over from last year's Founders' Day float parade. What did Appleton want, anyway? Maybe he'd realized he'd been too harsh on her and was ready to apologize. Maybe he wanted to reinstate her class rank or let her do the play after all. The drama club had planned to perform *The Tempest*, but right before winter break, Rosewood Day told Christophe Briggs, the senior director, that he wasn't allowed to use water or pyrotechnics onstage to replicate the play's signature storm. Christophe, kicking up a tempest of his own, had shut down *The Tempest* for good and started casting for *Hamlet*. Since everyone was learning new parts, Spencer hadn't even missed any rehearsals.

When she carefully closed Appleton's door behind her and turned around, her blood turned to ice. Her parents were sitting side by side in stiff leather chairs. Veronica Hastings was in a black wool dress, her hair pulled back with a velvet headband, her face puffy and red with tears. Peter Hastings was in a three-piece suit and shiny loafers. He was clenching the muscles in his jaw so tightly they looked as though they might snap.

'Ah,' Appleton blustered, rising from his desk. 'I'll leave you three alone.' He huffed out of the office and shut the door.

Spencer's ears rang in the silence. 'W-what's going on?' she asked, slowly lowering herself into a chair.

Her dad shifted uncomfortably. 'Spencer, your grand-mother died this morning.'

Spencer blinked. 'Nana?'

'Yes,' Spencer's mother said quietly. 'She had a heart attack.' She folded her hands in her lap, clicking into business mode. 'Her will reading is tomorrow morning because your dad needs to fly to Florida to take care of the estate before her funeral next Monday.'

'Oh my God,' Spencer whispered faintly.

She sat very still, waiting for the tears to come. When had she last seen Nana? They'd just been to Nana's house in Cape May, New Jersey, a couple months ago, but Nana had been in Florida – she hadn't come up north in years. The thing was, Spencer had struggled through so many other deaths lately, and of people much younger. Nana had lived a rich, happy ninety-one years. Plus, Nana hadn't always been the *warmest* of grandmothers. Sure, she'd generously built Spencer and Melissa an enormous playroom in her Cape May manse, outfitting it with dollhouses and My Little Ponies and big trash buckets of Legos. But Nana always used to stiffen when Spencer tried to hug her, never wanted to see the sloppy birthday cards Spencer made for her, and grumbled about the Lego airplanes Spencer carried out of the playroom and left on top of Nana's Steinway baby grand piano. Sometimes, Spencer wondered if Nana even liked children or whether the playroom had just been a way to get Spencer and her sister out of her hair.

Mrs. Hastings took a big swig of her Starbucks latte. 'We were in a meeting with Appleton when we got the news,' she said after swallowing.

Spencer stiffened. Her parents had *already* been here? 'Were you meeting about me?'

42

'No,' Mrs. Hastings said tightly.

Spencer let out a loud sniffle. Her mother closed her purse and stood, and her father followed. Mr. Hastings checked his watch. 'Well, I've got to get back.'

An ache rippled through Spencer's body. All she wanted was for them to comfort her, but they'd been acting cold to her for months, all because of the Golden Orchid scandal. Her parents had known Spencer stole Melissa's work, but they'd wanted her to keep quiet about it and accept the award anyway. Not that they were admitting that now. When Spencer confessed the truth, her parents had pretended to be shocked by the news.

'Mom?' Her voice cracked as she spoke. 'Dad? Could you maybe ... stay a few more minutes?'

Her mother paused for a moment and Spencer's heart lifted. Then Mrs. Hastings looped her cashmere scarf around her neck, grabbed Mr. Hastings's hand, and turned for the door, leaving Spencer all alone in the office.

5
The Changing Of The Guard

At lunchtime on Monday, Hanna sauntered down the arts hall toward her advanced fabrics classroom. There was nothing like starting off a new semester looking absolutely fierce. She'd lost five pounds over the break and her auburn hair gleamed, thanks to the ylang-ylang deep-conditioning treatment she'd charged to her father's for-emergencies-only credit card. A group of boys in matching Rosewood Day ice hockey jerseys leaned up against their lockers, ogling her as she passed. One of them even whistled.

That's right, Hanna smirked, giving them a three-finger wave. She could still bring it.

Of course, there had been a few instances when she *hadn't* quite felt like she'd returned to fabulous Hanna-dom. Take right now: Lunch was *the* time of the school day to see and be seen, but Hanna wasn't sure where she should go. She'd assumed she would eat with Lucas, but he was at debate team practice. Back in the day, she and Mona used to camp out at Steam, sipping Americanos and critiquing everyone's handbags and shoes. Then, after they'd scarfed down their Splenda yogurts and Smart Waters, they would claim prime spots in front of the mirrors in the English wing's bathroom to touch up their makeup. But today she'd avoided both of those places. It seemed desperate to sit at a café table alone, and Hanna's makeup didn't really need fixing.

She sighed, gazing jealously at a group of happy girls on their way to the cafeteria, wishing she could hang out with them for at least a few minutes. But that had always been the problem with her friendship with Mona – there had never been room for anyone else. And now Hanna couldn't shake the nagging feeling that the whole school thought of her as That Girl Whose Best Friend Tried to Kill Her.

'Hanna!' a voice called. 'Hey!'

Hanna paused and squinted down the hall at the tall, thin figure waving at her. A sour taste filled her mouth. *Kate.*

It was beyond nauseating to see Kate in a Rosewood Day-issue navy blue blazer and plaid skirt. Hanna wanted to run in the other direction, but Kate approached at break-neck speed, navigating deftly in her three-inch-heeled boots. Kate's face was as earnest and cheerful as a Disney cartoon character's, and her breath smelled like she'd eaten about eight Listerine breath strips. 'I've been looking all over for you!'

'Huh,' Hanna grunted, searching around for someone to interrupt them. She'd have settled for that smart-ass Mike Montgomery, or even her prudish, virginity-pledging ex, Sean Ackard. But the only people in the hall were the members of the Rosewood Day madrigal choir, and they'd just broken into an impromptu Gregorian chant. *Freaks.* Then, out of the corner of her eye, she saw a tall, beautiful raven-haired girl in enormous Gucci sunglasses sweep around the corner, a golden retriever guide dog at her side.

Jenna Cavanaugh.

A shiver went through Hanna. There was so much about

Jenna she'd never known. Jenna and Mona had been friends, and Mona had been walking over to the Cavanaughs' house to visit Jenna the night she was blinded by the firework. That meant Mona had known about the horrible thing they'd accidentally done to Jenna the entire time she and Hanna were best friends. It was almost inconceivable to imagine. All those hours Mona had spent at Hanna's house, all those spring break trips to the Caribbean, all those bonding shopping and spa sessions ... and never once had Hanna suspected that the firework that had blinded Jenna had burned Mona too.

'What are you doing for lunch?' Kate chirped, making Hanna jump. 'Is this a good time for a tour?'

Hanna started walking again. 'I'm busy,' she said haughtily. Screw her father and his 'treat Kate like family' lecture. 'Go to the office and tell them you're lost. I'm sure they could draw you a map.'

With that, she tried to steer around Kate, but Kate stayed right with her. Hanna got a noseful of Kate's peach-scented shower gel. Fake peach, Hanna decided, was her least favorite scent in the whole world.

'How about coffee?' Kate said firmly. 'I'll buy.'

Hanna narrowed her eyes. Kate had to be an idiot if she thought Hanna would so easily be swayed by ass-kissing. When she and Mona had become friends at the beginning of eighth grade, Mona had won Hanna over by kissing her ass – and look what happened *there*. But even though Kate's expression was irritatingly friendly, it was obvious she wasn't going to take no for an answer. Something occurred to Hanna: If she was enough of a bitch, Kate might tattle on her again, Le Bec-Fin style.

Hanna let out a blustering sigh and threw her hair over her shoulder. 'Fine.'

They backtracked to Steam, which was only a few doors away. Panic at the Disco was on the stereo, both espresso machines were running, and the tables bustled with students. The drama club was meeting in the corner, talking about holding auditions for *Hamlet*. Now that Spencer Hastings had been barred from the play, Hanna had heard that a talented sophomore named Nora had a good shot at Ophelia. There were a few younger girls gaping at an old flyer for the Rosewood Stalker, who hadn't resurfaced since the whole A thing ended – the police figured it had most likely been Mona. A group of soccer boys leaned against one of the computer consoles. Hanna thought she felt their eyes burning into her back, but when she turned to wave, they weren't looking at her at all. They were looking at pretty, skinny, round-butt, C-cup *Kate*.

As they took their place in line and Kate studied the menu board, Hanna heard loud whispers on the other side of the room. She whirled around. Naomi Zeigler and Riley Wolfe – her oldest, nastiest enemies – stared at Hanna from the big wooden four-top that used to be Hanna and Mona's favorite table.

'Hi, Hanna,' Naomi teased, waving. She'd gotten a short and shaggy haircut over the break. The style was similar to Agyness Deyn's, but the supermodel's trademark cut made Naomi look like a pinhead.

Riley Wolfe, whose penny-colored hair was wound into a tight, ballet dancer-style bun, waved too. Her eyes zeroed right in on the Z-shaped scar on Hanna's chin.

Hanna's insides burbled, but she resisted covering the scar with her hands. No amount of foundation, powder, or mega-expensive laser treatments had been able to make it disappear completely.

Kate followed Hanna's gaze across the room. 'Oh! That

blond girl's in my French class. She seems super nice. Are they friends of yours?'

Before Hanna could say, *Absolutely not,* Naomi was waving to Kate and mouthing *hello.* Kate flounced across the room to their table. Hanna lingered a few paces behind, pretending to be really interested in the Steam menu board, even though she had it memorized. It wasn't like she *cared* what Naomi and Riley said to Kate. It wasn't like they *mattered.*

'You're new, right?' Naomi asked Kate as she approached.

'Yep,' Kate said with a huge smile. 'Kate Randall. I'm Hanna's stepsister. Well, stepsister-to-*be.* I just moved here from Annapolis.'

'We didn't know Hanna had a stepsister-to-be!' Naomi's grin reminded Hanna of a creepy jack-o'-lantern.

'She does.' Kate spread her arms out dramatically. '*Moi.*'

'I love those boots.' Riley pointed to them. 'Are they Marc Jacobs?'

'Vintage,' Kate admitted. 'I got them in Paris.'

Oh, I'm so special, I've been to Paris, Hanna mimicked in her head.

'Mason Byers was asking about you.' Riley gave Kate a sly look.

Kate's eyes glittered. 'Which one is Mason?'

'He's really hot,' Naomi said. 'You wanna sit?' She swiveled around and stole a chair from a table of band girls, carelessly tossing someone's backpack to the floor.

Kate glanced at Hanna over her shoulder, raising one eyebrow as if to say, *Why not?* Hanna took a big step away, shaking her head forcefully.

Riley pursed her shimmery lips. 'Are you too good to sit with us, Hanna?' Her voice dripped with sarcasm. 'Or are you on a friends-free diet, now that Mona's gone?'

'Maybe she's on a friend *purge*,' Naomi suggested, nudging Riley slyly.

Kate glanced at Hanna, then back to Naomi and Riley. It looked as if she were debating whether or not to laugh. Hanna's chest felt tight, like her bra had shrunk three sizes too small. Trying her best to ignore them, she whirled around, tossed her hair, and strutted into the crowded hall.

But once she was safe amid the throng of people streaming out of the cafeteria, her composure crumpled. *Friends-free diet. Friends purge.* Leave it to Kate to bond immediately with the bitches she hated most. Right now, Naomi and Riley were probably telling Kate about the time A had made Hanna tell them she had a little binging and purging problem *and* that Sean Ackard had turned her down cold when she propositioned him for sex at Noel Kahn's field party. Hanna could just picture Kate throwing her head back in laughter, all of them insta-BFFs.

Hanna angrily made her way down the hall back to the fabrics room, elbowing slow freshmen out of her way. Even though she was supposed to despise Mona these days, Hanna would have given anything to have her back right then. A few months ago, when Naomi and Riley had teased Hanna about purging, Mona had quickly stepped in, stomped the rumor flat, and reminded them who was truly in charge at Rosewood Day. It had been beautiful.

Unfortunately, there was no best girlfriend to get Hanna's back today. And maybe there would never be one, ever again.

6

Emily's Church Miracle

Monday evening after swim practice, Emily clomped up the stairs to the bedroom she and her sister Carolyn shared, shut the door, and flopped down on the bed. Practice hadn't been that grueling, but she felt so *tired*, like all of her limbs were weighted down with bricks.

She flipped on the radio and spun the dial. As she passed a news station, she heard a chilling, familiar name and paused.

'Ian Thomas's trial begins on Friday morning in Rosewood,' a clipped, efficient-sounding newswoman said. 'However, Mr. Thomas staunchly denies involvement in Alison DiLaurentis's death, and some sources close to the district attorney's office are saying his case might not even go to trial due to insufficient evidence.'

Emily sat up in bed, feeling dizzy. *Insufficient evidence?* Of course Ian was denying brutally killing Ali, but how could anyone believe him? Especially with Spencer's testimony. Emily thought about an online interview she had discovered a few weeks ago that Ian had given from inside the Chester County jail. He'd kept repeating, 'I didn't kill

Alison. Why would people think I killed her? Why would someone *say* that?' Beads of sweat clung to his brow, and he looked pale and gaunt. At the very end of the interview, right before the clip ended, Ian ranted, 'Someone *wants* me here. Someone's concealing the truth. They're going to pay.' The next day, when Emily went online to watch the interview again, the clip had mysteriously vanished.

She turned up the volume, waiting to hear whether the newscaster would say anything else, but the station had already moved on to a Shadow Traffic report.

There was a soft knock on the bedroom door. Mrs. Fields stuck her head in. 'Dinner's ready. I made homemade mac and cheese.'

Emily pulled her favorite stuffed walrus to her chest. Usually she could eat a whole pot of her mom's homemade mac and cheese in one sitting, but today her stomach felt swollen and angry. 'I'm not hungry,' she mumbled.

Mrs. Fields walked into the room, wiping her hands on her chicken-printed apron. 'Are you okay?'

'Uh-huh,' Emily lied, trying to muster a brave smile. But all through the day, she'd fought the urge to burst into tears. She'd tried to be strong when they'd done the Ali-purge ritual yesterday, but not so deep down, she hated that all of a sudden Ali was supposed to be dead and gone. Over. The end. Finito. Emily couldn't even count how many times she'd felt the overwhelming need to run out of school, drive to Spencer's house, dig up her Ali coin purse, and never let it out of her sight again.

More than that, being back at Rosewood Day just felt ... uncomfortable. Emily had spent the whole day dodging Maya, afraid of a confrontation. And she was just going through the motions at swim team. She hadn't been able to shake off the lingering feelings of wanting to quit, and her ex-boyfriend Ben and his best friend, Seth Cardiff, had kept giving her smirking, dirty looks, clearly bitter that she preferred girls to guys.

Mrs. Fields pursed her lips, making her *I'm not buying that* face. She squeezed Emily's hand. 'Why don't you come to the Holy Trinity fund-raiser with me tonight?'

Emily raised a suspicious eyebrow. 'You want me to go to something at the *church*?' From what Emily had gathered, Catholic churches and lesbians went together about as well as stripes and plaids.

'Father Tyson asked about you,' Mrs. Fields said. 'And *not* because of the gay thing,' she quickly added. 'He was worried about how you were doing after everything that happened with Mona last semester. And the fund-raiser will be fun – they're going to have music and a silent auction. Maybe you'll feel peaceful just being back there.'

Emily leaned appreciatively on her mom's shoulder. Just a few months ago, her mother wouldn't even speak to her, let alone invite her to church. She was thrilled to be sleeping in her comfy bed in Rosewood instead of on a foldout cot in her über-puritan aunt and uncle's drafty farmhouse in Iowa, where Emily had been sent to exorcise her so-called gay demons. And she was so happy that Carolyn was sleeping in their shared bedroom again, too, not shying away from Emily because she might get lesbian germs. It hardly mattered that Emily was no longer in love with Maya. Nor did it matter that the whole school knew she was gay or that most of the boys followed her around hoping they might catch her randomly making out with a girl. Because, you know, lesbians did that all the time.

What was important was that her family was going out of their way to accept her. For Christmas, Carolyn had given Emily a poster of the Olympic champion Amanda Beard in a two-piece TYR racing suit as a replacement for Emily's old poster of Michael Phelps in a teensy Speedo. Emily's father had given her a big tin of jasmine tea because he'd read on the Internet that 'uh, ladies like you' preferred tea to coffee. Jake and Beth, her older brother and sister, had pooled together and gotten her the complete *L Word* series on DVD. They'd even offered to watch a few episodes with Emily after Christmas dinner. Their efforts made Emily feel a little awkward – she cringed at the thought of her dad reading about lesbians on the Internet – but also really happy.

Her family's 180-degree attitude adjustment made Emily want to try harder with them, too. And maybe her mom was onto something. All Emily wanted was for her life to go back to the way it had been before all this A stuff happened. Her family had been going to Holy Trinity, Rosewood's biggest Catholic church, ever since she could remember. Maybe it *could* help her feel better. 'Okay,' Emily said, climbing out of bed. 'I'll come.'

'Good.' Mrs. Fields beamed. 'I'm leaving in forty-five minutes.' With that, she padded out of the room.

Emily stood up and walked to her big bedroom window, resting her elbows on the sill. The moon had risen above the trees, the dark cornfields behind her house were blanketed in untouched snow, and a thick sheet of ice covered the roof of her neighbors' castle-shaped swing set.

Suddenly, something white streaked through a row of dead cornstalks. Emily stood up straight, her nerves tingling. She told herself it was just a deer, but it was impossible to know for sure. Because when she squinted harder, there was only darkness.

Holy Trinity was one of the oldest churches in Rosewood. The church building was made of crumbling stone, and the little cemetery out back had messily arranged headstones that reminded Emily of rows of crooked teeth. Around Halloween in seventh grade, Ali had told them a ghost story about a girl who haunted her younger sister's dreams. She'd dared Emily and the others to sneak into this very cemetery at midnight and chant, 'My dead sister's bones,' twenty times without screaming and running away. Only Hanna, who would've streaked naked through the Rosewood Day commons to prove to Ali that she was cool, had been able to do it.

The inside of the church smelled just like Emily remembered, a strange mix of mildew, pot roast, and cat pee. The same beautiful but slightly scary stained-glass windows, all depicting biblical stories, lined the walls and the ceiling. Emily wondered if God, whoever he or she was, was looking down on them, horrified that *Emily* was in such a holy place. She hoped he wouldn't send Rosewood a locust attack for this. Mrs. Fields waved to Father Tyson, the kindly, white-haired priest who had baptized Emily, taught her the Ten Commandments, and gotten her hooked on the *Lord of the Rings* trilogy. Then she grabbed two coffees from the bar that had been set up next to a large statue of Mary and led Emily toward the stage.

As they settled in behind a tall man and his two young children, Mrs. Fields looked at the music program. 'Up now is a band called Carpe Diem. Oh, fun! The people in the band are juniors at Holy Trinity Academy.'

Emily groaned. Between fourth and fifth grades, her parents had sent her to Camp Long Pines, a sleepaway Bible camp. Jeffrey Kane, one of her counselors, had a band, and they performed the last night of camp. They covered Creed songs, and Jeffrey made the goofiest, most contorted faces, like he was having some sort of godly epiphany. She could only imagine what a Catholic school band called Carpe Diem would be like.

Twangy chords began to fill the room. Their view of the stage was partially obscured by a large amplifier, so Emily saw only a scruffy-haired guy playing drums. As the instrumental progressed, Carpe Diem sounded more emo rock than Creed II. And when the singer started the first verse, Emily was surprised that his voice sounded ... good.

She pushed around the man next to her and his kids to get a better look at the band. A lanky guy stood in front of the microphone, a honey-colored acoustic guitar slung across his chest. He wore a threadbare oatmeal-colored T-shirt, black jeans, and the same burgundy Vans skater shoes Emily had on. It was a nice surprise – she'd expected the singer to be a Jeffrey Kane clone.

A girl next to Emily started mouthing along to the words. Listening to the lyrics, Emily instantly realized the band was covering her favorite Avril Lavigne song, 'Nobody's Home.' She'd listened to it over and over on the plane ride to Iowa, feeling like *she* was the confused, empty girl Avril was singing about.

When the band finished the song, the singer stepped back from the microphone and peered out into the crowd. His clear, light blue eyes landed on Emily, and he smiled. Suddenly, electricity rushed through her, starting at the top of her head and zipping down to her feet. It felt like her coffee was pumped with ten times its usual amount of caffeine.

Emily glanced surreptitiously around. Her mother had wandered over to the coffee kiosk to talk to her choir friends, Mrs. Jamison and Mrs. Hart. A bunch of older ladies sat upright in the pews as if it were a church service, staring confusedly at the stage. Father Tyson was by the confession area, doubling over laughing at something an older man had just said. It was amazing no one had witnessed what had just happened. She'd felt this lightning strike only twice before. The first time was when she kissed Ali in her tree house in seventh grade. The second time was when she kissed Maya in Noel Kahn's photo booth last fall. But it was probably just a reaction to swimming so hard at practice today. Or an allergic reaction to the new flavor of PowerBar she'd eaten before practice.

The singer set his guitar on a stand and waved to the crowd. 'I'm Isaac, and this is Keith and Chris,' he said, gesturing to his bandmates. 'We're going to take a quick break, but we'll be back.' As Isaac stood up, he glanced at Emily again and took a step toward her. Emily's heart hammered and she lifted her hand to wave at him, but just then his drummer dropped one of his cymbals. Isaac turned back to his band.

'You moron,' Isaac said with a laugh, punching the drummer in the shoulder before following the other guys through a pale pink curtain that led to the church's makeshift backstage.

Emily clenched her teeth. Why had she *waved*?

'Do you know him?' an envious-sounding voice behind her asked.

Emily turned. Two girls dressed in the Holy Trinity Academy uniform – white blouses and crisply pleated black skirts – were staring at her.

'Uh, no,' Emily answered.

The girls turned back to each other, satisfied. 'Isaac's in my math class,' gushed the blonde to her friend. 'He's *so* mysterious. I didn't even know he had a band.'

'Does he have a girlfriend?' her dark-haired friend murmured.

Emily shifted from one foot to the other. They were

Catholic school versions of Hanna Marin: super thin, with long, glossy hair, perfect makeup, and matching Coach bags. Emily touched her own limp, chlorine-frizzed hair, and smoothed her Old Navy khakis, which were at least a size too big. She suddenly regretted not putting on any makeup – not that she usually wore it.

There wasn't, of course, any reason to feel competitive with these girls. It wasn't like Emily *liked* this Isaac guy. That electric feeling that had passed through her, and still resonated in her fingertips, had just been a ... fluke. A blip. Yep, that was it. Just then, Emily felt a tap on her shoulder. She jumped and turned around.

It was Isaac. And he was smiling at her. 'Hi.'

'Uh, hi,' Emily said, ignoring the fluttering in her chest. 'I'm Emily.'

'Isaac.' Up close, he smelled a little like Body Shop orange shampoo – the very same stuff Emily had used for years.

'I loved your cover of "Nobody's Home,"' Emily said before she could stop herself. 'That song really helped me get through this trip I took to Iowa.'

'Iowa, huh? I guess it can be pretty rough there,' he joked. 'I went with my youth group once. Why did you go?'

Emily hesitated, scratching the back of her neck. She could feel the Catholic school girls staring. Maybe it had been a mistake to bring up Iowa – or that she identified with such desperate, hopeless lyrics. 'Oh, just visiting family,' she finally answered, fiddling with the plastic top to her coffee cup. 'My aunt and uncle live outside of Des Moines.'

'Gotcha,' Isaac said. He stepped aside to let a bunch of kindergarten-age kids playing tag dart past. 'I hear you about identifying with the song. I got made fun of when I first started singing about a girl, but I think the song applies to everyone. It's like ... all those feelings of "Where do I fit in?"

57

and "Why can't I find anyone to talk to?" I think everyone feels that from time to time.'

'Me too,' Emily agreed, feeling grateful that someone else felt the same way she did. She glanced over her shoulder at her mother. She was still deep in conversation with her friends by the coffee kiosk. Which was good – Emily wasn't sure if she could handle her mother's scrutiny right now.

Isaac drummed his fingers on the worn church pew next to them. 'You don't go to Holy Trinity.'

Emily shook her head. 'Rosewood Day.'

'Ah.' Isaac lowered his eyes shyly. 'Listen, I have to go back onstage in a minute, but maybe you'd want to talk about music and stuff some other time? Get dinner? Go for a walk? You know, like a date.'

Emily almost choked on a sip of coffee. Like a ... *date*? She wanted to correct him – she didn't date guys – but it was as if the muscles in her mouth didn't know how to form those words. 'A walk, in this weather?' she blurted out instead, gesturing to the piles of snow lining the stained-glass windows.

'Why not?' Isaac shrugged. 'Maybe we could go sledding. I have a couple of snow tubes, and there's a great hill behind Hollis.'

Emily widened her eyes. 'You mean the big hill behind the chemistry building?'

Isaac pushed his hair off his forehead and nodded. 'That's the one.'

'I used to drag my friends there all the time.' Some of Emily's fondest winter memories were of when she, Ali, and the others sledded down Hollis Hill. Ali had deemed sledding dorky after sixth grade, though, and Emily had never found anyone else who wanted to go with her.

After a deep breath, Emily said, 'I'd love to go sledding with you.'

Isaac's eyes gleamed. 'Great!'

They exchanged phone numbers, the Holy Trinity girls gaping. As Isaac waved good-bye and Emily drifted over to her mother and her choir friends, she wondered what on earth she'd just agreed to. She couldn't have just made a *date* with him. They were going sledding just as friends. She'd set him straight – so to speak – the next time she saw him.

Only, as Emily watched Isaac drift away through the crowd, stopping every so often to talk to other kids or members of the congregation, she wasn't sure if she *wanted* to just be friends. Suddenly, she wasn't sure what she wanted at all.

7
One Big Happy Hastings Family

Early Tuesday morning, Spencer followed her sister up the steps of the Rosewood courthouse, the wind whipping at her back. Her family and relatives were meeting Ernest Calloway, the Hastings family lawyer, for the reading of Nana's will.

Melissa held the front door for her. The courthouse hallway was drafty and dim, lit only by a few yellow hallway lights – it was way too early for anyone who worked here to have arrived yet. Spencer shivered with dread – the last time she'd been here was for Ian's arraignment. And the next time she'd be here would be at the end of this week, to testify at his trial.

Their footsteps echoed on the hard marble floors as they climbed the stairs. The conference room where Mr. Calloway had scheduled the reading was still locked tight; Spencer and Melissa were the first to arrive. Spencer slid down the hallway's wall to the Oriental rug, staring at a large oil painting of a constipated-looking William W. Rosewood, who had founded the town in the seventeenth century with a bunch of other Quakers. For more than a hundred years, the town of Rosewood had belonged to only three farming families and had had more cows than people. The King James Mall had been built on top of an enormous old dairy pasture.

Melissa slumped against the wall next to her, pressing yet another pink Kleenex to her eyes. She'd been crying on and off since Nana had died. Both the sisters listened to the wind pressing against the windows, making the whole building creak. Melissa took a sip of the cappuccino she'd grabbed from Starbucks before they arrived. She caught Spencer's eye. 'Want some?'

Spencer nodded. Melissa had been especially nice lately, a bizarre shift from the sisters' usual pattern of cat-fighting and one-upmanship – with Melissa generally winning. It was probably because their parents were peeved at Melissa, too. She'd lied to the police for years, saying that she and Ian, who was her boyfriend at the time, had been together the whole night Ali went missing. Truthfully, Melissa had woken up at one point and found Ian gone. She'd been too afraid to say anything because she and Ian had been smashed, and Little Miss Perfect Valedictorian didn't do such tawdry things as get drunk and share a bed with her boyfriend. Still, Melissa seemed *extra* charitable this morning, which was setting off little warning bells in Spencer's head.

Melissa took a long sip of her coffee and eyed Spencer carefully. 'Have you heard some of the news stories? They're saying there's not enough evidence for Ian to be convicted.'

Spencer tensed. 'I heard a report about that this morning.' But she'd also heard a rebuttal from Jackson Hughes, the Rosewood D.A., saying there was *plenty* of evidence, and that the people of Rosewood deserved to have this horrible crime put to rest. Spencer and her old friends had met with Mr. Hughes countless times to discuss the trial. Spencer had met with Jackson a few more sessions than the others because, according to Mr. Hughes, her testimony – that she remembered seeing Ali and Ian together the split second before Ali vanished – was the most important piece of evidence of all. He'd gone through what questions she was going to be asked, how she should respond, and how she should and shouldn't act. To Spencer, it didn't seem that different from performing a part in a play, except instead of everyone clapping at the end, someone was going to go to prison for the rest of his life.

Melissa let out a small sniffle, and Spencer looked over. Her sister's eyes were lowered and her lips were pressed together in worry. 'What?' Spencer asked suspiciously. The alarm in her head was getting louder and louder.

'You know why they're saying there's insufficient evidence, right?' Melissa asked quietly.

Spencer shook her head.

'It's because of the Golden Orchid thing.' Melissa glanced at her out of the corner of her eye. 'You lied about the essay. So they aren't sure you're exactly ... trustworthy.'

Spencer's throat felt tight. 'But this is different!'

Melissa pressed her lips together and pointedly stared out the window.

'You believe me, don't you?' Spencer asked urgently. For a long time, she hadn't remembered anything about the night Ali vanished. Then little pieces began coming back to her, one by one. Her final suppressed memory was of two shadowy figures in the woods – one was Ali, and the other was definitely Ian. 'I know what I saw,' Spencer went on. 'Ian was *there*.'

'It's just talk,' Melissa mumbled. Then she glanced at Spencer, biting hard on her top lip. 'There's something else.' She swallowed. 'Ian sort of ... called me last night.'

'From jail?' Spencer felt the same sensation she had the time Melissa pushed her out of the big oak in their backyard –

first shock, and then, when she hit the ground, searing pain. 'W-what did he say?'

It was so quiet in the hall, Spencer could hear her sister's gulping swallow. 'Well, his mom is really sick, for one.'

'Sick ... like how?'

'Cancer, but I don't know what kind. He's devastated. Ian was so close to his mom, and he's afraid that his conviction and the trial brought it on.'

Spencer flicked a piece of lint off her cashmere coat, apathetic. *Ian* had brought the trial on himself.

Melissa cleared her throat, her red-rimmed eyes round. 'He doesn't understand why we did this to him, Spence. He begged us not to testify against him in the trial – he kept saying it was all a misunderstanding. He didn't kill her. He sounded so ... desperate.'

Spencer's mouth dropped open. 'Are you saying you're not going to testify against him?'

A vein in Melissa's swanlike neck fluttered. She fiddled with her Tiffany key chain. 'I just can't get over it, that's all. If Ian *did* do it, we would have been *dating* at the time. How could I not have suspected anything?'

Spencer nodded, suddenly exhausted. Despite everything, she understood Melissa's perspective. Melissa and Ian had been the model couple in high school, and Spencer remembered how upset Melissa had been when Ian broke up with her halfway into their college freshman year. When Ian blew back into Rosewood this fall to coach Spencer's hockey team – *creepy!* – he and Melissa quickly got back together. Outwardly, Ian had seemed like the ideal boyfriend: attentive, sweet, honest, and genuine. He was the kind of guy who'd help old ladies cross the street. It would be like if Spencer and Andrew Campbell were dating and he got arrested for dealing meth out of his Mini Cooper.

A snowplow grumbled outside, and Spencer looked up sharply. Not that she and Andrew would ever *be* a couple. It was merely an example. Because she didn't *like* Andrew. He was simply another example of a Rosewood Day Golden Boy, that was all.

Melissa started to say something else, but the main doors downstairs opened, and Mr. and Mrs. Hastings strode into the vestibule. Spencer's uncle Daniel, her aunt Genevieve, and her cousins Jonathan and Smith followed behind. Daniel, Genevieve, Jonathan, and Smith all looked weary, as if they'd driven across the country to get here, when in fact they lived in Haverford, only fifteen minutes away.

Mr. Calloway was the last person through the door. He bounded up the stairs, unlocked the boardroom, and ushered everyone inside. Mrs. Hastings swept past Spencer, tugging off her suede Hermès gloves with her teeth, Chanel No. 5 wafting behind her.

Spencer sat in one of the leather swivel chairs around the large, cherry conference table. Melissa pulled out the seat next to hers. Their dad settled on the other side of the room, and Mr. Calloway sat down next to him. Genevieve wriggled out of her sable coat while Smith and Jonathan powered off their BlackBerrys and straightened their Brooks Brothers ties. Both boys had been prissy ever since Spencer could remember. Back when the families celebrated Christmas together, Smith and Jonathan always carefully sliced their presents' wrapping paper at the seams so they wouldn't rip it.

'Let's start, shall we?' Mr. Calloway shoved his tortoise-shell glasses higher up on his nose and pulled a thick document out of a manila file. The overhead light glinted off the top of his bald head as he read through the opening preamble of Nana's last will and testament, indicating that she was of sound mind and body when she composed it. Nana stated that she would divide her Florida mansion, the Cape May beach house, and her Philadelphia penthouse apartment along with the bulk of her net worth between her children: Spencer's father, uncle Daniel, and aunt Penelope. When Mr. Calloway said Penelope's name out loud, everyone looked startled. They gazed around, as if Penelope were there and no one had noticed. Of course, she wasn't.

Spencer wasn't sure when she'd last seen Aunt Penelope. The family always grumbled about her. She was the baby of the family and had never married. She'd bounced from career to career, trying her hand at fashion design, then moving to journalism, even starting an online tarot card-reading site out of her beach house in Bali. After that, she'd disappeared, traveling the world, eating up her trust fund, and neglecting to visit for years. It was pretty clear that everyone was horrified that Penelope had been bequeathed anything at all. Spencer suddenly felt a kinship with her aunt – maybe every Hastings generation needed a black sheep.

'As for Mrs. Hastings's other assets,' Mr. Calloway said, flipping a page, 'she bequeaths two million dollars to each of her natural-born grandchildren as follows.'

Smith and Jonathan leaned forward. Spencer gaped. *Two million dollars?*

Mr. Calloway squinted at the words. 'Two million dollars to her grandson Smithson, two million dollars to her grandson Jonathan, and two million dollars to her granddaughter Melissa.' He paused, his eyes landing momentarily on Spencer. An awkward look fluttered over his face. 'And ... okay. We just need everyone to sign here.'

'Uh,' Spencer started. It came out like a grunt, and everyone looked over. 'I-I'm sorry,' she stammered, selfconsciously touching her hair. 'I think you forgot a grandchild.'

Mr. Calloway opened his mouth and closed it again, like one of the goldfish that swam in the Hastingses' backyard reflecting pond. Mrs. Hastings stood up abruptly, doing the goldfish thing with her mouth too. Genevieve cleared her throat, pointedly staring down at her three-carat emerald ring. Uncle Daniel flared his enormous nostrils. Spencer's cousins and Melissa gathered over the will. 'Right here,' Mr. Calloway said quietly, pointing to the page.

'Uh, Mr. Calloway?' Spencer goaded. She whipped her head back and forth between the lawyer and her parents. Finally, she let out a nervous laugh. 'I *am* mentioned in the will, aren't I?'

Her eyes wide, Melissa grabbed the will from Smith and handed it to Spencer. Spencer stared at the document for a moment, her heart like a jackhammer.

There it was. Nana had left two million dollars to Smithson Pierpont Hastings, Jonathan Barnard Hastings, and Melissa Josephine Hastings. Spencer's name was nowhere to be found.

'What's going on?' Spencer whispered.

Her father stood up abruptly. 'Spencer, maybe you should wait in your car.'

'What?' Spencer squeaked, horrified.

Her father took her arm and began to guide her out of the room. 'Please,' he said under his breath. 'Wait for us there.'

Spencer wasn't sure what else to do but to obey. Her father shut the door fast, the slam reverberating off the courtroom's quiet marble walls. Spencer listened to her own breathing for a few moments, and then, suppressing a sob, she wheeled around, sprinted to her car, gunned the ignition, and peeled out of the parking lot. Screw waiting. She wanted to be as far away from this courthouse – from whatever had just happened – as she possibly could.

8

Isn't Internet Dating Great?

Early Tuesday evening, Aria sat on a cloth stool in her mother's bathroom, her floral-printed Orla Kiely makeup bag in her lap. She glanced at Ella in her mirror. 'Oh my God, *no*,' she said quickly, widening her eyes at the orange stripes on Ella's cheeks. 'That's way too much bronzer. You're supposed to look sun-kissed, not sun-*broiled*.'

Her mother frowned and wiped her cheeks with a Kleenex. 'It's the dead of winter! What idiot is sun-kissed right now anyway?'

'You want to look like you did when we were in Crete. Remember how tan we all got from that puffin-watching boat cruise? And –' Aria halted abruptly. Maybe she shouldn't have brought up Crete. Byron had been on that trip, too.

But Ella didn't seem fazed. 'Tan skin screams melanoma.' She touched the pink, spongy roller in her hair. 'When do we take these out?'

Aria checked her watch. Ella's big Match.com date, the Rolling Stones-loving mystery man named – *shudder* – Wolfgang, would be here in fifteen minutes. 'Now, I guess.' She unclipped the first roller. A lock of Ella's dark hair cascaded down her back. Aria undid the rest, shook the can of Rave, and gave her mother's head a quick spritz. 'Voilà.'

Ella sat back. 'It looks great.'

Hair and makeup normally weren't Aria's thing, but not only had styling Ella for her big date been fun, it had also been the most time they'd spent together since Aria moved back in. Even better, Ella's makeover had been a good distraction from thinking about Xavier. Aria had obsessed over their conversation at the gallery for the past two days, trying to pick apart whether it had been flirtatious banter or friendly chitchat. Artists were so touchy-feely – it was impossible to tell what they actually meant. Still, she hoped he would call. Aria had signed her first name and cell number in the gallery's register, putting an asterisk by it. Artists looked at those register books, didn't they? She couldn't help but picture their first date – it would start with finger-painting and end with a messy make-out session on Xavier's studio floor.

Ella picked up a mascara wand and leaned in to the mirror. 'Are you sure you're okay with me going on a date?'

'Of course.' But the truth was that Aria wasn't sure how promising this date was going to be. The guy's name was Wolfgang, for God's sake. What if he spoke in rhymes? What if he was the guy who impersonated Wolfgang Amadeus Mozart for the Hollis Conservatory's Great Composers of History festival? What if he showed up in a doublet and hose and a powdered wig?

Ella stood up and walked back into the bedroom. Halfway across the carpet, she abruptly stopped. 'Oh.'

Her eyes were on the teal dress Aria had laid out on the queen-size bed. Earlier that afternoon, Aria had gone through Ella's closet for an appropriate date outfit, worried she wouldn't find anything among the dashikis, tunics, and Tibetan prayer robes Ella typically wore. The dress had been stuffed in the back, still wrapped in dry-cleaning plastic. It was simple and slimming, with just the tiniest scalloping at the neck. Aria had thought it was a perfect choice ... but judging by her mother's face, she suddenly wasn't so sure.

Her mother sat down next to the dress, touching its silky fabric. 'I forgot I had this,' she said in a small voice. 'I wore it to a Hollis benefit when Byron finally got tenure. It was the same night you slept over at Alison DiLaurentis's house for the first time. We had to run out and get you a sleeping bag because you didn't have one, remember?'

Aria sank down in the striped wing chair in the corner of the room. She remembered the first sleepover at Ali's house perfectly. It was right after Ali had approached Aria at the Rosewood Day charity drive and asked for her help in sorting through the luxury items. Aria's first instinct had been that Ali had done it on a dare. Just the week before, Ali had asked Chassey Bledsoe to try a spritz of a new perfume she'd discovered. It turned out that the 'perfume' was actually murky, poop-filled water from the Rosewood duck pond.

Ella cradled the dress in lap. 'So I guess you know about Byron's – that Meredith's ...' She cupped her hands near her stomach, miming a pregnant belly.

Aria bit her lip and nodded silently, her heart aching. This was the first time Ella had mentioned Meredith's condition. She'd tried her hardest to steer Ella away from all pregnancy references in the past month, but it was foolish to think she could avoid it forever.

Ella sighed, her jaw tense. 'Well, I guess it's time to create a new memory in this dress. It's time to move on.' She glanced at Aria. 'How about you? Have you moved on?'

Aria raised an eyebrow. 'From Byron?'

Ella pushed her wavy hair over her shoulder. 'No. I meant your teacher. Mr. ... Fitz.'

'You ... *know* about that?'

Ella traced her finger down the dress's side zipper. 'Your dad told me.' She smiled uncomfortably. 'I guess Mr. Fitz went to Hollis. Byron heard something about him being asked to leave Rosewood Day ... because of you.' She glanced at Aria again. 'I wish you would've come to me about this.'

Aria stared across the room at a large abstract painting Ella had done of Aria and Mike floating through outer space. She hadn't reached out to Ella at the time because Ella hadn't been answering her calls.

Ella's eyes lowered sheepishly, as if she'd just realized this too. 'He didn't ... take advantage of you, did he?'

Aria shook her head, hiding behind her hair. 'No. It was pretty innocent.'

She thought about the few times she'd actually spent with Ezra – the dark, sticky make-out session in the bathroom at Snooker's, a kiss in his school office, a few stolen hours at his apartment in Old Hollis. Ezra had been the first guy Aria thought she loved, and it had seemed that he loved her, too. When he'd told Aria to look him up in a few years, Aria had figured that meant he would wait for her. But someone who was waiting for her would have called every once in a while, right? She wondered if she'd been really naïve.

Aria took a deep breath. 'Maybe we weren't right for each other. But I might've met someone new.'

'Really?' Ella sat down on the bed and began to remove her slippers and socks. 'Who?'

'Just ... someone,' Aria said lightly. She didn't want to jinx things. 'I'm not sure about it yet.'

'Well, that's great.' Ella touched the top of Aria's head so lovingly, tears came to Aria's eyes. They were finally talking. Maybe things were becoming normal between them again.

Ella lifted up the dress by its hanger and carried it in the bathroom. As she shut the door and turned on the tap, the doorbell rang.

'Shit.' Ella poked her head out of the bathroom door, her smoky eyes wide. 'He's early. Will you get it?'

'Me?' Aria squeaked.

'Tell him I'll be down in a second.' Ella slammed the door shut.

Aria blinked. The doorbell rang again. She rushed over to the bathroom. 'What should I do if he's really ugly?' she whispered loudly through the door. 'What if he has hair growing out of his ears?'

'It's only one date, Aria,' Ella laughed. Aria squared her shoulders and walked to the foot of the stairs. She could see a shadowy figure shifting back and forth through the mottled glass of the front door.

Taking a deep breath, she whipped the door open. A guy with short hair stood on the stoop. For a moment, Aria couldn't speak.

'... Xavier?' she finally squeaked.

'Aria?' Xavier narrowed his eyes suspiciously. 'Are ... *you* ...?'

'Hello?' Ella glided down the stairs behind them, fastening a hoop earring in her ear. The teal dress fit her perfectly, and her dark hair spilled down her back. 'Hi!' Ella chirped to Xavier, grinning widely. 'You must be Wolfgang!'

'Oh God, no.' Xavier's hand flew to his mouth. 'That's my profile name.' His eyes darted from Aria to Ella. A smile bloomed across his lips, almost like he was trying not to laugh. Standing under the light in the foyer, he looked quite a bit older – probably in his early thirties, at least. 'My name is Xavier, actually. And you're Ella?'

'Yes.' Ella put her hand on Aria's shoulder. 'And this is my daughter, Aria.'

'I know,' Xavier said slowly.

Ella looked confused. 'We met on Sunday,' Aria quickly interjected, still not able to shake the baffled tone from her voice. 'At that gallery opening. Xavier was one of the artists.'

'*You're* Xavier Reeves?' Ella cried gleefully. 'I was going to go to your show, but I gave my invite to Aria instead.' She looked at Aria. 'I was so busy today I didn't even ask you about it! Was it good?'

Aria blinked rapidly. 'I ...'

Xavier touched Ella's arm. 'She can't say anything bad about it with me standing here! Ask her after I'm gone.'

Ella chortled as if this was the funniest thing anyone had ever said. Then she slung her arm around Aria's shoulders. Aria could feel her mother's forearm shaking. *She's nervous*, Aria thought. Ella had totally fallen for Xavier at first sight.

'This is a crazy coincidence, huh?' Xavier said.

'It's a *wonderful* coincidence,' Ella corrected.

She turned to Aria expectantly. Aria felt the need to paste the same dumb smile on her face. 'It's wonderful,' she echoed. Wonderfully *weird*.

9

You're Not Paranoid If He's Really After You

Later that same Tuesday, Emily slammed the door to her mom's Volvo and walked across Spencer's enormous front yard. She'd skipped the second half of swim practice to meet with her old friends, as Marion had suggested, to check in with one another and talk.

Just as she was about to ring the bell, her Nokia chimed. Emily dug it out of her bright yellow ski parka and looked at the screen. Isaac had sent her a ringtone. When she opened it up, she heard her favorite Jimmy Eat World song, the one that included the line, *Can you still feel the butterflies?* She'd listened to it a lot last September when she was falling for Maya. *Hey Emily*, said the accompanying text. *This song reminds me of you. See you at Chem Hill tomorrow!*

Emily blushed, pleased. She and Isaac had texted back and forth all day. He'd filled her in on the details of his religion class – taught by none other than Father Tyson, who'd gotten Isaac into the *Lord of the Rings* books too – and Emily had recapped the horror that had been her oral report on the Battle of Bunker Hill for history. They'd compared favorite books and TV shows and discovered they both liked

M. Night Shyamalan movies, even though he was terrible at dialogue. Emily had never been one of those girls who was glued to her phone during school hours – and anyway, it was technically forbidden at Rosewood Day – but whenever she heard her phone make a low-pitched little *ping*, she felt the urge to write back to Isaac immediately.

She'd asked herself several times that day exactly what she was doing and grappled to assess her feelings. Did she *like* Isaac? Was she even *capable* of that?

A branch cracked nearby, and Emily looked down Spencer's front walk to the dark, quiet street. The air smelled cold, like nothing. A thick coating of ice had turned the Cavanaugh mailbox flag from red to white. Down the street was the Vanderwaals', eerily unoccupied – Mona's family had disappeared from town after she died. A shiver ran up Emily's spine. A had lived just steps away from Spencer the whole time, and none of them had known.

Shuddering, Emily dropped her phone back into her jacket pocket and pressed Spencer's front bell. There were foot-steps, and then Spencer flung open the door, her dirty-blond hair spilling down her shoulders. 'We're back in the media room,' she mumbled.

The smell of butter permeated the air, and Aria and Hanna were perched on the edge of the couch, picking at a big plastic bowl of microwave popcorn. The TV was tuned to *The Hills*, the sound on mute. 'So,' Emily said, flopping onto the chaise. 'Are we supposed to call Marion, or what?'

Spencer shrugged. 'She didn't really say. She just said we should ... *talk*.'

They all looked around at one another, silent.

'So, girls, are we all doing our *chants*?' Hanna said in a fake-concerned voice.

'*Ommmmm*,' Aria hummed, erupting into giggles.

74

Emily picked at a loose thread on her navy blue Rosewood Day blazer, kind of wanting to defend Marion. She was trying to help. She gazed around the room, noticing something propped up against the base of a large wire sculpture of the Eiffel Tower. It was the black-and-white photograph of Ali standing in front of the Rosewood Day bike racks, her school blazer slung over her arm – the one Emily had asked Spencer not to burn.

Emily studied the candid. There was something very sharp and realistic about it. She could practically feel the crisp autumn air and smell the crabapple trees on Rosewood Day's front lawn. Ali was staring at the camera dead-on, her mouth open in laughter. There was a piece of paper in her right hand. Emily squinted at the words. *Time Capsule Starts Tomorrow! Get Ready!*

'Whoa.' Emily leapt off the chaise and held up the photo for the others to see. Aria read the flyer and widened her eyes too. 'Do you remember that day?' Emily asked. 'When Ali announced that she was going to find one of the pieces of the flag?'

'What day?' Hanna unfolded her long legs and walked over to them. 'Oh. Huh.'

Spencer was behind them now, finally curious. 'The common was totally mobbed. Everyone saw the sign at once.'

Emily hadn't thought about that day in a long time. She'd been so excited when she'd seen the flyer about the Time Capsule game beginning. And then Ali had marched outside with Naomi and Riley, pushed through the crowd, torn down the sign, and announced that one of the pieces was as good as hers.

Emily looked up, startled by the memory of what had happened next. 'Guys. Ian came up to her. Remember?'

Spencer nodded slowly. 'He teased her that she shouldn't brag that she was going to find a piece, because someone might try to steal it from her.'

Hanna's hand fluttered to her mouth. 'And Ali said there was no way that could be true. Whoever wanted her piece would have to ...'

'... kill her to get it.' Spencer's face was ashen. 'And then Ian said something like, "Well, if that's what it takes."'

'*God,*' Aria whispered.

Emily's stomach rumbled. Ian's words had been so eerily prophetic, but how could they have known to take him seriously? Back then, the only thing Emily had known about Ian Thomas was that he was Rosewood Day's go-to guy if they needed an upperclassman representative to help out at the elementary school's field day or corral kids in the cafeteria when a big snowstorm made the buses late. That day, after Ali strolled away with her posse, Ian had turned and walked casually to his car. It didn't seem like the behavior of someone who was planning murder ... which made the whole thing creepier.

'And then the next morning she was so smug, everyone knew she'd found the piece,' Spencer said with a frown, like it still bothered her that Ali had found the flag instead of her.

Hanna stared at the photo. 'I wanted Ali's piece of the Time Capsule flag so badly.'

'Me too,' Emily admitted. She glanced over at Aria, who shifted uncomfortably and seemed to be studiously avoiding everyone's eyes.

'We all wanted to win.' Spencer sat back down on the couch and hugged a blue satin pillow to her chest. 'Otherwise we wouldn't have shown up in her yard two days later to steal it.'

'Isn't it weird someone *else* stole Ali's piece first?' Hanna asked, turning a chunky turquoise bracelet around and around her wrist. 'I wonder whatever happened to it?'

Suddenly, Spencer's sister, Melissa, burst into the room. She wore a baggy beige sweater and wide-leg jeans. Her round face was ashen. 'Guys.' Her voice shook. 'Turn on the news. *Now.*' She pointed to the TV.

Emily and the others stared at Melissa for a beat without moving. Frustrated, Melissa grabbed the remote and keyed in channel four herself. The screen showed a crowd of people thrusting microphones in someone's face. The news camera wobbled, as if it was constantly being jostled around. Then, some of the heads parted. First, Emily saw a guy with a strong jaw and stunning green eyes. It was Darren Wilden, Rosewood's youngest cop, the officer who had helped them find Spencer when Mona had kidnapped her. When Wilden stepped away, the camera fixed on someone in a rumpled suit. His floppy golden hair was unforgettable. Emily's whole body went limp.

'Ian?' she whispered.

Aria grabbed Emily's hand.

Spencer stared at Melissa, her face completely white. 'What's going on? Why isn't he in prison?'

Melissa shook her head helplessly. 'I don't know.'

Ian's blond hair shone like that of a polished bronze statue, but his face looked sallow. The screen switched to a News 4 reporter. 'Mr. Thomas's mother has been diagnosed with aggressive pancreatic cancer,' she explained. 'There has just been an emergency hearing, and Thomas has been granted temporary bail to visit her.'

'*What?*' Hanna screamed.

A banner at the bottom of the screen said: JUDGE BAXTER RULES ON THOMAS BAIL REQUEST. Emily's heart hammered in her ears. Ian's lawyer, a silver-haired man in a pin-striped suit, pushed to the front of the crowd and stood in front of the cameras. Flashbulbs flared in the background. 'It was my client's mother's dying wish to spend her last days with her son,' he announced. 'And I'm thrilled we won the motion for temporary bail. Ian will be under house arrest until his trial starts on Friday.'

Emily felt faint. 'House arrest?' she repeated, dropping Aria's hand. Ian's family lived in a big Cape Cod-style house less than a mile from the Hastingses' farmhouse. Once, back when Ali was still alive and Ian and Melissa were dating, Emily had overheard Ian telling Melissa that he could see the Hastingses' windmill from his bedroom window.

'This can't be happening,' Aria said in a catatonic voice.

The reporters thrust microphones in Ian's face. 'How do you feel about the decision?' they asked. 'What has the county jail been like for you?' 'Do you feel you've been wrongfully accused?'

'Yes, I've been wrongfully accused,' Ian said, in a strong, angry voice. 'And jail has been exactly what you'd expect – hell.' He pursed his lips together, glaring right into the camera lens. 'I'm going to do everything in my power never to go back there.'

A chill ran up Emily's spine. She thought of Ian on that online interview she'd seen before Christmas. *Someone wants me here. Someone's concealing the truth. They're going to pay.*

The reporters chased Ian as he walked to a waiting black limousine. 'What do you mean, you're not going back there?' they cried. 'Did someone else do it? Do you know something we don't?'

Ian didn't answer. He just let his lawyer guide him toward the waiting limo. Emily looked around at the others. Hanna's face was green. Aria was chewing on the collar of her sweater.

Melissa ran out of the room, letting the door slam shut behind her. Spencer stood up and faced all of them.

'We're going to be okay,' she said forcefully. 'We can't freak out.'

'He might come looking for us,' Emily whispered, her heart booming. 'He's so angry. And he blames *us*.'

A tiny muscle near Spencer's mouth quivered.

The TV camera zoomed in on Ian as he climbed into the backseat of the limo. For a moment, it seemed like his deranged eyes were looking through the camera lens, like he could see Emily and her friends. Hanna let out a small 'eep.'

The girls watched as Ian settled into the leather seat and reached for something in his jacket pocket. Then Ian's lawyer slammed the door shut behind him, and the camera pulled away, switching back to the News 4 reporter. Below her the banner now read: JUDGE BAXTER GRANTS THOMAS TEMPORARY BAIL.

Suddenly, Emily's phone beeped, making her jump. At the same time, a chime sounded from Hanna's purse.

Then, there was a *bleep*. Aria's Treo, which was sitting in her lap, lit up. Spencer's Sidekick rang, two loud bleats like an old British telephone.

The TV flickered in the background. All they could see were the taillights of Ian's limo, pulling into the street and slowly driving away. Emily exchanged glances with her friends, all the blood slowly draining from her head.

Emily stared at her phone's LCD window, ONE NEW TEXT MESSAGE.

Her hands shook as she hit Read.

Honestly, bitches ... did you really think I'd let you off that easy? You haven't gotten nearly what you deserve. And I can't wait to give it to you. Mwah! – A

10
Blood Is Thicker Than Water...
If You're Really Family, That Is

Seconds later, Spencer was on the phone with Officer Wilden. She put the call on speaker so her friends could hear. 'That's right,' she barked into the mouthpiece. 'Ian just sent us a threatening text.'

'Are you sure it's Ian?' Wilden's voice crackled on the other end.

'Positive,' Spencer said. She looked at the others, and they nodded. Who else could have sent this, after all? Ian had to be furious at them. Their evidence had sent him to jail, and their testimony – specifically *her* testimony – at his upcoming trial would put him in prison for the rest of his life. Plus, he'd reached into his pocket just as the limo door had closed, as if searching for a cell phone ...

'I'm a couple miles from your house,' Wilden replied. 'I'll be there in a sec.'

They heard his car pulling into the driveway a minute later. Wilden wore a heavy, down-filled Rosewood PD jacket that smelled slightly of mothballs. There was a gun in his holster and his ever-present walkie-talkie. When he took off his black wool hat, his hair was matted.

'I can't believe the judge let him out.' Wilden's voice was razor-sharp. 'I seriously can't *believe* it.' He stormed into the foyer with a lot of pent-up energy, like a lion prowling around his habitat at the Philadelphia Zoo.

Spencer raised an eyebrow. She hadn't seen Wilden this keyed up since high school, when Principal Appleton had threatened to expel him for attempting to steal his vintage Ducati motorcycle. Even the night Mona died, when Wilden had had to tackle Ian in Spencer's backyard to make sure he didn't run, he'd remained stoic and unruffled.

But it was reassuring that he was as furious as they were. 'Here's the note,' Spencer said, thrusting her Sidekick under Wilden's nose. He frowned and studied the screen. His walkie made a few squawks and bleeps, but he ignored them.

Finally, Wilden handed the device back to Spencer. 'So you think this is from Ian?'

'Of *course* it's from Ian,' Emily urged.

Wilden pushed his hands into his pockets. He sank down on the rose-printed wingback living room couch. 'I know how this must look,' he started carefully. 'And I promise I will investigate this. But I want you guys to entertain the possibility that this is just from a copycat.'

'A *copycat*?' Hanna screeched.

'Think about it.' Wilden leaned forward, resting his elbows on his knees. 'Ever since your story has been on the news, there have been tons of people sending threatening notes, calling themselves A. And although we've tried to keep your cell numbers private, people have ways of getting hold of information.' He pointed to Spencer's phone. 'Whoever wrote that probably timed it with Ian's release, making it *look* like he'd sent it, that's all.'

'But what if it really *is* Ian?' Spencer squealed. She waved her hands toward the media room, where the TV was still playing. 'What if he wants to scare us into keeping quiet at his trial?'

Wilden gave her a slightly condescending, closed-mouth smile. 'I can see why you'd jump to that conclusion. But think about this from Ian's perspective. Even if he *is* mad, he's out of jail now. He wants to stay out. He wouldn't try something as blatantly stupid as this.'

Spencer ran her hand over the back of her neck. She felt like she had the time she'd gotten to try out one of the NASA astronaut training machines on a family trip to the Kennedy Space Center in Florida – nauseated and unsure which end was up. 'But he killed Ali,' she blurted out.

'Can't you just re-arrest him until his trial?' Aria suggested.

'Guys, the law doesn't work like that,' Wilden said. 'I can't just go around arresting anyone I please. It's not really for me to decide.' He gazed around at all of them, noting their dissatisfaction. 'I'll check Ian out personally, okay? And we'll try and track down where this text came from. Whoever is sending these will be stopped – I promise. Meanwhile, try not to worry. Someone's just messing with your heads. More than likely, it's just some dumb kid who has nothing better to do. Now, can we all take a deep breath and try not to think too hard about this?'

None of them said a word. Wilden tilted his head. '*Please?*'

A shrill ring sounded from his belt, making them all flinch. Wilden glanced down, unclipping his cell phone. 'I gotta take this, okay? I'll see you girls later.' He gave them all a small, apologetic wave, and let himself out.

The door closed quietly, filling the foyer with a burst of crisp, freezing-cold air. The room was silent except for the faraway murmurings of the television. Spencer turned her Sidekick over in her hands. 'I *guess* Wilden could be right,' she said quietly, not really believing her own words. 'Maybe it's just a copycat.'

'Yeah,' Hanna said, pausing to swallow. 'I've gotten a couple copycat notes.'

Spencer gritted her teeth. She had, too – but they'd been nothing like this.

'Same drill, I guess?' Aria suggested. 'If we get more notes, we tell each other?'

They all shrugged in agreement. But Spencer knew how well that plan had gone before – A had sent her plenty of devastatingly personal notes she hadn't dared tell the others about, and her friends hadn't shared theirs either. Only, those notes had been from Mona, who, thanks to Ali's diary, knew their darkest secrets, and had been able to skulk around, digging up dirt on them left and right. Ian had been in jail for more than two months. What could he really know about them, besides that they were afraid? Nothing. And Wilden had promised to look into it.

Not that any of this made her feel much better.

There was nothing to do except to usher her old friends out the front door. Spencer watched as they trudged down her front walk toward their cars in the carefully shoveled circular driveway. The world was absolutely still, stunned by winter. A patch of long, weapon-sharp icicles hung off the garage, glittering under the floodlights.

Something flickered near the thick line of black trees that separated part of Spencer's yard from Ali's. Then she heard a cough, and Spencer spun around and screamed. Melissa was standing behind her in the foyer, her hands clasped at her waist, a ghostly expression on her face. 'God,' Spencer said, pressing her hand to her chest.

'Sorry,' Melissa croaked. She moved quietly into the living room and brushed her hands along the top of the antique harp. 'I heard what you told Wilden. You guys got another note?'

Spencer raised a suspicious eyebrow. Had Melissa been hovering in the doorway, spying? 'If you were listening, why didn't you tell Wilden that Ian called you from prison and begged us not to testify?' Spencer demanded. 'Then Wilden might have believed that Ian wrote the note. He might have been able to re-arrest him.'

Melissa plucked a harp string. There was a helpless expression on her face. 'Did you see Ian on TV? He looked so … thin. It's like they didn't even let him eat when he was in jail.'

Rage and disbelief rushed through Spencer's body. Did Melissa actually feel sorry for him? 'Just admit it,' she sputtered. 'You think I'm lying about seeing Ian with Ali that night, just like I lied about the Golden Orchid. And you'd rather Ian *hurt* us than believe he could've killed her – *and* that he deserves to go back to jail.'

Melissa shrugged and plucked another string. A sour note filled the room. 'Of course I don't want anyone to hurt you. But … like I said. What if this is all a mistake? What if Ian didn't do it?'

'He *did*,' Spencer yelled, her chest burning. Interesting, she thought, that Melissa didn't admit whether she thought Spencer was lying or telling the truth.

Melissa waved her hand dismissively, as if she didn't feel like getting into it again. 'In any case, I do think Wilden's right about those notes. It's not Ian. He wouldn't be stupid enough to threaten you. Ian might be upset, but he's not an idiot.'

Spencer turned away from her sister, frustrated, and peered out over the cold, empty front yard just as her mother's car pulled into the driveway. Moments later, the door from the garage to the kitchen slammed, and Mrs. Hastings's high heels clacked across the kitchen floor. Melissa sighed and padded down the hall. Spencer heard them murmuring, then the crackle of grocery bags.

Spencer's heart began to pound. She had the urge to run upstairs, hide in her room, and try not to think about Ian or anything else, but this was her first opportunity to confront her mother about Nana's will.

Rolling back her shoulders, Spencer took a deep breath and walked down the long hallway into the kitchen. Her mother was leaning over the counter, pulling a fresh-baked rosemary bread loaf out of a Fresh Fields grocery bag. Melissa scuttled in from the garage, a case of Moët champagne in her arms.

'What's all that champagne for?' Spencer asked, wrinkling her nose.

'The fund-raiser, of course.' Melissa shot her a *duh* look.

Spencer frowned. 'What fund-raiser?'

Melissa lowered her chin, surprised. She glanced at their mother, but Mrs. Hastings continued unpacking organic vegetables and whole-wheat pasta, her lips pressed tightly together. 'We're having a Rosewood Day fund-raiser here this weekend,' Melissa explained.

A little squeak escaped from Spencer's throat. A fund-raiser? Event planning was something she and her mom always did together. Spencer organized the invitations, helped plan the menu, took RSVP calls, and even arranged the classical music playlist. It was one of the few things Spencer did better than Melissa – few people were OCD enough to create dossiers on each invitee, complete with information as to who didn't eat veal and who didn't mind sitting next to the vile Pembrokes at dinner.

Spencer turned to face her mother, her heart pounding. 'Mom?'

Spencer's mother whirled around. She touched her diamond tennis bracelet protectively, as if she thought Spencer might try to steal it.

'Do you ... need help with the fund-raiser?' Spencer's voice broke.

Mrs. Hastings tightly gripped the sides of a jar of organic blackberry preserves. 'I've got it covered, thank you.'

There was a cold hard knot at the pit of Spencer's stomach. She took a deep breath. 'I also wanted to ask you about Nana's will. Why was I left out? Is it even legal to give some grandchildren money and not others?'

Her mother placed the preserves on a pantry shelf and let out a chilling snicker. 'Of course it's legal, Spencer. Nana can do whatever she wants with her money.' She pulled her black cashmere cape around her shoulders and strode past Spencer to the garage.

'But ...' Spencer cried. Her mother didn't turn around. She slammed the door on her way out. The sleigh bells hanging from the doorknob jangled loudly, startling the two dogs from sleep.

Spencer's body went slack. So that was it. She was really, truly disowned. Maybe her parents had told Nana about the Golden Orchid debacle a few months ago. Maybe they'd even encouraged Nana to alter her will, deliberately leaving Spencer out because she'd disgraced the family. Spencer squeezed her eyes shut, wondering what her life would be like right now if she'd just kept quiet and accepted the Golden Orchid award. Could she have gone on *Good Morning America*, as the other Golden Orchid winners had done, and accepted everyone's congratulations? Could she seriously have attended a college that had given her early admission based on an essay she hadn't written – and didn't even really understand? If she'd just kept quiet, would there still be this chatter that Ian was going to be acquitted due to lack of reliable evidence?

She leaned against the granite-topped island and let out a small, pathetic whimper. Melissa dropped a folded grocery bag to the table and walked over to her. 'I'm so sorry, Spence,' she said quietly. She hesitated a moment and then wrapped her thin arms around Spencer's shoulders. Spencer was too numb to resist. 'They're being so awful to you.'

Spencer plopped into a seat at the kitchen table, reached for a napkin from the holder, and dabbed at her teary eyes.

Melissa sat down next to her. 'I just don't understand it. I've been going over and over it, and I don't know why Nana would leave you out of her will.'

'She hated me,' Spencer said flatly, her nose getting that peppery, about-to-sneeze feeling it always did whenever she was about to start bawling. 'I stole your paper. Then I admitted I stole it. I'm a huge disgrace.'

'I don't think it has anything to do with that.' Melissa leaned closer. Spencer could smell Neutrogena sunscreen – Melissa was so anal, she put on sunscreen even when she was going to be spending the entire day indoors. 'Something about it was really suspect.'

Spencer lowered the napkin from her eyes. 'Suspect … how?'

Melissa scraped the chair closer. 'Nana left money to each of her *natural-born grandchildren*.' She tapped the kitchen table three times to emphasize the last three words, and then stared at Spencer searchingly, as if Spencer was supposed to deduce something from this. Then Melissa glanced out the window, where their mother was still unloading groceries from the car. 'I think there are a lot of secrets in this family,' she whispered. 'Things you and I aren't allowed to know. Everything has to look all perfect on the outside, but ...' She trailed off.

Spencer squinted. Even though she had no idea what Melissa was talking about, a sick, swooping feeling began to wash over her. 'Will you just spit out what you're trying to say?'

Melissa sat back. '*Natural-born grandchildren*,' she repeated. 'Spence ... maybe you were adopted.'

11

If You Can't Beat Her, Join Forces With Her

Wednesday morning, Hanna burrowed under her down comforter, trying to drown out the sound of Kate singing scales in the shower. 'She's so sure she's going to get the lead in the play,' Hanna grumbled into her BlackBerry. 'I wish I could see her face when the director tells her it's Shakespeare, not a musical.'

Lucas chuckled. 'Did she seriously threaten to tell on you when you weren't going to give her a tour of the school?'

'Basically,' Hanna growled. 'Can I move in with you until we graduate?'

'I wish,' Lucas murmured. 'Although we'd have to share a bedroom.'

'I wouldn't mind,' Hanna purred.

'Me neither.' Hanna could tell he was smiling.

There was a knock at the door, and Isabel poked her head in. Before she'd gotten engaged to Hanna's father, she'd been an ER nurse, and she still wore hospital-issue scrubs to bed. *Yecch*. 'Hanna?' Isabel's eyes were even droopier than usual. 'No talking on the phone if you haven't made your bed, remember?'

Hanna scowled. '*Fine,*' she said under her breath. Seconds after Isabel had hauled in her Tumi luggage and replaced the custom-made plantation shutters with purple, crushed-velvet drapes, she'd laid down all these rules: No Internet after 9 P.M. No talking on cell phones if chores weren't finished. Absolutely no boys in the house when Isabel and Hanna's father weren't home. Hanna was basically living in a police state.

'I'm being forced to get off the phone,' Hanna said into her BlackBerry, loud enough for Isabel to hear.

'It's okay,' Lucas said. 'I need to get moving. Photography club meets this morning.'

He made a kissing sound and hung up. Hanna wiggled her toes, all of her irritations and worries melting away. Lucas was a way better boyfriend than Sean Ackard, and he almost made up for the fact that Hanna was essentially girlfriend-less. He understood how hard she was taking what Mona had done to her, and he always snickered at her evil Kate stories. Plus, with a new salon haircut and a Jack Spade messenger bag to replace his ratty JanSport backpack, Lucas wasn't half as dorky as he'd been when they first became friends.

Once Hanna was certain Isabel had retreated down the hall to the bedroom she and Hanna's father shared – double *ughh* – she crawled out of bed, haphazardly pulling up the covers so it looked like she'd made it. She then sat down at her makeup table and snapped on her LCD TV. The Action News Morning Report song blared out of the speakers. ROSE-WOOD REACTS TO IAN THOMAS'S TEMPORARY RELEASE flashed in big black block letters at the bottom of the screen. Hanna paused. As much as she didn't want to watch the report, she couldn't tear her eyes away.

A petite, redheaded news reporter was at the local SEPTA

train station, canvassing commuters for their thoughts about the trial. 'It's despicable,' said a thin, stately older woman in a high-necked cashmere coat. 'They shouldn't let that boy out for even a minute after what he did to that poor girl.'

The camera moved to a dark-haired girl in her twenties. Her name, Alexandra Pratt, appeared below her face. Hanna recognized her. She'd once been Rosewood Day's star field hockey player, but had graduated when Hanna was in sixth grade, a year ahead of Ian, Melissa Hastings, and Ali's brother, Jason. 'He's definitely guilty,' Alexandra said, not bothering to take off her enormous Valentino sunglasses. 'Alison occasionally played field hockey with a group of us on the weekends. Ian sometimes talked to Ali after the games. I never knew Ali that well, but I think he made her uncomfortable. I mean, she was so young.'

Hanna uncapped her Mederma scar cream. That wasn't how *she* remembered it. Ali's cheeks flushed and her eyes lit up any time Ian was around. At one of their sleepovers, when they were practicing kissing on the monkey pillow Ali had sewn in sixth-grade home ec, Spencer had made each of them confess which boy they wanted to kiss in real life. 'Ian Thomas,' Ali had blurted out, and then quickly covered her mouth.

Ian's senior picture was now on the screen, his smile so white, wide ... and fake. Hanna looked away. Yesterday, after another awkward dinner with her new family, Hanna had dug out Officer Wilden's business card from the bottom of her bag. She wanted to ask him how strict Ian's house arrest was going to be. Would he be chained to his bed? Would he have on one of those ankle bracelet thingies that Martha Stewart had to wear? She wanted to believe Wilden was right about yesterday's A note – that it was just a copy-cat – but every bit of reassurance would help. Plus, she thought

Wilden might give her a little extra info. He'd always tried to be buddy-buddy with her back when he and her mom were dating.

Only useless Wilden had said, 'Sorry, Hanna, but I'm really not allowed to discuss the case.' Then, as Hanna was about to hang up, Wilden had cleared his throat. 'Look, I want him to fry as much as you do. Ian deserves to be locked up for a long, long time for what he did.'

Hanna clicked off the TV as the morning news moved on to a story about an E. coli scare in local grocery store lettuce. After a few more layers of Mederma, foundation, and powder, Hanna decided her scar was as hidden as it was going to get. She spritzed herself with Narciso Rodriguez perfume, straightened her uniform skirt, threw all her crap into her Fendi-logo tote, and walked downstairs.

Kate was already at the breakfast table. When she saw Hanna, her whole face broke into a dazzling smile. 'Omigod, Hanna!' she cried. 'Tom brought this amazing organic honeydew at Fresh Fields last night. You *have* to try it.'

Hanna hated how Kate called her father *Tom*, like he was their age. It wasn't like Hanna called Isabel by her first name. Actually, she avoided calling Isabel anything at all. Hanna walked across the kitchen and poured herself a cup of coffee. 'I hate honeydew,' she said primly. 'It tastes like sperm.'

'*Hanna*,' her father scolded. Hanna hadn't noticed him by the kitchen island, finishing a slice of buttered toast. Isabel was next to him, still in those hideous puke-green scrubs, looking particularly faux-tan orange.

Mr. Marin approached the girls. He put one hand on Kate's shoulder and one hand on Hanna's. 'I'm off. See you girls tonight.'

'Bye, Tom,' Kate said sweetly.

Her father left, and Isabel clomped back upstairs. Hanna

stared at the front page of the *Philadelphia Inquirer* her father had left on the table, but unfortunately, all the headlines were about Ian's bail hearing. Kate kept eating her melon. Hanna wanted to just get up and leave, but why should *she* have to be the one to go? This was *her* house.

'Hanna,' Kate said in a small, sad voice. Hanna glanced up, giving Kate an arch look. 'Hanna, I'm *sorry*,' Kate rushed on. 'I can't do this anymore. I can't just ... sit here and not talk. I know you're mad about this fall – about what happened at Le Bec-Fin. I was such a mess back then. And I'm really sorry.'

Hanna flipped to the next page of the newspaper. The obituaries, good. She pretended to be fascinated by an article about Ethel Norris, eighty-five, choreographer of a modern dance troupe in Philadelphia. She'd died yesterday in her sleep.

'I'm finding this difficult too.' Kate's voice shook. 'I miss my dad. I wish he were still alive. No offense to Tom, but it's weird to see my mom with someone else. And it's weird to be all happy for both of them, just like that. They don't think about *us*, do they?'

Hanna was so outraged, she wanted to throw Kate's melon across the kitchen. Everything out of Kate's mouth was so scripted, it was like she'd downloaded some perfect *feel bad for me* speech off the Internet.

Kate took a breath. 'I'm sorry about what I did to you in Philly, but I had other stuff going on that day. Stuff I shouldn't have taken out on you.' There was a little *clink* as she set down her fork. 'Something really scary happened to me right before that dinner. I hadn't told my mom yet, and I was sure she was going to lose it.'

Hanna frowned, glancing at Kate for a split second. Trouble?

Kate pushed her plate away. 'I was going out with this guy, Connor, last summer. One night, one of the last weekends before school started, things went kind of ... far.' Her forehead wrinkled, and her bottom lip started to tremble. 'He broke up with me the next day. About a month later, I went to the gynecologist, and there were ... complications.'

Hanna widened her eyes. 'Were you *pregnant*?'

Kate shook her head quickly. 'No. It was ... something else.'

Hanna was pretty sure that if her mouth gaped open any farther, it would graze the top of the table. Her brain raced a million miles a minute, trying to figure out what *complications* meant. An STD? A third ovary? A funny-looking nipple? 'So ... are you okay?'

Kate shrugged. 'I am now. But it sucked for a while. It was really scary.'

Hanna narrowed her eyes. 'Why are you telling me all this?'

'Because I wanted to explain what was going on,' Kate admitted. Her eyes glistened with tears. 'Look, please don't tell anyone what I just told you. My mom knows, but Tom doesn't.'

Hanna took a sip of her coffee. She was floored by Kate's words – and also a little relieved. Perfect Kate had screwed up. And never in a zillion years did Hanna think she'd ever see Kate *cry*. 'I won't say anything,' Hanna said. 'We all have issues.'

Kate let out a big, dubious sniff. 'Right. What's *your* issue?'

Hanna set down her polka-dotted coffee cup, debating. If nothing else, she could learn whether Ali had told Kate her secret. 'Fine. But you probably already know it. The first time it happened was that time Alison and I came to Annapolis.'

She peeked at Kate, trying to gauge if she understood. Kate poked her fork into a piece of honeydew, shifting her eyes uneasily around the room. 'You're still doing that?' she asked quietly. Hanna felt a mixture of thrill and disappointment – so Ali *had* run back to the patio and told her.

'Not really,' Hanna mumbled.

They were silent for a moment. Hanna stared out the window at a big snowdrift in the neighbors' backyard. Even though it was the ass-crack of dawn, the bratty six-year-old twins were out in the snow, pitching icy snowballs at squirrels. Then Kate cocked her head quizzically. 'I meant to ask you. What's up with you and Naomi and Riley?'

Hanna gritted her teeth. 'Why are you asking me? Aren't they your brand-new BFFs?'

Kate thoughtfully pushed a strand of chestnut hair behind her ears. 'You know, I think they want to be friends. Maybe you should give them a chance.'

Hanna snorted. 'Sorry, I don't talk to girls who insult me to my face.'

Kate leaned forward on her elbows. 'They probably say that stuff because they're jealous of you. If you were nice to them, I bet they'd be nice back. And think about it – if we join up with them, we could be unstoppable.'

Hanna raised an eyebrow. '*We?*'

'Face it, Hanna.' Kate's eyes danced. 'You and I would *totally* rule their group.'

Hanna blinked. She gazed at the hanging rack over the kitchen island, which held a bunch of All-Clad pots and pans Hanna's mother had bought a few years ago at Williams-Sonoma. Ms. Marin had left most of her personal belongings behind when she left for Singapore, and Isabel had had no problem claiming them as her own.

Kate definitely had a point. Naomi and Riley were insecure

to the core – they had been ever since Alison DiLaurentis had dropped them for seemingly no reason in sixth grade and decided to be friends with Hanna, Spencer, Aria, and Emily instead. It certainly would be nice to have a clique again – especially one she could rule.

'Okay. I'm in,' Hanna decided.

Kate grinned. 'Awesome.' She raised her orange juice glass in a toast. Hanna clinked it with her coffee mug. They both smiled and sipped. Then Hanna glanced back down at the newspaper, which was still open in front of her. Her eyes went right to an ad for vacation packages to Bermuda. *All your dreams will come true*, the ad copy assured her.

They'd better.

12
It's All Just A Matter Of Perspective

Early Wednesday evening, Aria and Mike sat down at Rabbit Rabbit, the Montgomery family's favorite vegetarian restaurant. The room smelled like a mix of basil, oregano, and soy cheese. A Regina Spektor song played loudly over the stereo, and the place was bustling with families, couples, and kids her age. After Ian's chilling release and the new A note yesterday, it felt good to be surrounded by so many people.

Mike scowled around the dining room and pulled up the hood of his oversize Champion sweatshirt. 'I don't get why we have to meet this dude anyway. Mom's only gone out with him *twice*.'

Aria didn't quite understand either. When Ella had returned home from her date with Xavier last night, she'd raved about how wonderfully it had gone and how easily she and Xavier had connected. Apparently, Xavier had given Ella a studio tour this afternoon, and when she'd gotten home from school today, Aria had found a note from Ella on the kitchen table, asking that she and Mike clean themselves up and meet her at Rabbit Rabbit at 7 P.M. sharp. Oh yeah, and Xavier was coming. Who knew both her parents could fall in love again so easily? They weren't even officially divorced yet.

Aria felt happy for Ella, of course, but she also felt embarrassed for herself. She'd been so certain that Xavier was interested in *her*. It was mortifying that she'd read the situation at the gallery so wrong.

Mike sniffed loudly, breaking Aria from her thoughts. 'It smells like rabbit pee in here.' He made a retching noise.

Aria rolled her eyes. 'You're just pissed Mom picked a place that doesn't serve wings.'

Mike crumpled his napkin. 'Can you blame me? A virile man like me can't live on vegetables alone.'

Aria cringed, grossed out that Mike was referring to himself as both *virile* and a *man*. 'How was your date with Savannah the other day, by the way?'

Mike cracked his knuckles, thumbing through the menu. 'That's for me to know and for you to obsess about.'

Aria raised an eyebrow. 'Aha! You didn't immediately correct me that it *wasn't* a date.'

Mike shrugged, stabbing his fork into the cactus centerpiece. Aria picked up a cornflower blue crayon from the little cup in the middle of the table; Rabbit Rabbit put crayons on every table and encouraged its patrons to draw on the backs of their place mats. Finished drawings were hung on the restaurant's walls. These days, the walls were all covered, so the staff had started hanging place mats from the ceiling.

'You made it!' Ella cried as she walked through the doorway with Xavier. Ella's newly dyed hair shone. Xavier's cheeks were adorably pink from the cold. Aria tried to smile, but she had a feeling it came out more like a grimace.

Ella made a flourishing gesture at Xavier. 'Aria, you two have already met. But Xavier, this is my son, Michelangelo.'

Mike looked like he was going to puke. '*No one* calls me that.'

'I won't tell.' Xavier stuck out his hand. 'Nice to meet you.' He glanced at Aria. 'Good to see you again.'

Aria gave him a tight smile, too embarrassed to make eye contact. She gazed around the room, searching out the last place mat Ali had decorated before she vanished. Ali had come here with Aria's family and had drawn a cartoon girl and a guy holding hands, skipping off toward a rainbow. 'They're *secret* boyfriend and girlfriend,' she'd announced to the table, her eyes on Aria. This wasn't long after Ali and Aria had caught Byron with Meredith ... but looking back now, maybe Ali had been referring to her secret relationship with Ian.

Xavier and Ella shrugged out of their coats and sat down. Xavier looked around, clearly amused by all the drawings on the walls. Ella kept clucking nervously, fidgeting with her hair, her jewelry, her fork. After a few seconds of silence, Mike narrowed his eyes at Xavier. 'How old are you, anyway?'

Ella shot him a look, but Xavier answered, 'Thirty-four.'

'You know our mom is forty, right?'

'*Mike*,' Ella gasped. But Aria thought it was sweet. She'd never seen Mike be protective of Ella before.

'I know that.' Xavier laughed. 'She told me.'

Their waitress, a busty girl with dreadlocks and a pierced septum, asked what everyone wanted to drink. Aria ordered green tea, and Xavier and Ella ordered glasses of cabernet. Mike tried to order cabernet too, but the waitress just pursed her lips and turned away.

Xavier looked at Mike and Aria. 'So I heard you guys lived in Iceland for a while. I've been there a few times.'

'Really!' Aria exclaimed, surprised.

'And let me guess – you loved it,' Mike interrupted in a droll voice, fiddling with the rubber Rosewood Day lacrosse bracelet around his wrist. 'Because it's so *cultural*. And so *pristinely untouched*. And everyone's so *educated* there.'

Xavier rubbed his chin. 'Actually, I thought Iceland was weird. Who wants to bathe in water that smells like rotten eggs? And what's with the miniature horse obsession? I didn't get it.'

Mike's eyes boggled. He gaped at Ella. 'Did you tell him to say that?'

Ella shook her head, looking a bit dismayed.

Mike turned back to Xavier, ecstatic. '*Thank you*. That's what I've been trying to tell my family for years! But noooo, they all loved the horses! Everyone thought they were so cute. But do you know what would happen if one of those pansy-ass horses got in a smackdown with a Clydesdale from the Budweiser commercials? The Clydesdale would kick its ass. There wouldn't be anything of that gay little horse left!'

'Damn right.' Xavier nodded emphatically.

Mike rubbed his hands together, obviously thrilled. Aria tried to hide a smirk. She had her own suspicions about the real reason Mike hated Icelandic horses. A few days after they'd arrived in Reykjavik, she and Mike had gone on a riding tour on a volcanic trail. Even though the stable boy offered Mike the oldest, fattest, slowest Icelandic horse to ride, the minute Mike climbed in the saddle, his face went disturbingly pale. He claimed he had a leg cramp and should stay behind. Mike had never gotten a leg cramp before ... or since, for that matter, but he still refused to admit that he was scared.

The waitress delivered their drinks, and Mike and Xavier chattered on about all the other things they hated about Iceland: that one of the country's delicacies was rotten shark.

How Icelanders all believed that *huldufolk* – elves – lived in rocks and cliffs. How they all queerly went by first names only, because everyone descended from the same three incestuous Viking tribes.

Every so often, Ella glanced Aria's way, probably wondering why Aria wasn't defending Iceland. But Aria simply wasn't in the mood for talking.

At the end of the dinner, just as they were finishing a plate of the restaurant's famous homemade organic oatmeal cookies, Mike's iPhone rang. He looked at the screen and stood up. 'Hold on,' he mumbled evasively, ducking out the front door.

Aria and Ella exchanged a knowing look. Usually, Mike had no problem talking on the phone right at the dinner table, even if the conversation was about, say, the size of a girl's boobs. 'We suspect Mike has a girlfriend,' Ella stage-whispered to Xavier. She stood up. 'I'll be back in a minute,' she announced, walking toward the ladies' room.

Aria fiddled with the napkin in her lap, staring helplessly as Ella wove between the tables. She wanted to follow her mother, but she didn't want Xavier to know that she didn't want to be alone with him.

She could feel Xavier's eyes on her. He took a long, slow sip of his second glass of wine. 'You've been really quiet,' he pointed out.

Aria shrugged. 'Maybe I'm always this quiet.'

'I doubt that.'

Aria looked up sharply. Xavier smiled, but his expression wasn't particularly easy to read. He plucked a dark green crayon out of the cup and started scribbling on his place mat. 'So are you okay with this?' he asked. 'Me and your mom?'

'Uh-huh,' Aria answered quickly, fidgeting with the spoon

from her after-dinner cappuccino. Was he asking because he sensed she liked him? Or because she was Ella's daughter, and it was the polite thing to do?

Xavier put the green crayon back in the cup and dug around for a black one. 'So your mom said you're an artist too.'

'I guess,' Aria said distantly.

'Who are your influences?'

Aria chewed on her lip, feeling put on the spot. 'I like the surrealists. You know, Klee, Max Ernst, Magritte, M. C. Escher.'

Xavier grimaced. 'Escher.'

'What's wrong with Escher?'

He shook his head. 'Every kid at my high school had an Escher poster in their bedroom, thinking they were so deep. *Ooh*, birds morphing into fish. *Wow*, one hand drawing another. Different perspectives. *Trippy*.'

Aria leaned back in her chair, amused. 'What, did you know M. C. Escher personally? Did he kick you when you were a little boy? Steal your Big Wheel?'

'He died in the early seventies, I think,' Xavier said, snorting. 'I'm not *that old*.'

'Could've fooled me.' Aria raised an eyebrow.

Xavier smirked. 'It's just … Escher's a sellout.'

Aria shook her head. 'He was brilliant! And how can you be a sellout if you're dead?'

Xavier stared at her for a moment, slowly grinning. 'Okay then, Miss Escher Fan. How about a contest?' He twirled the crayon in his hands. 'We both draw something in this room. Whoever's drawing is better is right about Mr. Escher. *And* the winner gets that last oatmeal cookie.' He pointed at the plate. 'I've noticed you ogling it. Or haven't you taken it because you're secretly on a diet?'

Aria scoffed. 'I've never dieted in my life.'

'That's what every girl says.' Xavier's eyes glimmered. 'But they're all lying.'

'Like you know anything about girls!' Aria crowed, giggling at their banter. She felt like they were in her favorite old movie, *The Philadelphia Story*, where Katharine Hepburn and Cary Grant got off on bickering constantly.

'I'll take part in your little contest.' Aria reached for a red crayon. She never could resist showing off her sketching skills. 'But let's give it a time limit. One minute.'

'Got it.' Xavier checked the tomato-shaped clock over the bar. The second hand was at the twelve. 'Go.'

Aria searched around the room for something to sketch. She finally settled on an old man hunched at the bar, nursing a ceramic mug. Her crayon flew deftly over the place mat, capturing his weary-but-peaceful expression. After she filled in a few more details, the hand on the clock swept past the twelve again. 'Time,' she called.

Xavier covered his place mat with his hand. 'You first,' he said. Aria pushed her drawing toward him. He nodded, impressed, his eyes seesawing from the paper to the old man. 'How'd you do that in just one minute?'

'Years of practice,' Aria answered. 'I used to secretly sketch kids at my school all the time. So does that mean I get the cookie?' She poked Xavier's hand, which was still covering his drawing. 'Poor Mr. Abstract Painter. Is yours so bad you're embarrassed to show it?'

'No ...' Xavier slowly moved his hands away from his place mat. His drawing, all soft lines and deft shading, was of a pretty, dark-haired girl. She had big hoop earrings, just like Aria's. And that wasn't the only resemblance.

'Oh.' Aria swallowed hard. Xavier had even captured the little mole on her cheek and the freckles across her nose. It

103

was as if he'd been studying her this whole dinner, waiting for this moment.

The sharp odor of tahini floated out from the kitchen, making Aria's stomach roil. Taken one way, Xavier's drawing was sweet – her mom's boyfriend was trying to bond with her. But taken another ... it was kind of wrong.

'You don't like it?' Xavier asked, sounding surprised.

Aria was opening her mouth to reply when she heard a chime sound from inside her bag. 'Um, just a sec,' she mumbled. She pulled her Treo out of her purse's pocket: *Two new picture texts*. Aria cupped her hands around the phone's little window to cut the glare.

Xavier was still watching her carefully, so Aria struggled not to gasp. Someone had sent her a picture of Aria and Xavier at the art exhibit on Sunday. They were leaning close together, Xavier's lips almost grazing Aria's ear. The next photo opened immediately afterward, this one of Aria and Xavier at this very table at Rabbit Rabbit. Xavier was covering his drawing with his hands, and Aria was leaning across the table, poking him teasingly, trying to get him to show it off. The camera had managed to capture a split second where it looked as if they were happily holding hands. Both photos painted a pretty convincing picture.

And the second one had been taken just *seconds ago*. Her heart in her throat, she glared around the restaurant. There was Mike, still chatting animatedly outside. Her mom was just coming out of the bathroom. The man she had drawn was in the middle of a coughing fit.

Her phone buzzed one last time. With trembling hands, Aria opened her new text. It was a poem.

Artists like ménages a trois,
Mommy just might too.

But if you *ferme la bouche* about me,
I'll do the same for you.
– A

The cell phone slipped from Aria's fingers. She stood up abruptly, practically upending her water glass.

'I have to go,' she blurted out, snatching Xavier's drawing from the table and stuffing it into her bag.

'What? Why?' Xavier looked confused.

'Just … because.' She pulled her coat tight around her, and pointed at the cookie on the corn on the cob-shaped plate. 'It's yours. Good job.' Then she whirled around, nearly colliding with a waitress carrying a big tray of tofu stir-fries. Copycat A or not, the photos proved one thing: The farther she stayed away from her mom and her new relationship, the better.

13

Strange Chemistry On Chemistry Hill

At the same time on Wednesday, just as the moon rose over the trees and the big Hollis parking lot floodlights snapped on, Emily stood at the top of Chemistry Hill, holding a donut-shaped snow tube in her mittened hand. 'You sure you want to race me?' she teased Isaac, who was holding his own snow tube. 'I'm the fastest sledder in all of Rosewood.'

'Says who?' Isaac's eyes sparkled. 'You've never raced *me* before.'

Emily grabbed the snow tube's purple handles. 'The first one to that big tree at the bottom wins. Ready ... set ...'

'Go!' Isaac preempted her, jumping on his snow tube and whizzing down the hill.

'Hey!' Emily yelled, belly flopping on her own tube. She bent her knees, picking up her boots so they wouldn't drag on the ground, and angled her tube toward the steepest part of the hill. Unfortunately, Isaac was steering his tube in that direction too. Emily approached him at a hurtling speed, and they collided in the middle of the hill, rolling off their sleds into the soft snow.

Isaac's snow tube continued down the hill without him,

heading straight into the woods. 'Hey!' he cried, pointing to the tube as it drifted past the tree they'd designated as the finish line. 'Technically, I won!'

'You *cheated*,' Emily grumbled good-naturedly. 'My brother used to start races before me too. It drove me crazy.'

'Does that mean I drive you crazy too?' Isaac smiled impishly.

Emily stared down at her red fleece mittens. 'I don't know,' she said in a quieter voice. 'Maybe.'

Color began to rise to her already pink cheeks. The moment Emily had pulled into the chemistry building parking lot and seen Isaac standing next to his truck with two sleds in his hands, her heart had started pounding wildly. Isaac looked even cuter all dressed up for playing in the snow than he did in his emo-rock T-shirt and jeans. His navy wool hat was pulled low on his forehead, smushing his hair over his ears and making his eyes look extra blue. Both his mittens had reindeer knitted on the palms. He'd sheepishly admitted his mom made him a new pair every year. And there was something about how his scarf was looped twice around his neck, covering every inch of skin, that made him seem both cuddly and vulnerable.

Emily wanted to think the zingy, snappy feelings inside her were merely excitement over making a new friend ... or maybe side effects of acute hypothermia, as the little thermometer inside her mom's Volvo said it was only nineteen degrees out. But really, she had no idea what was going on with her emotions.

'I haven't been here in ages.' Emily broke the silence, gazing at the brick chemistry building at the bottom of the hill. 'My brother and sister found this place. They're in college now, in California. I don't understand how they could've gone somewhere where it never snows.'

'You're lucky to have brothers and sisters,' Isaac admitted. 'I'm an only child.'

'I used to wish I was an only child.' Emily groaned. 'There were always way too many people at my house. And I never got new clothes – only hand-me-downs.'

'Nah, being an only child is lonely,' Isaac said. 'When I was little, my family lived in a neighborhood where there weren't many other kids nearby, so I had to entertain myself. I used to go on these walks all alone, pretending I was an explorer. I'd narrate what I did to myself. *Now the Great Isaac forges a mighty stream. Now the Great Isaac discovers a mountain.* I'm sure anyone who heard me thought I was crazy.'

'The Great Isaac, huh?' Emily giggled, finding it unbelievably cute. 'Well, siblings can be overrated. I'm not that close with my brothers and sisters. We've actually had some major issues recently.'

Isaac propped himself up on one elbow, facing her. 'Why?'

The snow was beginning to seep through Emily's jeans and long underwear to her skin. She was referring to how her family had reacted to the news that she liked Maya. Not only had Carolyn freaked, but Jake and Beth had taken her off their e-mail joke lists for a while.

'Oh, just normal family stuff,' she finally said. 'Nothing that interesting.'

Isaac nodded, then stood up and announced he'd better go down and rescue his snow tube from the woods before it got too dark. Emily watched him tromp down the hill, an uneasy, gnawing feeling coursing through her. Why hadn't she just told Isaac the truth about who she was? Why did it seem so ... difficult?

Then, her eyes moved to the empty chemistry building

108

parking lot. A car was making a wide circle around the parking spaces, coming to a stop under a spotlight at the bottom of Hollis Hill, not that far from where she and Isaac had crashed. *Rosewood PD* was printed on the car's side. Emily squinted, recognizing the driver's familiar brown hair. It was Officer Wilden.

Wilden's forehead was creased with worry, and he was barking something into his phone. Emily watched for a moment. Back when she was younger, she and Carolyn used to haul the portable kitchen TV into their bedroom and watch late-night horror movies at ultra-low volume. Emily's lipreading was rusty, but she was pretty sure she'd just caught Wilden telling whoever was on the phone to 'just stay away.'

Emily's heart knocked in her chest. *Just stay away?* At that very moment, Wilden noticed Emily on the hill. He widened his eyes. After a second, he gave her a tight nod and then looked down sharply.

Emily shifted uncomfortably, wondering if Wilden had come here to get a little privacy to deal with something personal. It was silly to think that his entire life revolved around the Ali case.

When her phone, which was tucked into a little zippered pocket in her parka, began to ring, Emily let out a yelp. She pulled it out of her pocket, her body electrified. Aria's name flashed on the caller ID. 'Hey,' Emily sighed, relieved. 'What's up?'

'Have you gotten any more weird texts?' Aria demanded.

As Emily shifted her weight, the snow beneath her crunched. She watched Isaac disappear into the thick pine forest, in search of his snow tube. 'No ...'

'Well, I did. Just now. Whoever it is took a picture of me, Emily. *Tonight.* The person writing these notes knows where we are and what we're doing.'

A gust of wind knifed across Emily's face, bringing tears to her eyes. 'Are you sure?'

'I called Wilden at the station twenty minutes ago,' Aria went on, 'but he said he was going into an important meeting there and couldn't talk.'

'Wait.' Emily rubbed her numb jaw, confused. 'Wilden isn't at the station. I just saw him a second ago.' She gazed back down the hill. The spot where Wilden's car had been was now empty. The knot in her belly tightened. Wilden must have told Aria he'd be driving around, not going into a meeting. She'd probably just heard him wrong.

'Where are you anyway?' Aria asked.

Isaac emerged from the woods with his tube. He looked up at her and waved. Emily swallowed hard, her heart pounding. 'I have to go,' she said abruptly. 'I'll call you back.'

'Wait!' Aria sounded worried. 'But I haven't –'

Emily snapped her phone closed, cutting Aria off. Isaac raised the snow tube over his head, triumphant. 'The Great Isaac had to wrestle this back from a bear!' he yelled. Emily forced a giggle, trying to settle down. There had to be a logical explanation for Aria's text. It couldn't be anything serious.

Isaac plopped down on his sled and examined her carefully. 'So we never decided what my prize is for winning the race down the hill.'

Emily sniffed, allowing herself to relax into the moment. 'How about the title of World's Biggest Cheater? Or a snowball, right in the face?'

'Or how about this?' Isaac asked. Before she knew it, Isaac was leaning in to her, kissing her softly on the lips. When he pulled away, Emily put her hands to her mouth. She tasted the wintergreen Tic Tac Isaac had been sucking on, and her lips tingled, as if they'd just been stung.

110

Isaac's eyes widened, registering Emily's expression. 'Was that ... okay?'

Emily smiled goofily. 'Yeah,' she said slowly. And as soon as the words left her lips, she knew that somehow, it *was* okay.

Isaac grinned as he took her mittened hand in his. Emily's head spun like it had just been on a few rounds of a carnival Tilt-a-Whirl ride.

Suddenly, her phone chirped again. 'Sorry. My friend just called,' she explained, reaching for it. 'It's probably her calling back.' She turned slightly away and looked at the screen: *One new text message.*

Emily's heart leapt to her throat. She looked around the vast, dark hill, but she and Isaac were the only people there. Slowly, she opened the text.

Hi, Em! Doesn't the Bible say good Christian boys shouldn't kiss girls like you? So WWAD – What Would A Do? I won't confess *your* sins if you don't confess *mine.* XX, A

14
Viva La Hanna!

A little later that Wednesday evening, Hanna hovered in the entrance of Rive Gauche, the King James Mall's French bistro, balling up her fists and releasing them. Serge Gainsbourg lilted out of the carefully hidden speakers, and the air smelled like steak frites, melted goat cheese, and Dior J'Adore. If Hanna shut her eyes, she could almost imagine it was last winter and Mona was at her side. Nothing had gone wrong yet – Ali's body hadn't turned up in that awful hole, there was no garish scar on her chin, no creepy Ian out on temporary bail, no new fake A notes. Hanna and Mona were still BFFs, checking out their reflections in the antique mirrors that hung over the booths and ogling the newest copies of *Elle* and *Us Weekly*.

She'd come to Rive Gauche since Mona, of course – Lucas worked here on the weekends, and he always slipped Hanna free Diet Cokes with the teensiest splash of rum. But it wasn't Lucas standing next to her tonight either. It was ... Kate.

Kate looked good – fabulous, even. Her chestnut hair was held back by a black silk headband. She wore a vermilion empire-waist dress with a pair of dark brown Loeffler Randall boots. Hanna was wearing her favorite black patent leather Marc Jacobs heels, a fuchsia cashmere cowl-neck, skinny jeans, and her favorite ultra-red Nars lipstick. Together, they looked a gazillion times better than Naomi and Riley, who were huddled like ugly garden gnomes at *Hanna*'s rightful table.

Hanna glowered. Naomi's super-short hair and stumpy neck made her look like a turtle. Riley's ratlike nose twitched as she wiped her nonexistent lips with a napkin.

Kate glanced at Hanna, registering what was happening. 'They're not your frenemies anymore, remember?' she said out of the corner of her mouth.

Hanna let out a sigh. In theory, she backed Kate's *if you can't beat 'em, join 'em* plan. But in reality ...

Kate faced Hanna. She was three inches taller than Hanna, so she had to look down at her when she talked. 'We need them as friends,' Kate said calmly. 'Strength in numbers.'

'It's just –'

'Do you even *know* why you hate them?' Kate snapped.

Hanna shrugged. She hated them because they were bitchy ... and because Ali had hated them. Only, Ali had never explained the odious thing Naomi and Riley had done that had made her drop them cold. And it wasn't like Hanna could've asked Naomi and Riley about what they'd done. Ali made Hanna and the others promise never to speak to Naomi and Riley, *ever*.

'Come on.' Kate put her hands on her hips. 'Let's do this.'

Hanna groaned, glowering at her soon-to-be stepsister. There was a tiny indication of a blemish at the corner of Kate's lip. Hanna wasn't sure if it was just a pimple ... or something else. She'd been obsessing over the puzzling secret Kate had alluded to yesterday at breakfast – that she'd slept with a guy, but it had led to a *complication*. Herpes was certainly a complication, wasn't it? And didn't herpes lead to cold sores?

'Fine, let's go,' Hanna snarled. Kate smiled, grabbed her hand again, and proceeded toward Naomi and Riley's table. The girls noticed them, waving at Kate but looking at Hanna suspiciously. Kate marched right up to the banquette and plopped down on the plushy red seat. 'How *are* you guys!' she squealed, giving them air kisses.

Naomi and Riley fawned over Kate for a few moments, admiring her dress, bracelet, and boots, pushing their uneaten fries in her direction. Then Naomi glanced at Hanna, who had remained standing by the dessert cart. 'What's *she* doing here?' she said in a low voice.

Kate pushed a fry into her mouth. She was, Hanna had observed, the kind of girl who could super-size everything and not gain an ounce. *Bitch*. 'Hanna's here because she has something to say to you guys,' Kate announced.

Riley raised an arched eyebrow. 'She does?'

Kate nodded, folding her hands. 'She wants to apologize for all the mean things she's done to you over the years.'

What? Hanna was too stunned to speak. Kate had said they should be *nice*, not sell out. Why should *she* apologize to Naomi and Riley? They'd done just as much to Hanna over the years as Hanna had done to them.

Kate continued. 'She wants to start fresh with you guys. She told me she didn't even know why you were fighting in the first place.'

Hanna shot Kate a look that could have frozen molten lava. But Kate didn't flinch. *Trust me*, her expression said. *This will work*.

Hanna faced forward, running her hand through her hair. 'Fine,' she mumbled, lowering her eyes. 'I'm sorry.'

'Good!' Kate crowed. She faced the others encouragingly. 'So, truce?'

Naomi and Riley glanced at each other, then smiled. 'Truce!' Naomi exclaimed loudly, making the diners at the next table look over in annoyance. 'Mona screwed us over, too. She acted all BFF and then dumped us after your car accident. For no reason at all!'

'Well, *now* we know the reason,' Riley corrected, raising a finger. 'She wanted to ditch us to get back on your good side so, like, no one would suspect that she hit you with her car.'

'God.' Riley pressed her palm to her chest. '*So* evil.'

Hanna winced. Did they really need to get into all that right now?

'Anyway, we feel so awful for what you had to go through, Hanna,' Naomi simpered. 'And we're sorry, too, about our fight. So truce, definitely!' She jiggled up and down excitedly.

'Great!' Kate cried. She nudged Hanna, and Hanna mustered a smile too.

'So sit, Hanna!' Naomi said. Hanna sat cautiously, feeling like a Chihuahua who had walked into a testy Rottweiler's yard. This seemed way too easy.

'We were just looking at the new *Teen Vogue*,' Riley announced, shoving a dog-eared magazine toward them. 'There's that benefit this weekend, after all. We have to beat all those ugly bitches to the best dresses.'

Hanna raised a suspicious eyebrow, noticing the date on the *Teen Vogue* cover. 'I thought this issue didn't come out for another few weeks.'

Riley took a sip of her seltzer and cranberry juice. 'My cousin works there. This is just a mock-up, but the issue's already been put to bed. She sends me early issues all the time. Sometimes she even sends me local sample-sale invites, stuff the public never gets invited to.'

Kate's blue eyes were saucers. 'Nice.'

Riley leafed through a few pages of the magazine and pointed at a flirty black cocktail dress. 'Omigod, this would look so beautiful on you, Hanna.'

'Who makes that?' Hanna leaned forward curiously.

'And this would look awesome with your eyes, Kate.' Naomi pointed at a robin's egg blue sheath by BCBG. 'Prada makes these gorgeous satin shoes in the exact same color. Have you been to the Prada store yet? It's just over there.' She pointed.

Kate shook her head. Naomi clapped her hand over her mouth, mock horrified.

Kate giggled and then glanced down at the magazine again. 'I bet we're supposed to bring dates to this benefit, right?' she said, touching the glossy pages. 'I don't even *know* any guys here.'

'You have nothing to worry about.' Naomi rolled her eyes. 'Every guy in school has been talking about you.'

Riley flipped a page. 'And Hanna, you already have a date.'

Hanna immediately tensed. Was that sarcasm she detected in Riley's voice? And what was with that ugly smile on Naomi's face? Suddenly, it hit her – they were going to make a snarky crack about Lucas. About his afterschool-club obsession, maybe, or about the queer vest he had to wear when he bussed tables at Rive Gauche, or that he wasn't a lacrosse player. There was even that ridiculous – and very untrue – rumor Ali had seeded years ago that Lucas was a hermaphrodite.

Hanna clenched her fists, waiting. She'd known this for-give-and-forget thing was too good to be true.

But Naomi simply gave Hanna a benign smile. Riley clucked her tongue. 'Lucky bitch.'

A model-thin waitress laid down the leather booklet with the check at the corner of the table. Across the room, a young couple in their twenties was sitting under Hanna's favorite old French poster, a green devil dancing with a bottle of absinthe. Hanna peeked at Naomi and Riley, the girls who had been her enemies for as long as she could remember. The things she and Mona used to tease them about suddenly didn't seem so valid anymore. Riley's love of leggings was actually pretty fashion-forward – she'd started wearing them before Rachel Zoe picked them out for Lindsay Lohan. And Naomi's new haircut *did* make her look chic, and she definitely got credit for trying something so daring.

She stared down at the magazine, suddenly feeling magnanimous. 'Riley, you'd look stunning in this Foley and Corrina,' she said, pointing to an emerald green gown.

'I was thinking the same thing!' Riley agreed, giving Hanna a high five. Then she got a cunning look on her face. 'You know, the mall's still open for another hour. Wanna hit Saks?'

Naomi's eyes lit up. She gazed at Hanna and Kate. 'What do you say, girls?'

Hanna suddenly felt like someone had wrapped her in a big, cozy cashmere scarf. Here she was at Rive Gauche with a group of girls, getting ready to hit all her favorite stores. It made everything she'd been worried about just minutes ago ooze away. Who had time to be bitter or afraid when there was shopping to be done with her new BFFs? Hanna thought of the dream she'd had when she was in the hospital after her accident, where Ali leaned over Hanna's hospital bed and told her everything was going to be okay. Maybe Dream Ali had been referring to *this* moment.

As she reached down to grab her bag to follow the others out, she noticed her BlackBerry was flashing with a new text. Hanna glanced up. Kate was busy shrugging into her princess-seamed coat, Naomi was signing the bill, and Riley was reapplying her lip gloss. The waiters swirled around Rive Gauche, taking orders and clearing plates. She tossed her hair behind her shoulders and opened the text.

Dear Little Piggy,
Those who don't remember the past are doomed to repeat it. Remember your unfortunate 'accident'? Tell anyone about little ol' moi, and this time I'll make sure you don't wake up. But just to show that I'm willing to play nice, here's a helpful hint: Someone in your life isn't what they seem.
Love ya! – A

'Hanna?'

Hanna covered the BlackBerry's screen fast. Kate was a few paces away, waiting by the marble-topped bar. 'Everything okay?'

Hanna took a deep breath, and slowly, the spots in front of her eyes receded. She let her cell phone slip back into her bag. *Whatever.* Screw knockoff A – anyone could have heard about that Little Piggy stuff and her accident. She was back on top where she belonged, and she wasn't about to let some stupid kid mess with her.

'Everything's perfect,' Hanna chirped, zipping up her bag. Then she strode across the restaurant and joined the others.

15
Even Libraries Aren't Safe

Spencer watched blankly as steam from her stainless-steel coffee carafe evaporated into the air. Andrew Campbell sat across from her, flipping a page of their massive AP econ textbook. He tapped a highlighted chart.

'Okay, this is talking about how the Federal Reserve controls the money supply,' Andrew explained. 'Like, if the Fed worries that the economy is going into a recession, it lowers its reserve requirements and interest rates for borrowing money. Remember when we talked about this in class?'

'Uh-huh,' Spencer mumbled vaguely. The only thing she knew about the Federal Reserve was that when it lowered interest rates, her parents got all excited because that meant their stocks would go up and her mother could redecorate the living room – *again*. But Spencer didn't recall talking about this in class at all. She felt the same frustrated, helpless feeling about AP econ as she did about her recurring dream of being trapped in an underground room that was slowly filling with water. Every time she tried to dial 911, the numbers on the phone kept moving around on her. And then the buttons turned to gummy bears and the water rose over her mouth and nose.

It was after 8 P.M. on Wednesday night, and Spencer and Andrew were sitting in one of the Rosewood Public Library's private, book-lined study rooms, going over the latest econ unit. Because she'd plagiarized an econ paper, Rosewood Day had mandated that if she didn't get an A this semester, she would be removed from the class permanently. Her parents certainly weren't going to shell out the money for a tutor – and they still hadn't reopened Spencer's credit card accounts – so Spencer had broken down and called Andrew, who had the highest grade in the class. Weirdly, Andrew had been happy to meet with her, even though they had tons of AP English, calculus, and chemistry homework tonight.

'And then there's the monetary equation of exchange here,' Andrew said, tapping the book again. 'You remember this? Let's do some chapter problems using it.'

A piece of Andrew's thick blond hair fell over his eyes as he reached for his calculator. She thought she detected the chestnutty smell of Kiehl's Facial Fuel, her favorite guy soap smell. Had he always used that, or was it something new? She was pretty sure he hadn't worn it to Foxy, the last time she'd been this close to him.

'Earth to Spencer?' Andrew waved his hand in front of her face. 'Hello?'

Spencer blinked. 'Sorry,' she stammered.

Andrew folded his hands over the textbook. 'Have you heard anything I've said?'

'Sure,' Spencer assured him, although when she tried to remember, her brain called up other things instead. Like the A note they'd received after Ian was released on bail. Or the news reports about Ian's upcoming trial on Friday. Or that her mother was planning a fund-raiser without her. Or, the clincher, that Spencer might not truly have been to the Hastings manor born.

Melissa didn't have much to back up the theory she'd blurted out Tuesday night. Her only proof that Spencer was possibly adopted was that their cousin Smith had teased her about it once when they were little. Genevieve had quickly spanked him and sent him to his room. And, come to think of it, Melissa couldn't remember their mother actually being pregnant with Spencer for nine months, either.

It wasn't much, but the more Spencer thought about it, the more it felt like an important puzzle piece snapping into place. Except for their similarly colored dirty-blond hair, she and Melissa looked nothing alike. And Spencer always wondered why her mom had acted so spazzy when she caught Spencer, Ali, and the others playing We Are All Secretly Sisters in sixth grade. They'd made up this fantasy that their birth mother was really worldly, rich, and connected, but she'd lost her five beautiful daughters in the Kuala Lumpur airport (mostly because they liked the words *Kuala Lumpur*) because she was schizo (mostly because they liked the word *schizo*). Usually Mrs. Hastings pretended Spencer and her friends didn't exist. But when she'd heard what they were doing, she'd quickly interjected, saying it wasn't funny to joke about mental illness or mothers abandoning their children. But hello? It was a *game*.

It explained a lot of other things, too. Like why her parents always favored Melissa over Spencer. Why they were always so disappointed in her. Maybe it wasn't disappointment at all – maybe they were snubbing her because she wasn't really a Hastings. But why hadn't they admitted it years ago? Adoption wasn't scandalous. Kirsten Cullen was adopted; her birth mother was from South Africa. The first show-and-tell of every elementary school year, Kirsten would bring in pictures from her summer trip to Cape Town, her birthplace, and every girl in Spencer's class would ooh with jealousy. Spencer used to wish she'd been adopted too. It seemed so exotic.

Spencer stared through the study room's porthole window at the enormous blue modern art mobile hanging from the library ceiling. 'Sorry,' she admitted to Andrew. 'I'm a little stressed.'

Andrew furrowed his brow. 'Because of econ?'

Spencer breathed in, ready to shoo him away and tell him it was none of his business. Only, he was looking at her so eagerly, and he *was* helping her. She thought more about that horrible night at Foxy. Andrew had been really excited when he thought they were actually going on a date, but had become dejected and angry when he found out Spencer was just using him. All that A and Toby Cavanaugh stuff had happened right after Andrew found out that she was dating someone else. Had Spencer even properly apologized?

Spencer began capping her multicolored highlighters and putting them back in their plastic sleeve, careful to make sure the markers were all turned the exact same way. Just as she slid the electric blue pen back in its place, everything inside her started to fizz, like she was a science-fair volcano about to bubble over.

'I got this application to Yale's pre-college summer program in the mail yesterday, and my mother threw it away before I could even look at it,' she blurted out. She couldn't tell Andrew about Ian or A, but it felt good to at least say *something*. 'She said there was no chance in hell Yale would be letting me in to their summer program. And ... and my parents are planning a Rosewood Day fund-raiser this weekend, but my mom didn't even tell me about it. Usually I help her plan them. And then my grandmother died on Monday, and –'

'Your grandmother died?' Andrew's eyes widened. 'Why didn't you say anything?'

Spencer blinked, thrown off track. Why *would* she tell Andrew her grandmother died? It wasn't as if they were friends. 'I don't know. But anyway, she left a will, and I wasn't in it,' she went on. 'At first I thought it was because of this Golden Orchid mess, but then my sister was talking about how the will said *natural-born grandchildren*. I didn't believe her right away, but then I started thinking about it. It makes perfect sense. I should've known.'

'Slow down,' Andrew said, shaking his head. 'I don't understand. You should've known ... what?'

Spencer took a breath. 'Sorry,' she said softly. '*Natural-born grandchildren* means that one of us is *not* naturally born. It means I'm ... adopted.'

Spencer tapped her nails against the wood-grain patterns in the study room's big mahogany desk. Someone had etched *Angela is a slut* into the surface. It felt weird for Spencer to say the words out loud – *I'm adopted.*

'Maybe it's a good thing,' Spencer mused, stretching her long legs under the table. 'Maybe my real mother would actually care about me. And maybe I could get out of Rosewood.'

Andrew was silent. Spencer glanced at him, wondering if she'd said something offensive. Finally he turned and looked straight into her eyes.

'I love you,' Andrew announced.

Spencer's eyes popped out. '*Excuse* me?'

'It's a Web site,' Andrew went on, unfazed. His chair creaked as he leaned back. 'I love you dot com. Or maybe *you* is just the letter *u*, I'm not sure. It matches adopted kids

123

to their birth mothers. This girl I met on the trip to Greece told me about it. She wrote me the other day saying it worked. She's meeting her birth mother next week.'

'Oh.' Spencer pretended to smooth down her already perfectly ironed skirt, feeling a little flustered. Of course she hadn't thought Andrew was actually saying he loved *her* or anything.

'Do you want to register for it?' Andrew began to load his books into his backpack. 'If you're not adopted, they just won't find a match. If you are ... maybe they will.'

'Um ...' Spencer's head spun. 'Okay. Sure.'

Andrew made a beeline through the library for the computer lab, and Spencer followed. The main reading room was mostly empty save for a few late-night studiers, two boys hovering around the copier, no doubt contemplating whether to copy their faces or their butts, and what looked like a cult meeting – every single middle-aged woman was in some sort of blue hat. Spencer thought she saw someone quickly duck behind one of the autobiography shelves, but when she looked again, no one was there.

The computer lab was at the front of the library, surrounded on all sides by large glass windows. Andrew sat down at a console and Spencer pulled out a chair next to him. He wiggled the mouse, and the screen flickered on. 'Okay.' Andrew started typing and tilted the screen toward Spencer. 'See?'

Reconnecting families, announced flowery pink script at the top of the page. On the left of the screen were a series of pictures and testimonials from people who had already used the service. Spencer wondered if Andrew's little Greece friend was pictured – and if she was pretty. Not that she would have been jealous or anything.

Spencer clicked on a link that said, *Sign up here*. A new

page popped up, asking her to answer various questions about herself, which the site would then use to match Spencer with her potential mother.

Spencer's eyes floated back to the testimonials. *I thought I would never find my son!* Sadie, age forty-nine, wrote. *Now we're reunited and best friends!* A girl named Angela, twenty-four, exclaimed, *I always wondered who my true mother was. Now I've found her, and we're starting an accessories business together!* Spencer knew the world wasn't this innocent and naïve – things didn't work out this easily. But she couldn't help but hope all the same.

She swallowed hard. 'What if it actually works?'

Andrew pushed his hands into his blazer pockets. 'Well, that's good, right?'

Spencer rubbed her jaw, took a deep breath, and started to type her name, cell phone number, and e-mail address. She filled in the blanks of where and when she'd been born, any health problems she'd had, and her blood type. When she got to the question that asked, *Please explain why you're conducting this search*, her fingers hovered over the keyboard, searching for the appropriate answer. *Because my family hates me*, she wanted to type. *Because I mean nothing to them.*

Andrew shifted over her shoulder. *Curiosity*, Spencer finally typed. Then she took a deep breath and hit Send.

'Twinkle, Twinkle, Little Star' tinkled over the computer's tiny speakers, and onto the screen floated an animated picture of a stork flying around the world, as if diligently searching for Spencer's match.

Spencer cracked her knuckles, numb to what she'd just done. As she looked around, everything suddenly seemed unfamiliar. She'd been coming to this library all her life, but she'd never noticed that all the oil paintings on the computer

125

room's walls were of woodsy landscapes. Or that the big sign on the back of the door said, LIBRARY USERS: WHEN ON INTERNET, NO FACEBOOK OR MYSPACE EVER! She'd never really looked at the sand-colored wood floors, or the huge, pentagon-shaped lamps that hung majestically from the library ceiling.

When she glanced at Andrew, he was kind of unfamiliar too – in a good way. Spencer blushed, feeling vulnerable. 'Thank you.'

'You're welcome.' Andrew stood up and leaned against the doorjamb. 'So, you feel less stressed?'

She nodded. 'Yeah. I do.'

'Good.' Andrew smiled and checked his watch. 'I have to go, but I'll see you in class tomorrow.'

Spencer watched as he strode through the library, waved to Mrs. Jamison, the librarian, and pushed out through the turnstile. She then turned back to the computer, logging into her e-mail. The adoption site had sent her a welcome message, stating that she would most likely hear results in anywhere from the next few days to six months. As she was about to log out, a new e-mail popped up in her inbox. The sender's name was a jumble of letters and numbers, and the subject line read, *I'm watching*.

Prickles ran up Spencer's back. She opened the e-mail and squinted at the words.

I thought we were friends, Spence. I send you a sweet little note, and you call the cops ... What do I have to do to keep you girls quiet? Actually, don't tempt me! – A

'Oh my God,' Spencer whispered.

A thumping noise sounded behind her. Spencer turned, her

126

muscles rigid. No one else was in the computer room. A spotlight shone on the courtyard behind the library, but there wasn't a single footprint in the bright white snow. Then Spencer noticed something on the outside of one of the windowpanes – a quickly fading smudge from someone's breath.

Spencer's blood turned cold. *I'm watching*. Someone had been right there just seconds ago ... and she hadn't had any idea.

16
Weirdos Attract

The next morning, Aria walked downstairs, rubbing her eyes. The smell of the organic coffee Ella bought at the farmer's market – one of the few items she paid premium price for without complaining – lured her to the kitchen. Ella had already left for work, but Mike was at the table, inhaling a bowl of Fruity Pebbles and Twittering on his iPhone. When Aria saw who was sitting next to Mike, she let out a startled cry.

'Oh.' Xavier looked up, alarmed. 'Hey.'

Xavier was wearing a plain white T-shirt and very familiar plaid pajama pants. At first, Aria thought they might be ones Byron had left behind, but then she realized they were *Ella's*. Byron's favorite old Hollis College coffee mug sat in front of Xavier's place, as did today's *Philadelphia Inquirer* cryptoquote. Aria pressed her arms tightly and chastely against her chest. She hadn't thought she needed to put on a bra for breakfast.

A horn honked outside. The chair made an angry scrape as Mike stood up, milk dribbling from his chin. 'That's Noel.' He grabbed his enormous bag of lacrosse gear and regarded Xavier. 'Wii tonight, right?'

'I'll be there,' Xavier answered.

Aria looked at her watch. 'It's seven twenty.' School started in an hour, and Mike usually procrastinated until the very last second.

'We're getting a prime seat at Steam so we can check out Hanna Marin and her hot stepsister.' Mike's eyes goggled. 'Have you *seen* that Kate girl? I can't believe the two of them live together! You talk to Hanna sometimes – do you know if they sleep in the same bed?'

Aria gave him an exasperated look. 'Do you honestly expect me to answer that?'

Mike hefted his bag over his shoulder and sauntered into the hall, knocking over the enormous frog-faced totem pole Ella had found at a junk shop in Turkey. The front door slammed heavily. Aria heard an engine gunning ... and then nothing.

The house was maddeningly still. The only thing Aria heard was the Indian sitar music Ella always listened to before work – she often left it on all day, maintaining that it was soothing for their cat, Polo, and the plants.

'Do you want a part of the paper?' Xavier broke the silence.

He held up the front page. Splayed across the top was the headline *Ian Thomas Vows to Find Real DiLaurentis Killer Before Trial Tomorrow*. Aria shuddered. 'That's okay.' She quickly poured herself a cup of coffee and headed back toward the stairs.

'Wait,' Xavier said loudly. Aria stopped so abruptly, some of her coffee spilled to the floor. 'I'm sorry if I might have made you uncomfortable at the restaurant last night,' Xavier said solemnly. 'That's the last thing I meant to do. And I wanted to be gone before you came down today – I didn't want to skeev you out more. I know how weird this must be.'

129

Aria wanted to ask if he meant that it must be weird because he knew she had been interested in him, or because he was dating her not-yet-divorced mom.

'It's … fine.' Aria set her coffee down on the telephone table next to the door. It was littered with a whole bunch of flyers and postcards of Xavier's recent shows – Ella must have been boning up on his work. Then she adjusted her way-too-short gray terry-cloth pajama shorts. If only she hadn't been wearing the ones with the enormous pink Pegasus silk-screened across the butt.

She thought about the A note she'd received at Rabbit Rabbit yesterday. Wilden had promised to call her once he traced the origin of her latest A note. She hoped she'd hear from him today so she could put the whole thing behind her.

Aria had debated just explaining the photos of her and Xavier to Ella before A had the chance. She tried to picture it. *The thing is, I kind of liked Xavier before you started dating him*, she could say. *But it's not like I do now! So if anyone sends you a note or pictures, ignore them, okay?* But their relationship was just too fragile to broach something like this – especially if she didn't need to.

In truth, Wilden was probably right. The notes had to be from some dumb kid. And there wasn't much of a reason to be angry at Xavier – all he'd done was draw a sketch of her – a really *good* sketch. That was it. Even if Ella saw the pictures A had sent Aria, Xavier would jump in to explain that nothing had been going on. He probably hadn't even realized the message he'd sent, drawing Aria's portrait in such detail. Xavier was an *artiste*, after all, and artists weren't the most socially adept creatures in the world. Take Byron: When he'd held cocktail parties for his Hollis under-grad students, he'd often hidden up in the bedroom, forcing Ella to entertain.

Xavier stood up, wiping his chin with a napkin. 'How about I make it up to you? I'll go get dressed and then give you a ride to school.'

Aria lowered her shoulders. Ella had taken the car to work that morning, and getting a ride definitely beat taking the Rosewood Day bus, which was filled with elementary school boys who never got tired of farting contests. 'Okay,' she agreed. 'Thanks.'

Twenty minutes later, Aria was shrugging into the black bouclé coat she'd bought at a vintage shop in Paris and stepping out onto the front porch. Xavier's car, a pristinely restored, late-sixties BMW 2002, chugged in the driveway. Aria slid into the front seat, admiring the sleek chrome interior. 'Now *this* is how an old car should look.' She whistled, impressed. 'Have you seen my mom's ancient Honda? There's mold growing on the seats.'

Xavier chuckled. 'My dad had one of these when I was growing up.' He began to back out of the driveway. 'After my parents divorced and he moved to Oregon, I missed the car more than him.'

He glanced at Aria, giving her a sympathetic look. 'I really *do* know how weird this is, you know. My mom started dating right away after she got divorced. I hated it.'

So that's what he'd meant. Aria stared pointedly in the other direction, watching a couple of younger public school students crunch clumsily over the quickly melting snowdrifts at the bus stop. The last thing she wanted to hear was another *I've been there* story. Sean Ackard, who she'd gone out with for about a minute this fall, had earnestly revealed his struggles with his mom's death and his dad's remarriage. And Ezra had bemoaned that when his parents divorced, he'd smoked tons of pot. Woo-hoo, everyone else's lives sucked ass too. It didn't really make Aria's problems any easier.

'All my mom's boyfriends tried to bond with me,' Xavier went on. 'Every single one of them brought me sports equipment, like baseball gloves, basketballs, once even a whole hockey uniform, complete with pads and stuff. If they'd *really* attempted to learn anything about me, they would've known to bring me a handheld mixer. Or Bundt cake pans. Or muffin tins.'

Aria looked over, intrigued. 'Muffin tins?'

Xavier smiled sheepishly. 'I was really into baking.' He hit the brakes at a crosswalk, waiting for a bunch of little kids to pass. 'It helped to calm me down. I was especially good at meringues. This was before I discovered art. I was the only guy in my school's home ec club. Actually, that's where my Match.com nickname comes from – Wolfgang. I was obsessed with Wolfgang Puck when I was in high school. He had this restaurant in L.A. called Spago, and this one time, I drove down there from Seattle, where I went to high school, thinking I could just walk in without reservations.' He rolled his eyes. 'I ended up eating at Arby's.'

Aria looked at him, noting his serious expression. She burst out laughing. 'You are *such* a girl.'

'I know.' Xavier ducked his head. 'I wasn't very popular in high school. No one really got me.'

Aria ran her fingers through her long, black ponytail. 'I used to be really unpopular too.'

'You?' Xavier waved his hand. 'Nah.'

'It's true,' Aria said quietly. 'No one understood me at all.'

She sat back in the seat, thrust into thought. Aria had always tried very hard not to dwell on the lonely, friendless years before she'd become friends with Ali, but seeing that black-and-white photo of her the other day – the one from when Time Capsule was announced – had jostled a whole bunch of memories free.

132

When Aria was in fourth grade, everyone in her Rosewood Day class was friends with everyone else. But in fifth, things suddenly ... changed. Tight-knit cliques cropped up literally overnight, and everyone knew their place. It was like a game of musical chairs: after the music stopped, all her classmates easily found a seat, while Aria was still floundering around, chairless.

Aria tried to find a group of friends. One week, she dressed in black and Doc Martens and loitered around the hooligans that shoplifted from Wawa and shared cigarettes behind the dragon-shaped slide before school. But she had nothing in common with them. They all despised reading, even fun things like *Narnia*. Another week, she dug out her frilly vintage clothes and tried to hang with the prissy girls who loved Hello Kitty and thought boys were gross. But they were so high-maintenance. One of the girls cried for *three hours* because she'd accidentally stepped on a ladybug at recess. No group fit her, so Aria eventually stopped trying. She spent a lot of time by herself, ignoring everyone else as best she could.

Everyone, that was, except Ali. Sure, Ali was a Typical Rosewood Girl, but something about her fascinated Aria. The day Ali strolled out of the school and announced she was going to win Time Capsule, Aria couldn't help but sketch Ali's beautiful, heart-shaped face and stunning smile. She envied how effortless Ali was around boys – even older ones like Ian. But the thing Aria liked most about Ali was Ali's gorgeous, sensitive older brother.

The day Jason strutted up to Ian and told him to leave Ali alone, Aria had already developed a full-blown, unbridled, very painful crush on him. For weeks, she'd been sneaking over to the high school library during her free periods to watch him studying with his German class. She would hide behind a tree that overlooked the soccer fields to spy on him as he stretched near the goalie pen. Sometimes she would leaf through old yearbooks in the yearbook room to find out all the information she could about Jason. It was one of the few times Aria was glad not to have any friends. She could enjoy her unrequited crush in peace, without having to explain it to anyone.

Right after Time Capsule was announced, Aria slipped Byron's signed copy of *Slaughterhouse-Five* in her knapsack – one of the things she'd read about Jason in an old yearbook was how much he loved Kurt Vonnegut. Aria's heart pounded as she waited for Jason to emerge from the Journalism Barn after his Principles of Newspaper Writing class. When she saw him, she reached into her bag for the book, hoping to show it to him as he walked by. When Jason found out Aria liked Vonnegut too, maybe he'd realize they were soul mates.

But Mrs. Wagner, the high school's head secretary, cut in front of Aria at the last minute and grabbed Jason's arm. There was an important call for him in the office. 'A girl,' Mrs. Wagner explained. Jason's face clouded. He brushed past Aria without even looking at her. Aria dropped the book back into her bag, embarrassed. The girl on the phone was probably Jason's age and stunningly beautiful, while Aria was just some sixth-grade freak. The day after that, Aria, Emily, Spencer, and Hanna had all shown up in Ali's backyard at the same time. They'd clearly all had the same hope and plan: to snag Ali's Time Capsule flag. By that point, Aria didn't care so much about stealing Ali's flag – she just wanted another opportunity to see Jason. Little did she know at the time that she'd finally get her wish. Xavier pulled up the old BMW's brake, jolting Aria back to reality. They were in a parking space right in front of Rosewood Day. 'I still don't feel like people get me,' Aria concluded, staring at the stately brick school in front of them. 'Even now.'

'Well, maybe that's because you're an artist,' Xavier said gently. 'Artists never feel understood. But that's what makes you special.'

Aria ran her fingers along the sides of her yak-fur bag. 'Thanks,' she said, really appreciating his words. Then she added with a smirk, '*Wolfgang.*'

Xavier winced. 'Later.' He waved and drove away.

Aria watched as his BMW snaked down the long drive and out to the street. Then, she heard what sounded like a giggle, close in her ear. She whipped around, trying to figure out where it was coming from, but no one was looking at her. The school's parking lot was packed with kids. Devon Arliss and Mason Byers were trying to shove each other into a dirty patch of slush. Scott Chin, the yearbook photographer, was aiming his camera at the gnarled bare upper branches of a tree, and beyond him, Jenna Cavanaugh and her guide dog were standing on the slippery walk. Jenna's head was held high, her pale skin shone, and her dark hair fanned out over her red wool trench. If it weren't for the white cane and the service dog, Jenna would've been a gorgeous Typical Rosewood.

Jenna had paused just a few yards from Aria, seemingly staring right at her.

Aria paused for a moment. 'Hi, Jenna,' she called quietly.

Jenna cocked her head – not hearing, and certainly not seeing – before she pulled on the dog's collar and continued down the path into the school.

Goose bumps began to rise up on Aria's arms and legs, and an icy shiver went from the top of her head all the way down to her feet. Even though it was frigid outside, Aria was pretty sure neither response was due to the weather.

17

Oh, The Sacrifices To Be Popular

'Something about Kirsten Cullen looks fatter,' Naomi whispered in Hanna's ear. 'Is it her upper arms?'

'Definitely,' Hanna whispered back. 'But that's what happens when you drink full-calorie beer at Christmas parties.' She watched as Sienna Morgan, a pretty sophomore, walked past, her prized monogrammed Vuitton tote swinging. 'And you guys know the truth about Sienna's bag, right?' She looked around at the others, pausing for dramatic effect. 'She got it at an *outlet*.'

Naomi clapped her hand over her mouth. Riley stuck out her tongue, disgusted. Kate flicked her chestnut hair over her shoulder, reaching inside her own, bona fide Vuitton bag for lipstick. 'I hear the stuff at outlets is fake,' Kate murmured.

It was Thursday morning before school, and Hanna was sitting with Kate, Naomi, and Riley at Steam's best table. Classical music began to play over the loudspeakers, which meant it was time to get moving to homeroom. Hanna and Kate stood up and linked arms, and Naomi and Riley brought up the rear. They were a four-girl parade, with a small entourage of guys following. Hanna's auburn hair bounced. Naomi looked fashion-forward in her forest green ankle boots. Normally flat-chested Riley looked rather buxom today, thanks to the Wonderbra they'd made her get at the King James yesterday. It had definitely been the best shopping spree Hanna had been on in a long time. No wonder the small knot of sophomore girls by the lost-and-found were gazing at them with envy. No wonder Noel Kahn, Mike Montgomery, James Freed, and the rest of the lacrosse team had been ogling them from a table at the back of the café. Only a handful of hours had passed since Hanna apologized to Naomi and Riley, but everyone in school already understood that *they* were the people to envy, the girls to know. And it felt *so* frickin' good.

Suddenly, Hanna felt a hand on her arm. 'Do you have a sec?'

Spencer twitched against the lockers. Her dirty-blond hair was pulled off her face and her eyes darted back and forth. It seemed as if the little mechanical key in her back had been wound way too tight. 'Uh, I'm busy,' Hanna said, trying to walk past.

Spencer pulled her into the water fountain alcove anyway. Kate glanced over her shoulder, raising an eyebrow, but Hanna waved her on. She turned back to her old friend. 'God, *what*?' she snapped.

'I got another note last night.' Spencer shoved her Sidekick under Hanna's nose. 'Look.'

Hanna read the text silently. *I thought we were friends, Spence!* Blah, blah, blah. 'So?' she snapped.

'I was in the Rosewood library at the time. And when I turned around, I saw steam on the window. *Breath marks.* I swear to God it's Ian. He's watching us.'

Hanna sniffed. This probably would be the time to

mention her own A note from yesterday, but that would mean she believed the notes were something to be afraid of. 'Wilden told us it's just a copycat,' she whispered. 'Not Ian.'

'It's got to be Ian!' Spencer shrieked so shrilly that a pack of younger girls dressed in winter cheerleading uniforms looked over in alarm. 'He's out of jail. He doesn't want us to testify against him, so he's trying to scare us. It totally makes sense, doesn't it?'

'Ian's under lockdown,' Hanna reminded her. 'This is probably just from some loser kid from Rosewood who saw you on the news, thought you were hot, and thinks this is a way to get your attention. And you know what? He has your attention. He's won. The best thing you can do is just ignore him.'

'Aria got another note too.' Spencer whipped her head around and looked down the hall, as if Aria would miraculously materialize. 'Did she say anything about it to you? Do you know if Emily has gotten any?'

'Why don't you bother Wilden with this instead?' Hanna said hurriedly, taking a step back.

'Do you think I should?' Spencer put her finger to her chin. 'This note says I should keep quiet.'

Hanna groaned. 'You are so lame,' she said. 'It's. A. Fake.'

With that, she gave Spencer a parting shrug and whirled away. Spencer let out a squeak of disbelief, but Hanna ignored her. She was not about to let Knockoff A manipulate her – she would *not* be that scared, weak little girl from just a few months ago. Her life was different now.

Kate, Naomi, and Riley were clumped at the end of the hall near the big picture window that looked out onto the snowy soccer fields. Hanna rushed back to them, hoping she hadn't missed anything good. The three of them were chattering about what they were going to wear to the

Rosewood Day charity benefit at Spencer's house Saturday night. The plan was to spray-tan at Sun Land in the morning, get mani-pedis at Fermata in the afternoon, and then change and do makeup at Naomi's before hopping in a rented town car. They'd considered arriving in a stretch Hummer limo, but Kate had informed them that Hummers were *so* two years ago.

'Society photographers might be there, so I'm going to go for my Derek Lam halter dress.' Naomi swept a lock of long white-blond bangs out of her eyes. 'My mom said I had to save it for prom, but I know she'll forget in a week and let me get something else.'

'Or we could all dress alike,' Riley suggested, pausing to gaze into her Dior compact. 'What about those Sweetface dresses we saw at Saks yesterday?'

'Sweetface, blegh.' Naomi stuck out her tongue. 'Celebs should *not* be allowed to design clothes.'

'Those dresses are totally short and cute,' Riley urged, not giving up.

'Stop cat-fighting,' Kate said, bored. 'We'll go to the King James again this afternoon, okay? There are probably tons of stores we didn't hit. We'll all find something fabulous. What do you think, Hanna?'

'Done.' Hanna nodded. Naomi and Riley quickly straightened up and agreed.

'And we need to find you a boyfriend, too, Kate.' Naomi wound her arm around Kate's waist. 'There are so many cuties in this town.'

'What about Noel's brother Eric?' Riley suggested, edging her scrawny butt against the heat vents by the windowsill. 'He's so hot.'

'He went out with Mona, though.' Naomi glanced at Hanna. 'Is that, like, weird?'

'Nah,' Hanna said quickly. For the first time, she didn't feel a twinge at hearing Mona's name.

'Eric *would* be perfect for Kate.' Naomi widened her eyes. 'I heard that when he was dating Briony Kogan, they snuck off to New York and stayed in a penthouse at the Mandarin Oriental. Eric took her on a carriage ride around Central Park and bought her a love bracelet from Cartier.'

'I heard that *too*.' Riley swooned.

'Well, I certainly could use some romance like that,' Kate admitted. She shot Hanna a covert pout. Hanna nodded back, catching Kate's oblique reference to her secret, the disastrous, *complicated* relationship with Herpes Boy in Annapolis. Though Kate still hadn't confirmed it was herpes, she'd asked that Hanna not get into it with their new friends.

Hanna felt another hand on her arm and exasperatedly turned, thinking it was Spencer again. Instead, it was Lucas.

'Oh, hi.' Hanna coolly ran her hands through her hair. Over the past few days, she'd communicated with Lucas via only a few terse e-mails and texts, ignoring his repeated calls. But she'd been busy cultivating her new clique, which was as delicate an art as hand-beading a couture gown. Surely Lucas would understand.

Hanna noticed a tiny speck of what looked like pink donut frosting on the tip of Lucas's nose. Normally, she found Lucas's inability to get all of his food in his mouth cute, but with Kate, Naomi, and Riley here, it was embarrassing. She quickly wiped it off. She wished she could also tuck in his shirt, tie the laces on one of his Converse sneakers, and muss up his hair a little – it appeared he'd forgotten to use the Ceylon-scented styling gel she'd bought him at Sephora – but that might seem really high-maintenance.

Kate stepped forward, grinning broadly. 'Hi, Lucas. Nice to see you again.'

Lucas's eyes darted back and forth from Kate's arm, which was linked around Hanna's, to Hanna's face, then back to Kate's arm again. Hanna smiled dumbly, praying that Lucas would keep his mouth shut. The last time he'd seen Hanna and Kate together was over winter break, when he'd picked Hanna up to go skiing. Hanna hadn't even bothered to acknowledge Kate, pretending like she was merely another piece of living room furniture. She hadn't had time to tell him about the latest turn of events.

Kate cleared her throat, looking amused. 'Well. We should leave the lovebirds alone, girls.'

'I'll catch up with you,' Hanna said tightly.

'Bye, Lucas,' Kate trilled as she, Naomi, and Riley clacked down the hall.

Lucas shifted the books in his arms. 'So ...'

'I know what you're going to say,' Hanna interrupted, her vocal cords taut. 'I decided to give Kate a chance.'

'But I thought you said she was demonic.'

Hanna put her hands on her hips. 'What am I supposed to do? She lives in my house. My father basically told me that he'll disown me if I'm not nice to her. She apologized to me, and I decided to accept her apology. Why can't you just be happy for me?'

'Okay, okay.' Lucas stepped back in surrender. 'I *am* happy for you. I didn't mean for it to sound like I wasn't. I'm sorry.'

Hanna let out a long, fiery breath through her nose. 'It's fine.' But Lucas had killed her buzz. She strained to hear what Kate, Naomi, and Riley were saying, but they were too far away. Were they still talking about dresses, or had they moved on to shoes?

Lucas waved an arm in front of Hanna, a concerned look on his face. 'Are you okay? You seem kind of … weird.'

Hanna snapped back to him, mustering up the best smile she could. 'I'm fine. Great, actually. But we should go, right? We're going to be late to class.'

Lucas nodded, still looking at Hanna funny. Finally, he sighed, leaned over, and kissed her neck. 'We'll talk more about this later.'

Hanna watched Lucas as he loped down the hall to the science wing. Over the winter break, Hanna and Lucas had built a huge snowwoman in the snow, something Hanna hadn't done since she was little. Lucas had given the snow-woman big plastic surgery boobs, and Hanna had tied her Burberry scarf around the snowwoman's neck. After they finished, they had a snowball fight, then went inside and baked chocolate chip cookies. Hanna virtuously ate only *two*.

It had been Hanna's favorite winter break memory, but now she wondered if she and Lucas should've been doing something more mature. Like sneaking off to the Mandarin Oriental in New York City, for example, and shopping for jewelry on Fifth Avenue.

The halls were almost empty, and many of the teachers were shutting their classroom doors. Hanna started down the hall, tossing her hair and trying her hardest to snap out of her weirdness. A tiny beeping sound from inside her bag made her jump. Her cell phone.

A small seed of worry began to throb in the pit of Hanna's stomach. When she looked at the screen, she was relieved to see it was just from Lucas. *I forgot to ask*, he wrote. *Are we still hanging out this afternoon? Text me when you get this.*

The between-classes classical music went silent, meaning

Hanna was late. She'd forgotten that she'd offered to help Lucas pick out new jeans at the mall. But she hated the idea of Kate, Naomi, and Riley dress-shopping without her, and it seemed weird to have Lucas tag along.

Can't, she replied, typing while walking. *Sorry*.

She hit Send and clapped her phone shut. When she turned the corner, she saw her new BFFs standing at the end of the hallway, waiting for her. She smiled and caught up to them, pushing her sinking, guilty feelings out of her head. After all, she was Hanna Marin, and she was fabulous.

18
A Jury Of One

Thursday evening, Spencer sat at the dinner table all alone. Melissa had left with friends an hour ago, and her parents had made themselves scarce and then pointedly breezed out the front door, barely saying good-bye. She'd had to scavenge in the fridge for some leftover cartons of Chinese food for dinner.

She stared at the pile of mail on the kitchen table. Fenniworth College, some podunk school in central Pennsylvania, had sent her a catalogue and an accompanying letter saying they would be thrilled to show her around their campus. But the only reason Fenniworth was still willing to let Spencer apply was probably because of how much money her family had. Money she'd thought she was entitled to – until now.

Spencer pulled her Sidekick out of her pocket and checked her e-mail inbox for the third time in fifteen minutes. Nothing from the adoption site. Nothing else from that creepy new A. And, unfortunately, nothing from Wilden. At Hanna's suggestion, she'd called him about the note she'd received in the library, adding that she was positive someone had been watching her through the windows.

But Wilden had seemed distracted. Or maybe he didn't believe her – perhaps he thought Spencer was an unreliable witness too. He'd reassured her yet again that this was just some bored kid making trouble, and that he and the rest of the Rosewood PD were investigating the origin of the notes. Then he'd hung up on Spencer when she was in the middle of a sentence. She'd stared at the phone, peeved.

Candace, the family's housekeeper, started scrubbing the stove, filling the room with eucalyptus-scented cleaner. The latest season of *America's Next Top Model*, Candace's favorite show, droned on the little flat-screen TV above the cabinets. The caterers had just come to drop off some of the ingredients for Saturday's fund-raiser, and the alcohol distributor had brought in several cases of wine. A few magnum bottles sat on the kitchen island, constant reminders that Spencer was *not included* in these preparations. If she had been, she certainly wouldn't have ordered merlot – she would've gone for something classier, like Barolo.

Spencer looked up at the TV, staring as a bunch of pretty girls walked down a makeshift runway in a morgue, modeling what looked like crosses between bikinis and straitjackets. Suddenly, the TV went dark. Spencer cocked her head. Candace let out a frustrated grunt. A news logo flashed on the screen. 'We have breaking news from Rosewood,' said a voice-over. Spencer reached over to the remote and turned up the volume.

A bug-eyed reporter with a crew cut stood in front of the Rosewood courthouse. 'We have an update about the much-anticipated Alison DiLaurentis murder trial,' he announced. 'Despite speculation about lack of evidence, the D.A.'s office announced just minutes ago that the trial will take place as scheduled.'

Spencer pulled her cashmere cardigan closer around her,

letting out a huge sigh of relief. Then the broadcast cut to a shot of the front of Ian's house, a big, rambling compound with an American flag prominently over the front porch. 'Mr. Thomas has been released on temporary bail until his trial begins,' the reporter's voice announced off-camera. 'We spoke with him last night to see how he was doing.'

Ian's image swam onto the screen. 'I'm innocent,' he protested, his eyes wide. 'Someone else is guilty of this, not me.'

'Ugh,' Candace spat, shaking her head. 'I can't believe that boy was ever in this house!' She picked up a can of Febreeze and squirted it toward the TV camera, as if Ian's mere presence on the screen had let a bad odor into the room.

The report ended, and *ANTM* came back on. Spencer stood up, feeling dizzy. She needed to get some air ... and clear Ian from her head. She stumbled out the back door and onto the patio, a chilly gust of wind hitting her in the face. The heron-shaped thermometer that swung from a post next to the grill said the temperature was only thirty-five degrees, but Spencer didn't bother to go back inside to get a jacket.

It was quiet and dark on the porch. The woods behind the barn – the very last place Spencer had seen Ali alive – seemed darker than usual. When she turned and looked toward her front yard, a light in the Cavanaughs' house snapped on. A tall, dark-haired figure floated by the living room bay window. Jenna. She was pacing around, talking into her cell phone, her lips moving quickly. Spencer shuddered, uneasy. It was such a disconnect to see someone wearing sunglasses indoors ... and at night.

'Spencer,' someone whispered, very close.

Spencer whirled around toward the voice, and her knees buckled. Ian was standing on the other side of the deck. He wore a black North Face down jacket zipped up to his nose and a black ski hat pulled down to his eyebrows. The only thing Spencer could see was his eyes.

Spencer started to cry out, but Ian held up his hand. '*Shhhh*. Just listen for a sec.'

Spencer was so terrified, she could have sworn her heart was leaping around in her chest. 'H-how did you get out of your house?'

Ian's eyes glimmered. 'I have my ways.'

Spencer glanced into the back window, but Candace had left the kitchen. Spencer's Sidekick was only feet away, nestled in its mint green Kate Spade leather case on the wet patio table. She started to reach for it.

'Don't,' Ian pleaded, his voice softening. He unzipped his jacket slightly and took off his hat. It looked as if he'd lost weight in his face, and his tawny blond hair stood on end. 'I just want to talk to you,' he said. 'You and I used to be such good friends. Why did you do this to me?'

Spencer's mouth dropped open. 'Because you murdered my best friend, that's why!'

Ian rummaged in his jacket pocket, his eyes on her the whole time. Slowly, he pulled out a pack of Parliaments and lit one with a Zippo. It was something Spencer thought she'd never see. Ian used to do local public service ads for the Great American Smokeout with several other clean-cut Rosewood kids.

A plume of bluish smoke trailed out of his mouth. 'You know I didn't kill Alison. I wouldn't hurt a hair on her head.'

Spencer gripped the smooth wooden posts along the side of her deck for balance. 'You *did* kill her,' she reiterated, her voice wobbly. 'And if you think the notes you've sent us are going to scare us into not testifying against you, you're wrong. We're not afraid of you.'

Ian cocked his head, confounded. 'What notes?'

'Don't play dumb,' Spencer squeaked.

Ian sniffed, still acting confused. Spencer glanced at the hole in the DiLaurentises' yard. It was *so close*. Her eyes moved to the barn, the site of their very last sleepover. They'd all been so excited that seventh grade was over. Sure, there'd been some tension between all of them, and sure, Ali had done a lot of things that had pissed Spencer off, but Spencer had been certain that if they spent enough time together that summer, away from everyone else at Rosewood Day, they'd be as close as ever before.

But then she and Ali had had that stupid fight about closing the blinds so Ali could hypnotize them. Before Spencer knew it, the argument had spiraled out of control. She told Ali to leave ... and Ali did.

For a long time, Spencer felt terrible about what happened. If she hadn't told Ali to leave, maybe Ali wouldn't be dead. But now she knew that nothing she could've done would have made a difference. Ali had been planning to ditch them all along. She was probably dying to meet Ian to see what he'd decided – to break up with Melissa, or to let Ali tell the world about their oh-so-inappropriate relationship. Ali thrived on stuff like that, seeing just how far she could manipulate people. Still, that didn't give Ian permission to *murder* her.

Spencer's eyes brimmed with tears. She thought about that old picture they'd looked at just before the news came on announcing Ian's temporary bail, the one from the day Time Capsule was announced. Ian had had the audacity to stroll right up to Ali and tell her he was going to kill her. Who knew, maybe he'd wanted to even then. Maybe he'd had some death wish for Ali all along. And maybe he'd seen it as the perfect crime. *No one will ever suspect me*, he'd probably thought. *I'm Ian Thomas, after all.*

She glared at Ian, her body shaking. 'Did you really think

you'd get away with what you did? What was going through your head, even fooling around with Ali? Didn't you know it was wrong? Didn't you realize you were taking advantage of her?'

A crow cawed in the distance, loud and ugly. 'I wasn't taking advantage of her,' Ian said.

Spencer sniffed. 'She was in seventh grade – you were in twelfth. That doesn't seem weird to you?'

Ian blinked.

'So she pestered you with a stupid ultimatum,' Spencer went on, her nostrils flaring. 'You didn't have to take her seriously. You should've just told her you didn't want to see her anymore!'

'That's how you think it was?' Ian sounded truly astonished. 'That Ali liked me more than I liked her?' He laughed. 'Ali and I flirted a lot, but that was all. She never seemed interested in taking it further than that.'

'*Right*,' Spencer said through clenched teeth.

'But then ... suddenly ... she changed her mind,' Ian went on. 'At first I thought she was paying attention to me just to make someone else mad.'

A few slow seconds went by. A bird landed on the feeder on the back deck, pecking at the birdseed. Spencer put her hands on her hips. 'And I suppose that would be *me*, right? Ali decided to like you because it would make me mad?'

'Huh?' A stiff wind blew up the edges of Ian's black scarf.

Spencer snorted. Did she really have to spell it out? 'I. Liked. You. Back in seventh grade. I know Ali told you. She convinced you to kiss me.'

Ian breathed out, his brow still furrowed. 'I don't know. It was a long time ago.'

'Stop lying,' Spencer snapped, her cheeks burning. 'You killed Ali,' she repeated. 'Stop pretending you didn't.'

Ian opened his mouth, but no sound came out. 'What if I told you there's something you don't know?' he finally blurted.

An airplane rumbled softly overhead. A few houses down, Mr. Hurst started up his snowblower. 'What are you talking about?' Spencer whispered.

Ian took another drag of his cigarette. 'It's something big. I think the cops know about it too, but they're ignoring it. They're trying to frame me, but by tomorrow I'll have my hands on evidence that will prove my innocence.' He leaned closer to Spencer, blowing the smoke in her face. 'Believe me, it's something that will turn your life upside down.'

Spencer's entire body went numb. 'So tell me what it is.'

Ian looked away. 'I can't say yet. I want to know for sure.'

Spencer laughed bitterly. 'You expect me to just ... take your word for it? *I* don't owe *you* any favors. Maybe you should be talking to Melissa instead of me. I think she'll be more sympathetic to your little sob story.'

A wary look Spencer couldn't quite read passed over Ian's face, as if he didn't like that idea at all. The toxic smell of his cigarette settled over them like a shroud. 'I may have been drunk that night, but I know what I saw,' Ian said. 'I went out there *intending* to meet up with Ali ... but I saw two blondes in the woods instead. One of them was Alison. The other ...' He raised his eyebrows suggestively.

Two blondes in the woods. Spencer shook her head quickly, understanding what Ian was implying. 'It wasn't me. I followed Ali out of the barn. But then she left me – to find *you.*'

'It was another blonde, then.'

'If you saw someone, why didn't you say something to the cops when Ali first went missing?'

Ian's eyes darted left. He took another nervous drag.

150

Spencer snapped her fingers and pointed at him. 'You never said anything, because you *never saw anything*. There isn't any big secret the cops are ignoring … period. *You* killed her, Ian, and you're going to fry. End of story.'

Ian held her gaze for a long few seconds. Then, he moved his shoulder jerkily, flicking his cigarette butt into the yard. 'You've got it all wrong,' he said in a dead voice. And just like that, he whirled around and stomped off the deck, skulking through Spencer's side yard and slipping into the woods. Spencer waited until he was past the tree line before she collapsed weakly to her knees, barely noticing as the slush immediately soaked through her jeans. Hot, frightened tears slid down her face. Several long minutes passed before she noticed that her Sidekick, still sitting on the patio table, was ringing.

She leapt up and grabbed it. There was one new text in her inbox.

Question: If poor little Miss Not-So-Perfect suddenly vanished, would anyone even care? You told on me twice. Three strikes and we'll find out if your 'parents' will cry over the loss of your pathetic life. Tread softly, Spence. – A

Spencer looked up at the trees at the back of the property. 'Not sending notes, huh, Ian?' she screamed out into the emptiness, her voice raw. 'Come out where I can see you!'

The wind swirled silently. Ian didn't answer. The only evidence that he had been here at all was the angry, red-tipped ember of his cigarette butt, slowly dying in the middle of the yard.

19

Fortune Cookies Usually Never
Say Anything This Good

Thursday night after swimming, Emily stood in front of the full-length mirror in the Rosewood Day natatorium, examining her outfit. She had on her favorite pair of chocolate brown corduroys, a pale pink blouse with just a teensy bit of ruffle, and dark pink flats. Was the look appropriate for a dinner at China Rose with Isaac? Or was it too girly and un-Emily? Not that she knew what constituted 'Emily' these days.

'Why are you looking all cute?' Carolyn burst around the corner, making Emily jump. 'You got a date?'

'No!' Emily said quickly, horrified.

Carolyn cocked her head knowingly. 'Who is she? Anyone I know?'

She. Emily sucked her teeth. 'I'm just meeting a guy for dinner. A friend. That's all.'

Carolyn flitted over and adjusted Emily's collar. 'Is that the story you gave Mom, too?'

Actually, it *was* the story Emily had given her mother. She was probably the only girl in Rosewood who could tell her parents she was going out with a boy without getting any paranoid lectures about how sex is a serious thing and should be between two people who were much older and in love.

Ever since her kiss with Isaac yesterday, she'd been wandering around in a perplexed haze. She had no idea what had happened in any of her classes today. Her peanut butter and jelly sandwich at lunch could've been made with sawdust and sardines, for all she'd noticed. And she'd barely flinched when Mike Montgomery and Noel Kahn waved to her in the parking lot after swim practice, asking if she'd had a good Christmas break. 'Is there a lesbian version of Santa Claus?' Mike had yelled excitedly. 'Did you sit on her lap? Are there lesbian elves?'

Emily hadn't even been offended, and that worried her too – if gay jokes no longer bothered her, did that mean she wasn't gay? But wasn't that the big, scary thing she'd figured out about herself over the past few months? The reason her parents had shipped her off to Iowa? If she felt the same emotions for Isaac as she had for Maya and Ali, what did that make her? Straight? Bi? Confused?

As much as she wanted to tell her family about Isaac – he was, ironically, the model boy to bring home to her parents – she felt sheepish. What if they didn't believe her? What if they laughed? What if they got angry? She'd put them through a lot this fall. Now she liked a boy again, just like that? And her note from A had actually made a good point. She had no idea how conservative Isaac was or how he'd react to the secrets of her past. What if it made him uncomfortable and he never spoke to her again?

Emily slammed her locker shut, spun the dial, and then scooped up her canvas bag. 'Good luck,' Carolyn singsonged breezily as Emily left the locker room. 'I'm sure she'll love you.' Emily winced, but didn't correct her.

China Rose was a few miles down Route 30, a cheerful little stand-alone building next to a falling-down stone structure that used to be a spring. To get there, Emily had to drive through the parking lot of a Kinko's, a yarn store, and the Amish market, which sold homemade apple butter and paintings of farm animals on lacquered slabs of wood. When she got out of the car, the parking lot was eerily silent. *Too* silent? The hair on the back of her neck began to rise. Emily had never called Aria back last night to discuss New A. Frankly, Emily had been too afraid to talk to anyone about it, and decided that if she just didn't think about it, maybe it would go away. Aria hadn't called back either. Emily wondered if she was trying to block it out too.

The Rosewood Bowl-O-Rama was in the business complex too, although it was in the process of being remodeled into yet another Whole Foods.

Emily, Ali, and the others used to go bowling at this very alley on Friday nights at the beginning of sixth grade, right after they'd become friends. At first, Emily had thought it was strange. She'd assumed they'd be hanging out at the King James Mall, where Ali and her old posse used to go on the weekends. But Ali said she needed a break from the King James – and from everyone else at Rosewood Day. 'New friends need alone time, don't you think?' Ali told them. 'And no one from school will find us here.'

It had been in this very bowling alley that Emily asked Ali her one and only question about the Time Capsule game – and the spooky thing Ian had said to Ali that day. They had been fooling around in a lane, getting a sugar rush off fountain sodas from the snack bar and seeing if they could knock down more pins by bowling between their legs. Emily felt extra brave that night, more willing to delve into the past that they all tried so hard to avoid. When Spencer got up to bowl and Hanna and Aria ran off to the vending machines, Emily turned to Ali, who was busy drawing cartoon smiley faces in the margins of the scorecard.

'Do you remember that fight Ian Thomas and your brother got into that day Time Capsule was announced?' Emily asked casually, as if she hadn't been thinking about it for weeks.

Ali laid down the nubby scorecard pencil and stared at Emily for nearly a minute. Finally she leaned over and retied her already tight shoelace. 'Jason's a freak,' she mumbled. 'I teased him about it when he gave me a ride home that day.'

But Jason *hadn't* given Ali a ride home that day – he'd sped away in a black car, and Ali and her posse had headed toward the woods. 'So that fight didn't upset you, then?'

Ali looked up, grinning. 'Easy there, Killer! I can take care of myself!' It was the first time Ali had ever called her Killer – as in, her personal, protective pit bull – and the name had stuck.

Looking back on it now, Emily wondered if Ali had gone to meet Ian that day and covered it up with her lie about riding home with Jason. Shaking all thoughts of Ali from her head, Emily slammed the door of the Volvo, put her keys in her pocket, and made her way down the little brick path to China Rose's front door. The inside of the restaurant was decorated to look like a thatch-roofed hut, with bamboo sheaths covering the ceiling and a big aquarium filled with bloated, silvery goldfish. Emily wove around the takeout waiting area, the smell of ginger and green onions tickling her nose. A bunch of cooks hovered over enormous woks in the chaotic open kitchen. Thankfully, she didn't see anyone she recognized from Rosewood Day.

155

Isaac was waving at her from a table toward the rear. Emily waved back, wondering if her face was contorted with nerves. Feeling wobbly, she walked toward him, trying not to bump into any of the tightly grouped tables.

'Hi,' Isaac said. He was wearing a dark blue button-down that brought out his eyes. His hair was pushed back from his face, showing off his chiseled cheekbones.

'Hi,' Emily answered. There was a pregnant pause as she sat down.

'Thanks for coming,' Isaac said, rather formally.

'You're welcome.' Emily tried to sound shy and demure.

'I missed you,' Isaac added.

'Oh,' Emily squeaked, having no clue how to respond. She took a sip of water so she wouldn't have to answer.

A waitress interrupted, handing them menus and towels for their hands. Emily laid the towel over her wrists, trying to calm down. Feeling the moist heat against her skin made her think of the time she and Maya had gone swimming in the Marwyn trail stream in the fall. The creek water had been so warm from the midday sun, as soothing as a hot tub.

A pan clattered in the kitchen, shattering Emily's thoughts. Why on earth had *Maya* popped into her head? Isaac gazed at her curiously, as if he knew what she was thinking. It made her blush even more.

Emily stared down at the place mats of the Chinese zodiac, eager to get her mind off Maya. Along the place mat margins was the regular zodiac too. 'What's your sign?' she blurted.

'Virgo,' Isaac answered promptly. 'Generous, shy, and a perfectionist. What are you?'

'Taurus,' Emily answered.

'That means we're compatible.' Isaac gave her a little smile.

Emily raised an eyebrow, startled. 'You know about astrology?'

'My aunt's into it,' Isaac explained, running the hot towel over his palms. 'She's at our house all the time, and she does my chart a couple times a year. I've known all about my moon and rising sign since I was six. She'll do your chart, if you want.'

Emily grinned, thrilled. 'I'd love that.'

'But actually, did you know we're not really the astrological signs we think we are?' Isaac took a sip of his green tea. 'I saw something about it on the Science Channel. People created the zodiac thousands of years ago, but between then and now, the earth has slowly moved on its axis. The zodiac constellations and the months in which they appear in the sky are out of synch by one whole astrological sign. I didn't quite get all the logistics, but technically, you're not a Taurus. You're an Aries.'

Emily's mind boggled. *Aries?* That was impossible. Her whole life lined up perfectly with what was right for a Taurus, from choosing what colors to wear to what her best swimming stroke was. Ali used to tease that dependable, stubborn Tauruses always had the most boring horoscopes, but Emily liked her sign. The only thing she knew about Aries people was that they were impatient, had to be the center of attention, and were sometimes kind of slutty. Spencer was an Aries. Or was she really a Pisces?

Isaac leaned forward, pushing his menu to the side. 'And I'm a Leo. And we're *still* compatible.' He laid down his menu. 'So now that we've gotten the whole astrology thing out of the way, what else should I know about you?'

A niggling little voice inside of Emily's head said there were lots of things he *should* know, but she just shrugged. 'Why don't you tell me about you first?'

'Okay ...' Isaac took a sip of water, thinking. 'Well, besides playing the guitar, I also play the piano. I've taken lessons since I was three.'

'Wow,' Emily exclaimed. 'I took lessons when I was younger, but I found it way too boring. My parents used to yell at me because I never practiced.'

Isaac smiled. 'My parents forced me to practice, too. So ... what else? Well, my dad owns a catering company. And because I'm a nice guy and his son and therefore cheap labor, I work a lot of his events.'

Emily grinned. 'So you can cook?'

Isaac shook his head. 'Nope, I'm pathetic – I can't even make toast. All I do is serve. Next week I'm working a fundraiser at this burn rehab place. It's a plastic surgery hospital too, but hopefully the party isn't to raise money for any of *that*.' He made a face.

Emily widened her eyes. There was only one burn rehab/ plastic surgery clinic around here. 'You mean the William Atlantic?'

Isaac nodded, smiling questioningly.

Emily looked away, gazing blankly at the big bronze gong near the hostess stand. Some little boy with two missing front teeth was trying desperately to kick it while his dad held him back. The William Atlantic – or Bill Beach, as a lot of people called it – was where Jenna Cavanaugh had been treated for her burns after Ali accidentally blinded her with the firework. Or maybe Ali burned her on purpose ... Emily didn't know what was true anymore. Mona Vanderwaal had been treated there for the burns she'd received that same night.

Isaac's eyebrows lowered. 'What's the matter? Did I say something wrong?'

Emily shrugged. 'I, uh, I know the kid whose dad founded the burn clinic.'

'You know David Ackard's son?'

'He goes to my school.'

Isaac nodded. 'Right. Rosewood Day.'

'I'm on partial scholarship,' Emily said quickly. The last thing she wanted was for him to think she was one of the privileged, spoiled rich kids.

'You must be really smart,' Isaac said.

Emily ducked her head. 'Nah.'

A waitress passed by, balancing multiple plates of General Tso's Chicken. 'My dad is catering a Rosewood Day fund-raiser on Saturday. It's at some ten-bedroom farmhouse.'

'Oh yeah?' Emily's stomach burbled. Isaac was obviously talking about the event at Spencer's house – there'd been an announcement about the fund-raiser that morning in home-room. Nearly every parent attended school fund-raisers, and most students went too, as no one could resist an opportunity to dress up and sneak glasses of champagne while their parents weren't watching.

'So will I see you there?' Isaac's face lit up.

Emily pressed the tines of her fork into her palm. If she went, people were bound to ask questions about why they were together. But if she *didn't go* and Isaac asked around about her, someone might tell him the truth about her past. Like Noel Kahn or Mike Montgomery, or maybe even Ben, Emily's old boyfriend. Maybe New A would be there, too.

'I guess you will see me there,' she decided.

'Great.' Isaac smiled. 'I'll be the one in the caterer's tuxedo.'

Emily blushed. 'Maybe you can serve me personally,' she flirted.

'Done,' Isaac said. He squeezed her hand, and Emily's heart did a somersault.

Suddenly, Isaac looked beyond Emily's head, smiling at something behind her. When Emily swiveled around, her heart dropped to her knees. She blinked several times, hoping the girl standing there was just a mirage.

'Hey, Emily.' Maya St. Germain pushed a curly lock of hair out of her tiger yellow eyes. She was wearing a heavy white sweater, a denim skirt, and white cable-knit tights. Her eyes kept ping-ponging back and forth from Emily to Isaac, trying to figure out what they were doing together.

Emily pulled her hand away from Isaac's. 'Isaac,' she croaked, 'this is Maya. We go to school together.'

Isaac stood up halfway, offering his hand. 'Hi. I'm Emily's date.'

Maya widened her eyes and took a step back, as if Isaac had just said that he was made of cow manure. 'Right,' she joked. 'Her *date*. Good one.'

Isaac's eyebrows knitted together. 'I'm ... sorry?'

Maya's forehead furrowed. And then time seemed to slow down. Emily saw the precise moment when the realization rolled over Maya's face – it *wasn't* a joke. A slow, amused smile grew across her lips. *You're on an actual date with him.* Maya's eyes gleamed nastily. *And you haven't told him what you are, just like you didn't tell Toby Cavanaugh.* Emily realized how angry Maya must be with her – Emily had jerked Maya around all autumn, cheated on her with Trista, a girl she'd met in Iowa, accused Maya of being A, and hadn't said a word to her for months. Here was Maya's big chance to get Emily back for all of that.

As Maya opened her mouth to speak, Emily leapt up, ripped her jacket off the back of her chair, grabbed her purse, and began weaving around the tables toward the door. There was no point being here when Maya told Isaac. She didn't want to see the disappointment – and most certainly disgust – on Isaac's face.

The freezing air whipped around her. When she reached

160

her car, she leaned over the hood, trying to regain her balance. She didn't dare look back inside the restaurant. It would be best if she just got in the car, drove away, and never came to this shopping village again.

Wind swirled around the desolate parking lot. A big streetlight above Emily's head flickered and swayed. Then something rustled behind a massive Cadillac Escalade. Two spots down Emily stood on her tiptoes. Was that a shadow? Was someone *there*? She rifled for her car keys, but they were lost in the depths of her purse.

Her cell phone beeped, and Emily let out a muffled scream. She fumbled for it in her pocket, her hands trembling. *One new text message*. She stabbed at her keypad, opening it up.

Hi Em – Don't you just hate it when your ex shows up
and ruins your romantic night? I wonder how she
knew where to find you . . . Let this be a warning. Talk,
and your past will be the least of your problems. – A

Emily ran her hands over her hair. It made perfect sense – A had sent Maya a text that she was at the restaurant, and Maya, wanting revenge, had taken the bait. Or, even worse, maybe Maya *was* New A.

'Emily?'

She whirled around, her heart racing. Isaac stood behind her. He wasn't wearing his coat, and his cheeks flared red from the cold. 'What are you doing out here?' he asked.

Emily stared at the fluorescent lines that demarcated the parking spaces, unable to meet his eyes. 'I-I thought it would be better if I left.'

'*Why?*'

She paused. Isaac didn't sound angry. He sounded . . . *confused*. She glanced through the windows of the restaurant,

161

watching as the waitresses walked up and down the rows of tables. Was it possible Maya hadn't said anything?

'I'm sorry about what I said in there,' Isaac went on, shivering. 'That I was your date. I didn't mean to define tonight like that.'

His face was full of earnest shame. Suddenly, Emily saw it from his perspective – what *he'd* blurted out, the delicate mistake he thought he'd made. 'Don't apologize,' she burst out, steadying his chilled hands. 'God, *please* don't apologize!'

Isaac blinked. One corner of his mouth pulled up into a tentative smile.

'I wanted this to be a date,' Emily breathed. As soon as she said it, she knew it was the absolute truth. 'In fact, that Rosewood Day fund-raiser you're working? You should see if your dad will let you off for the night. I'd love it if you could come with me ... as *my* date.'

Isaac grinned. 'I think he could let me off work just this once.' Then he squeezed her hands hard and pulled her close. Then, as an afterthought, he murmured, 'So who was that girl in the restaurant, anyway?'

Emily stiffened, a sharp feeling of guilt prodding her side. She should just tell Isaac the truth before A did. Would it really be so bad? Hadn't she spent the entire fall coming to terms with being out in the open about this?

But no – the deal was if Emily kept her mouth shut about A, A would keep quiet to Isaac. Right? The hug was so cozy and warm, and it seemed a shame to ruin the moment. 'Oh, just this girl who goes to my school,' she finally answered, pushing the truth down deep. 'No one important at all.'

20
So Much For A New Father Figure

An hour later on Thursday, Aria sat rigidly on the couch in her den. Mike sat beside her, clicking through the setup windows of his Wii, which Byron had bought him for Christmas as an attempt to apologize for wrecking the family and impregnating Meredith. Mike was making yet another Mii character, flipping through the options for eyes, ears, and noses. 'Why can't I make my biceps bigger?' he grumbled, assessing his character. 'I look so puny.'

'You should make your *head* bigger,' Aria grumbled.

'Want to see the Mii Noel Kahn made of you?' Mike clicked back to the main screen, tossing Aria a *someone still likes you* look. Noel had had a thing for Aria back in the fall. 'He made one of himself, too. You guys could get it on in Wii-land.'

Aria just slumped down in the couch, reached into the big plastic bowl that sat in the middle of the couch for another cheese curl, and said nothing.

'Here's the Mii Xavier made.' Mike clicked over to a large-headed character with short hair and big brown eyes. 'That dude kills at bowling. But I kicked his ass at tennis.'

Aria scratched the back of her neck, an ambivalent heaviness in her chest. 'So you ... like Xavier?'

'Yeah, he's pretty cool.' Mike clicked back to the Wii's main menu. 'Why, don't you?'

'He's ... okay.' Aria licked her lips. She wanted to point out that Mike suddenly seemed to be taking their parents' divorce in stride, considering that after they'd split up, he'd obsessively played lacrosse in the rain. But if she said something like that, Mike would roll his eyes and ignore her for a week.

Mike glared at her, turning off the Wii and switching the television back to the news. 'You're acting like you're on drugs or something. Are you nervous about the trial tomorrow? You're going to rock on that witness stand. Just do some Jäger shots before you go up there. It'll be all good.'

Aria sniffed and stared at her lap. 'Tomorrow's just opening statements. I won't be testifying until late next week at least.'

'So? Do a shot of Jäger tomorrow anyway.'

Aria shot him a weary look. If only a Jäger shot could cure all her problems.

The six o'clock news was on. The screen showed yet another shot of the Rosewood courthouse. A reporter was getting more civilians' thoughts about the start of tomorrow's big murder trial. Aria buried her head into the pillow, not wanting to watch.

'Hey, don't you know that chick?' Mike asked, pointing at the TV.

'What chick?' Aria asked, her voice muffled by the pillow.

'That blind chick.'

Aria whipped her head up. Sure enough, Jenna Cavanaugh was on television, a microphone thrust under her chin. She was wearing her fabulous, oversize Gucci sunglasses and

164

a bright red wool coat. Her seeing-eye golden retriever was standing obediently by her side.

'I hope this trial is over quickly,' Jenna said to the reporter. 'I think it's bringing a lot of bad press to Rosewood.'

'You know, she's pretty sexy for a blind chick,' Mike remarked. 'I'd do her.'

Aria groaned and smacked her brother with a pillow. Then, Mike's iPhone bleated, and he jumped up and rushed out of the room. As he clomped up the stairs, Aria turned her attention back to the television. Ian's mug shot popped up. His hair was a mess and he wasn't smiling. After that, a camera panned over the snowy hole in the DiLaurentises' backyard where Ali's body had been found. The wind made the police tape flap and dance. A blurry shadow shimmered between two enormous pine trees. Aria leaned forward, her pulse suddenly racing. Was that ... a *person*? The picture changed again, back to another shot of the reporter in front of the courthouse. 'The case is proceeding as planned,' the reporter said, 'but many are still saying the evidence is too thin.'

'You shouldn't put yourself through this torture.'

Aria whirled around. Xavier leaned against the doorway. He was wearing an untucked striped button-down, baggy jeans, and Adidas sneakers. A chunky watch dangled from his left wrist. His eyes flicked from the TV screen to Aria's face.

'I, um, think Ella is still at the gallery,' Aria said. 'She had to work a private show.'

Xavier took a step into the room. 'I know. We had coffee before she had to go back. There's no electricity at my place, though – I guess ice knocked down some power lines. She said I could hang out here until we're sure it's back on.' He grinned. 'Is that okay? I could make dinner.'

Aria ran her hands through her hair. 'Sure,' she said, trying to act natural. Things were fine between them, after all. She scooted to the corner of the couch and put the bowl of cheese curls on the coffee table. 'You want to sit?'

Xavier plopped down two cushions away. The news was walking through their projection of the night of Ali's murder, complete with reenactments. '*Ten thirty* P.M., *Alison and Spencer Hastings get into an argument. Alison leaves the barn,*' a voice-over said. The girl who played Spencer looked pinched and sour. The petite blond girl who played Ali wasn't nearly as pretty as the real Ali was. '*Ten forty* P.M., *Melissa Hastings wakes up from a nap and notices that Ian Thomas is missing.*' The girl who played Spencer's sister looked like she was about thirty-five.

Xavier looked at her hesitantly. 'Your mom said you were with Alison that night.'

Aria winced and nodded. '*Ten fifty* P.M., *Ian Thomas and Alison are near the hole in the DiLaurentises' backyard,*' continued the voice-over. A shadowy Ian fought with Ali. '*It's alleged that there was a struggle, Thomas pushed DiLaurentis in and was back inside the house by eleven-oh-five.*'

'I'm so sorry,' Xavier said softly. 'I can't even imagine what this must be like.'

Aria bit her lip, hugging one of the couch's chenille throw pillows to her chest.

Xavier scratched his head. 'I gotta say, I was really surprised when they announced Ian Thomas was their suspect. It seems like that kid had it all.'

Aria bristled. So what if Ian was a groomed, well-mannered rich kid? It didn't make him a saint.

'Well, he *did*,' Aria snapped. 'End of story.'

Xavier nodded sheepishly. 'I didn't mean for it to come out

like that. Goes to show that you don't really know anything about anyone, huh?'

'You can say that again,' Aria groaned.

Xavier took a long sip from his water bottle. 'Is there anything I can do to help?'

Aria stared blankly across the room. Her mother still hadn't taken down any of the family photos with Byron in them, including Aria's favorite, one of all four of them standing on the edge of the Gullfoss waterfall in Iceland. They'd walked all the way out to the slippery edge of the cliff above the waterfall.

'You could beam me back to Iceland,' Aria said wistfully. 'Because, unlike you and my brother, *I* loved it there. Puny horses and all.'

Xavier smirked. His eyes twinkled. 'Actually, I have a secret for you. I really like Iceland too. I said that stuff to get on Mike's good side.'

Aria's eyes widened. 'I can't believe it!' She smacked him with her pillow. 'You're such a kiss-ass!'

Xavier grabbed the pillow on his side of the couch and held it menacingly over his head. 'A kiss-ass, huh? You'd better take that back!'

'Okay, okay.' Aria giggled, raising a finger. 'Truce.'

'It's too late for that,' Xavier cackled.

He lowered down to his knees, his face close. *Too* close. And all of a sudden, his lips were pressed to hers.

It took Aria a few stunned seconds to realize what was going on. Her eyes bulged. Xavier held her shoulders, his hands digging into her skin. Aria let out a small squeak and wrenched her head away. 'What the hell?' she gasped.

Xavier shot back. For a moment, Aria was too baffled to move. Then she shot up as fast as she could.

'Aria …' Xavier's face crumpled. 'Wait. I'm …'

167

She couldn't answer. Her knees buckled out from under her, and she nearly twisted her ankle as she climbed off the couch. 'Aria!' Xavier called again.

But Aria kept going. As she reached the top of the stairs, her Treo, which was sitting on the desk in her bedroom, started to chime. *One new text message*, the screen taunted.

Gasping, she pounced on it and opened it up. The text was one simple word: *Gotcha!*

And, as usual, it was punctuated with a crisp, concise letter *A*.

21
Spencer Holds Her Breath

The flyer was pinned above the bike rack for everyone to see. *Time Capsule Starts Tomorrow*, it said in big black letters. *Get ready!*

The final bell of the day rang. Spencer noticed Aria sitting on the stone wall, scribbling. Hanna stood next to Scott Chin, her cheeks round and puffy. Emily was whispering to some other swimmers, Mona Vanderwaal was unlocking her scooter, and Toby Cavanaugh was crouched under a distant tree, shoving a stick into a small pile of dirt.

Ali pushed through the crowd and snatched down the flyer. 'Jason's hiding one of the pieces. And he's going to tell me where it is.'

Everyone cheered. Ali pranced through the throng of kids and gave Spencer a high five. Which was startling – Ali had never paid attention to Spencer before, even though they lived next to each other.

But today, it appeared they were friends. Ali bumped Spencer's hip. 'Aren't you excited for me?'

'Uh, sure,' Spencer stammered.

Ali narrowed her eyes. 'You're not going to try and steal it, are you?'

Spencer shook her head. 'No! Absolutely not!'

'Yeah, she is,' said a voice behind them. A second, older Ali stood on the sidewalk. She was a little taller and her face was a little thinner. A blue string bracelet was tied around her wrist – the very bracelet Ali had made for them after The Jenna Thing – and she wore a pale blue American Apparel T-shirt and a rolled-up-at-the-waist hockey kilt. It was the same outfit Ali had worn to the end-of-seventh-grade sleep-over in Spencer's barn.

'She's totally going to try and steal it from you,' the second Ali confirmed, giving Younger Ali a sidelong glance. 'But she doesn't. Someone else does.'

Younger Ali narrowed her eyes. '*Right*. Someone's going to have to kill me to get my flag.'

The crowd of Rosewood Day students parted, and Ian slipped through. He opened his mouth, an evil look on his face. *If that's what it takes*, he was about to tell Ali. But when he breathed in to speak, he made a fire engine sound instead, shrill and piercingly loud.

Both Alis covered their ears. Younger Ali took a step back.

Older Ali put her hands on her hips, kicking Younger Ali with the side of her foot. 'What's wrong with you? Go flirt with him. He's gorgeous.'

'No,' Younger Ali said.

'Yes,' Older Ali insisted. They were fighting as bitterly as Spencer and Melissa did.

Older Ali rolled her eyes and faced Spencer. 'You shouldn't have thrown it away, Spencer. Everything you needed was there. All the answers.'

'Thrown … *what* away?' Spencer asked, confused.

170

Younger Ali and Older Ali exchanged a glance. A frightened look washed over Younger Ali's face, like she suddenly understood what Older Ali was talking about. '*It*,' Younger Ali said. 'That was a huge mistake, Spencer. And it's almost too late.'

'What do you mean?' Spencer cried. 'What is *it*? And why am I almost too late?'

'You're going to have to fix this,' Younger Ali and Older Ali said in unison, their voices identical now. They joined hands and fused back into one Ali. 'It's up to you, Spencer. You shouldn't have thrown it away.'

Ian's siren grew louder and louder. A gust of wind kicked up, blowing the Time Capsule flyer right out of Ali's hands. It hung in the air for a moment, then blew straight for Spencer, smacking her square in the face hard, feeling more like a rock than a piece of paper. *Get ready!* it said, right in front of Spencer's eyes.

Spencer shot up in bed, sweat drenching her neck. Ali's vanilla body cream tickled her nose, but she wasn't in the Rosewood Day commons anymore – she was in her spotless, silent bedroom. The sun streamed through the window. Her dogs were racing around the front yard, filthy from the dirty slush. It was Friday, the first day of Ian's trial.

'Spencer?' Melissa's face swam into view. She hovered over Spencer's bed, her blunt-cut blond hair hanging down over her face, the strings of her blue-and-white striped hoodie almost grazing Spencer's nose. 'Are you okay?'

Spencer shut her eyes and remembered last night. How Ian had materialized on the porch, smoking that cigarette, saying all of those crazy, terrifying things. And then that note: *If Poor Little Miss Perfect were to suddenly vanish, would anyone even care? As* much as she wanted to, Spencer had been too afraid to tell anyone about it. Calling Wilden and telling him that Ian had broken his house arrest would probably have gotten him thrown back in jail, but Spencer was afraid that as soon as she told Wilden, something awful would happen to her – or to someone else. After what had happened to Mona, she couldn't bear to have any more blood on her hands.

Spencer swallowed hard, facing her sister. 'I'm going to testify against Ian. I know you don't want him to go to prison, but I'm going to have to tell the truth on the witness stand about what I saw.'

Melissa's face remained placid. Light bounced off her Asscher-cut diamond earrings. 'I know,' she said vaguely, like her mind was elsewhere. 'I'm not asking you to lie.'

With that, Melissa patted Spencer's shoulder and walked out of the room. Spencer stood up slowly, taking deep yoga fire breaths. Both Ali voices still bonged in her ears. She took one more careful look around her bedroom, half expecting one of them to be standing over her. But of course no one was there.

An hour later, Spencer pulled her Mercedes into a parking space at Rosewood Day and hurried to the elementary school. Most of the snow had melted, but there were still a couple of die-hard little kids outside, making pathetic little snow angels and playing Find the Yellow Snow. Her friends were waiting by the elementary school swings, their old secret meeting spot. Ian's trial was starting at 1 P.M., and they wanted to talk before it began.

Aria waved as Spencer jogged toward her friends, visibly shivering in her fur-lined hooded jacket. Hanna had purple circles under her eyes and was nervously tapping the pointy toe of her Jimmy Choo boot. Emily looked as if she was about to cry. Seeing them together in their old spot made something inside Spencer break. *You should tell them what happened*, she thought. It didn't feel right keeping Ian's visit a secret. But Ian's message was ever-present in her mind: *If you tell anyone about me ...*

'So, are we ready?' Hanna asked, chewing nervously on her lips.

'I guess,' Emily answered. 'It's going to be weird to ... you know. See Ian.'

'Seriously,' Aria whispered.

'Uh-huh,' Spencer stammered nervously, keeping her eyes glued on a zigzagging crack in the pavement.

The sun poked through a cloud, reflecting blindingly against the remaining snow. A shadow moved behind the jungle gym, but when Spencer turned, it was only a bird. She thought about the dream she'd had this morning. Younger Ali had seemed uninterested, but Older Ali had urged her to flirt with Ian – he was gorgeous. It was a lot like what Ian had said to Spencer yesterday. At first, Ali hadn't taken him very seriously. When she started liking him, it was instantaneous, like a light had switched on.

'Do you guys happen to remember Ali ever saying anything ... *negative* ... about Ian?' Spencer blurted out. 'Like maybe that she thought he was too old or too skeevy?'

Aria blinked, looking confused. 'No ...'

Emily shook her head too, her blondish-red ponytail swishing from side to side. 'Ali talked to me about Ian a couple times. She never said his name, only that he was older, and she was totally into him.' She shuddered, staring down at the muddy ground.

'That's what I thought,' Spencer said, satisfied.

Hanna ran her fingers over her scar. 'Actually, I heard something weird on the news the other day. They were interviewing people at the train station about Ian's bail hearing.

And this girl, Alexandra something, she said she was pretty sure Ali thought Ian was perverted.'

Spencer stared at her. 'Alexandra Pratt?'

Hanna nodded, shrugging. 'I think so. She's a lot older?'

Spencer let out a shaky breath. Alexandra Pratt had been a senior when Spencer and Ali were sixth-graders. As the captain of the varsity field hockey team, Alexandra had been the main student judge for JV tryouts. At Rosewood Day, sixth-graders were allowed to try out for JV, but only one would make the team any given year. Ali boasted she might have a leg up because she'd practiced with Alexandra and the other older players a couple of times in the fall, but Spencer had simply laughed it off – Ali wasn't nearly as good as she was.

For whatever reason, Alexandra didn't like Spencer. She was constantly critiquing Spencer's dribbling skills and telling her she held her hockey stick wrong – as if Spencer hadn't spent *every single summer* at field hockey camp, learning from the very best of the best. When the team was announced and Ali's name was on the list and Spencer's wasn't, Spencer stormed home in disbelief and rage, not bothering to wait for Ali to walk with her. 'You can always try out next year,' Ali simpered to Spencer on the phone later. 'And c'mon, Spence. You can't be the best at *everything*.'

And then she'd giggled gleefully. That very night, Ali had begun hanging her brand-new JV uniform in her bedroom window, knowing that Spencer would look out and see it.

It wasn't just field hockey. Everything between Spencer and Ali had been a competition. In seventh grade, they'd made a bet about who could hook up with the most older boys. Although neither of them would come out and say it, they both knew their number one target was Ian. Every time they were at Spencer's house and Melissa and Ian were there

174

too, Ali made a point of walking by Ian, hiking up her field hockey shirt or standing up straighter to stick out her boobs.

She certainly hadn't acted like she thought Ian was perverted. Alexandra Pratt obviously had her facts wrong.

A bus roared into the drop-off lane, making Spencer jump. Aria was staring at her curiously. 'Why are you asking that, anyway?'

Spencer swallowed hard. *Tell them*, she thought. But her mouth clamped closed.

'Just curious,' she finally answered. She sighed heavily. 'I wish there was something we could find – something concrete that would put Ian away for good.'

Hanna kicked at a hard clump of snow. 'Yeah, but what?'

'This morning, Ali kept saying I was missing something,' Spencer said thoughtfully. 'Like a big piece of evidence.'

'Ali?' Sunlight glinted sharply off Emily's small silver hoop earrings.

'I had a dream about her,' Spencer explained, shoving her hands in her pockets. 'Actually, there were two Alis in the dream. One Ali was in sixth grade, and one Ali was in seventh. They both were pissed at me, acting like there was something really obvious that I wasn't seeing. They said it was up to me ... and that soon it would be too late.' She pinched the bridge of her nose, trying to ease her pounding tension headache.

Aria chewed on her thumbnail. 'I had a dream about Ali a couple of months ago that was a lot like that. It was right when we realized she'd been secretly dating Ian, and she kept saying, *The truth is right in front of you, the truth is right in front of you.*'

'And I had that dream about Ali in the hospital,' Hanna

reminded them. 'She was standing right over me. She kept telling me to stop worrying. That she was okay.'

A cold shiver ran down Spencer's spine. She exchanged a glance with the others, trying to swallow the enormous lump in her throat.

More buses pulled up to the curb. Little kids skipped down the elementary sidewalks, their lunch boxes swinging, all of them talking at once. Spencer thought again of how Ian had smirked at her yesterday and then disappeared into the trees. It was almost like he thought this was all a game.

Just a few more hours, she reminded herself. The D.A. would get Ian to cave and admit he'd killed Ali after all. Maybe he'd even get Ian to confess to taunting Spencer and the others, pretending to be a new A. Ian had a lot of money – he could hire a whole team of A spies and direct the whole operation from house arrest. And it made sense why he was sending notes: He didn't want any of them to testify against him. He wanted to scare Spencer into recanting her statement, into saying she *hadn't* seen Ian with Ali that night she disappeared. That she had really made it all up.

'I'm glad Ian gets locked up again after today,' Emily breathed out. 'We can all relax at the benefit tomorrow.'

'I'm not going to feel calm until he's gone for good,' Spencer answered, her throat thick with tears. Her voice carried up beyond the gnarled tree branches, high into the turquoise blue winter sky. She twisted a lock of hair around her finger until it almost snapped. *Only a few more hours*, she repeated. But those few hours suddenly seemed like an eternity.

22
Déjà Vu All Over Again

Hanna shrugged out of her red Chloé leather jacket and tossed it into her locker as Dvorak's *New World Symphony* played loudly over the Rosewood Day hallway speakers. Naomi, Riley, and Kate were next to her, chattering about all the boys who had gotten instant crushes on Kate.

'Maybe you should keep your options open,' Naomi was saying, draining the last little bit of her hazelnut cappuccino. 'Eric Kahn is really sexy, but Mason Byers is *the* catch of Rosewood Day. Whenever he opens his mouth I want to tear off his clothes.' Mason's family had lived in Sydney for ten years, so he spoke with a slight Australian accent. He sounded like he'd spent his whole life on a sun-soaked beach.

'Mason's on the volleyball team.' Riley's eyes lit up. 'I saw a yearbook proof of him at a recent tournament – he had his shirt off. Gor-*geous*.'

'Doesn't the volleyball team practice after school?' Naomi rubbed her hands together excitedly. 'Maybe we all should make a special appearance as Mason's personal cheering section.' She looked at Kate for approval.

Kate gave her a high five. 'I'm game.' She turned to Hanna. 'What do you think, Han? You in?'

Hanna looked back and forth between them, flustered. 'I have to leave school early today ... I have that trial thing.'

'Oh.' Kate's face clouded. 'Right.'

Hanna waited, expecting Kate to say something more, but she, Naomi, and Riley just went back to gossiping about Mason. Hanna pressed her nails into her palm, feeling the teensiest bit hurt. Part of her had figured they'd come with her to Ian's trial as a show of moral support. Naomi was in the middle of cracking a joke about the size of Mason Byers's didgeridoo when Hanna felt someone tapping her shoulder.

'Hanna?' Lucas's face swam in front of her. As usual, he was carrying various paraphernalia from the clubs he took part in – a schedule for future chemistry club meetings, a list of names for the Stop Putting Sugary Drinks in the Vending Machine petition he was trying to get passed, and a blazer lapel pin that said *Future Politicians of America*. 'What's up?'

Hanna wearily pushed a lock of hair over her shoulder. Kate, Naomi, and Riley glanced at them and moved a few feet away. 'Not much,' she mumbled.

There was an awkward pause. Out of the corner of her eye, Hanna noticed Jenna Cavanaugh slipping into an empty classroom, her dog in tow. Every time Hanna saw Jenna around Rosewood Day, an uncomfortable sensation surged through her.

'I missed you yesterday,' Lucas was saying. 'I ended up not going to the mall – I wanted to wait to go with you.'

'Uh-huh,' Hanna murmured, only half listening. Her gaze moved to Kate and the others. They were now at the end of the hall near the Watercolor II class exhibit, whispering and chuckling. Hanna wondered what was so funny.

When she looked back at Lucas, he was frowning. 'What's going on with you?' he asked. 'Are you mad at me?'

'No.' Hanna fiddled with her blazer's cuff. 'I've just been ... busy.'

Lucas touched her wrist. 'Are you nervous about Ian's trial? Do you need a ride?'

Hanna's sudden irritation was palpable, like a hot poker shoved into her thigh. 'Don't go to the trial,' she snapped.

Lucas jumped back like she'd slapped him. 'But ... I thought you wanted me to go.'

Hanna turned away. 'It's not going to be that interesting,' she muttered, deflated. 'It's just opening statements. You'll be bored out of your mind.'

Lucas stared at her, ignoring the rush of students drifting past them. A bunch of them were kids heading to drivers' ed, their Pennsylvania driving rules booklets in their hands. 'But I want to be there for you.'

Hanna clenched her jaw and looked away. 'Seriously. I'll be fine.'

'Is there a *reason* you don't want me to go?'

'Just drop it, okay?' Hanna waved her arms in front of her, putting up a barrier between them. 'I have to get to class. I'll see you at the benefit tomorrow.'

With that, she slammed her locker shut and brushed past Lucas. She couldn't quite explain why she didn't just turn around, take his hand, and apologize for being bitchy. Why did she want Kate, Naomi, and Riley to accompany her to Ian's trial, but when Lucas offered – so loyally and sincerely – she just got annoyed? Lucas was her boyfriend, and the past few months with him had been awesome. After Mona had died, Hanna had gone around in a numb haze until she and Lucas got back together. Once they did, they'd spent all their time together, hanging out at his house, playing Grand Theft

Auto, and spending hours and hours skiing at Elk Ridge Mountain. Hanna hadn't been to a mall or a spa once during the entire nine days they'd had off at Christmas. Half the time she spent with Lucas, she didn't even put on makeup, except stuff to cover her scar.

These past few months with Lucas might have been the first time she'd felt purely, simply happy. Why wasn't that enough?

Only it just *wasn't*, and she knew it. When she and Lucas had reunited, she hadn't thought there was much chance of becoming Fabulous Hanna Marin ever again – and now there was. Being the most popular girl at Rosewood Day was threaded through every single molecule of Hanna's DNA. From fourth grade on, she'd memorized even the most minuscule designers in *Vogue, Women's Wear Daily,* and *Nylon.* Back then, she rehearsed snarky comments about girls in her class to Scott Chin, one of her only friends, who giggled gleefully that she was a perfect bitch-in-training.

In sixth grade, right after Time Capsule ended, Hanna had gone to the Rosewood Day charity drive and spotted a Hermes scarf that someone had foolishly placed in the fifty-cent pile. Mere seconds later, Ali sidled up to her, complimenting Hanna's keen eye. And then they'd started talking. Hanna was certain that Ali chose Hanna to be her new best friend not because Hanna was the prettiest, not because she was the thinnest, not even because she'd been ballsy enough to show up in Ali's backyard to steal her piece of the Time Capsule flag, but because Hanna was most qualified for the job. And because she wanted it the most.

Hanna smoothed her hair, trying hard to forget about everything that had just happened with Lucas. As she turned the corner, she saw Kate, Naomi, and Riley stare straight at her before bursting into nasty giggles.

Suddenly, Hanna's eyes began to blur, and all at once, it wasn't Kate standing there, laughing – it was Mona. It was just a few months ago, mere days before Mona's Sweet Seventeen party. Hanna would never forget the swirling feelings of disbelief when she'd seen Mona standing with Naomi and Riley, acting as if they were her brand-new BFFs, whispering about how much of a loser Hanna was.

Those who forget the past are doomed to repeat it. Kate, Naomi, and Riley weren't laughing at *her*, were they?

And then Hanna's vision cleared. Kate noticed Hanna and waved enthusiastically. *Meet at Steam next period?* she mouthed, pointing toward the coffee bar.

Hanna nodded feebly. Kate blew her a kiss and disappeared around the corner.

Whirling around, Hanna pushed into the girls' bathroom. Thankfully, it was empty. She rushed to one of the sinks and leaned over the basin, her stomach raging. The sharp, ammonia smell of cleaning products filled her nose. She stared in the mirror, getting close so she could see each and every pore.

They were not laughing at you. You're Hanna Marin, she mouthed to her reflection. *The most popular girl in school. Everyone wants to be you.*

Her BlackBerry, which was tucked into one of her purse's side pockets, began to buzz. Hanna flinched and pulled it out. *One new text message.*

The little mosaic-tiled bathroom was still. A droplet of water leaked from the sink. The chrome hand dryers made Hanna's face look bulbous and misshapen. She peeked underneath the stall doors for feet. No one.

She took a deep breath and opened the new text.

Hanna – A glutton for Cheez-Its . . . and punishment, too, it seems. Ruin her before she ruins you. – A

Rage coursed hotly through her veins. She'd had enough of Nouveau A. Hanna opened up a reply text and began to sloppily type. *Rot in hell. You don't know a thing about me.*

Her BlackBerry made an efficient little *ping* to indicate the text had been sent. Just as Hanna was sliding it back in its suede case, it chimed again.

I know that someone sometimes makes herself puke in the girls' bathroom. And I know someone's sad because she isn't daddy's only little girl anymore. And I know someone dearly misses her old BFF, even though she wanted her dead. How do I know so much? Because I grew up in Rosewood, Hannakins. Just like you.
— A

23

The Quietest Courtroom On
The Main Line

Aria stepped out of Spencer's Mercedes, gaping at the media circus in front of the Rosewood courthouse. The steps were crammed with reporters, cameras, and guys in quilted down jackets wielding booms and microphones. There were clusters of people with picket signs, too. Some conspiracy theorists were protesting the trial, saying it was a left-wing witch hunt – they were after Ian because his father was a CEO for a big pharmaceutical company in Philadelphia. Angry people on the other side of the steps demanded that Ian deserved to go to the electric chair for what he'd done. And there were, of course, the Ali Fans – people who came simply to hold up big pictures of Ali's face and signs that said, WE MISS YOU, ALI, even though most of them had never met her.

'Whoa,' Aria whispered, her stomach churning.

Halfway across the sidewalk, Aria noticed two people walking slowly from the auxiliary parking lot. Ella's arm was looped around Xavier's, and they were both in thick wool coats.

Aria hid under her big, fur-lined hood. Last night, after Xavier had kissed her, she'd run upstairs and locked herself in her room. When she'd finally emerged a few hours later, she found Mike at the kitchen table, eating an enormous bowl of Count Chocula. He scowled at her when she entered the room. 'Did you say something shitty to Xavier?' Mike spat. 'When I got off the phone, he was hightailing it out of here. Are you *trying* to screw it up for Mom?'

Aria had turned away, too ashamed to say anything. She was pretty sure the kiss had been a mistake, something done on a whim. Even Xavier had seemed surprised and regretful about what he'd just done. But she certainly didn't want Mike – or anyone else – to know. Unfortunately, someone did know: A. And Aria had crossed A by telling Wilden about her previous note. All night, Aria had anticipated a phone call from Ella, saying she'd received a mysterious message that said Aria had made a pass at Xavier and not the other way around. If Ella ever found out, Aria would probably be excommunicated from the family for the rest of her life.

'Aria!' Ella called, spying Aria under her hood. She started to wave, signaling for Aria to come over. Xavier had a sheepish expression on his face. As soon as Xavier got a second with her alone, Aria was certain he would apologize. But she was too overwhelmed to deal with it today, on top of everything else.

She grabbed Spencer's arm, turning away from her mother. 'Let's go in,' she said urgently. 'Now.'

Spencer shrugged. They faced the throng on the steps. Aria pulled her hood over her head again and Spencer covered her face with her sleeve, but the reporters still descended on them anyway. 'Spencer! What do you think will happen at today's trial?' they screamed. 'Aria! What kind of toll has all this taken on you?' Aria and Spencer clutched hands tightly, moving as fast as they could. A Rosewood cop stood at the courthouse door, holding it open for them. They ducked inside, breathing hard.

The hallway smelled like floor wax and aftershave. Ian and his lawyers hadn't arrived yet, so a lot of people were milling outside the courtroom. Many of them were Rosewood cops and city officials, as well as neighbors and friends. Aria and Spencer waved to Jackson Hughes, the distinguished-looking D.A. When Jackson stepped out of the way, Aria's minty gum slid down her throat. Ali's family was standing behind him. There was Mrs. DiLaurentis, Mr. DiLaurentis, and ... Jason. Aria had seen him not all that long ago – he'd come to Ali's memorial and Ian's arraignment – but each time she saw him she was floored by how gorgeous he still was.

'Hi, girls,' Mrs. DiLaurentis said, walking over. The lines by her eyes were more pronounced than Aria remembered, but she was still svelte and elegant. She assessed Aria and Spencer. 'You've both gotten so tall,' she said sadly, as if to imply that if Ali were still alive, she would've gotten taller too.

'Are you holding up okay?' Spencer asked in her best adult voice.

'Best we can.' Mrs. DiLaurentis smiled bravely.

'Are you staying in the city again?' Aria asked. The family had stayed in Philadelphia for Ian's arraignment a few months ago.

Mrs. DiLaurentis shook her head. 'We've rented a house a few towns over for the duration of the trial. We thought it might be too difficult to commute back here every day from the city. We'd rather be somewhere close.'

Aria raised an eyebrow, surprised. 'Is there anything we can do for you?' Aria asked. 'Like ... help around the house?

Do you need your driveway shoveled? My brother and I could come over.'

An ambiguous expression flickered over Mrs. DiLaurentis's face. Her hands fluttered to the freshwater pearl necklace at her throat. 'Thanks, dear, but that won't be necessary.' She gave them a tight, distracted smile and excused herself.

Aria watched Mrs. DiLaurentis walk back across the lobby to her family. She held her head so stiff and straight, as if she had a book balanced on top of it. 'She seemed ... weird,' Aria murmured.

'I can't imagine what this is like for her.' Spencer shivered. 'This trial is probably hell.'

They pushed through the heavy wooden doors into the courtroom. Hanna and Emily were already sitting in the second row, right behind the big tables for the lawyers. Hanna had taken off her Rosewood Day blazer and slung it over the back of her chair. Emily was picking at a piece of lint on her pleated plaid uniform skirt. Both girls nodded quietly at Aria and Spencer as they slid into seats next to them.

The courtroom filled up fast. Jackson had set up a bunch of folders and files on his table. Ian's lawyer arrived and took his place across the aisle. Off to the side the jury box was filled with twelve people Aria had never seen before, hand-picked by both lawyers. The actual courtroom was closed to the media and most of Rosewood, and only close family and friends were allowed in, along with police and witnesses. When Aria looked around, she saw Emily's parents, Hanna's dad and soon-to-be step-mom, and Spencer's sister, Melissa. On the other side of the courtroom Aria spied her father, Byron. He was slowly helping Meredith into a seat, even though she wasn't *that* pregnant.

Byron looked around the courtroom, as if he sensed Aria's gaze. He found her and waved. *Hi*, Aria mouthed. Byron smiled. Meredith noticed her too, widened her eyes, and mouthed, *You okay?* Aria wondered if Byron knew Ella was here – and that she'd brought her new boyfriend.

Emily poked Aria's side. 'You know the night you called me saying you got a note from New A? I got one that night too.'

A shiver ran up Aria's back. 'What did it say?'

Emily ducked her head, fiddling with a loose button on her blouse. 'Just ... nothing, really. Did Wilden ever get back to you about who they could be from?'

'No.' Aria scanned the courtroom, thinking Wilden might be here. She didn't see him. She peered around Emily to look at Hanna. 'Have you gotten any?'

Hanna's expression became guarded. 'I don't really want to talk about it right now.'

Aria frowned. Did that mean she had or she hadn't? 'What about you, Spencer?'

Spencer looked at them nervously. She didn't answer. A sour taste welled in Aria's mouth. Did this mean they'd *all* gotten more notes from this new A?

Emily chewed nervously on her bottom lip. 'Well, I guess it won't matter soon, right? If it's Ian, it'll be over as soon as he's back in jail ...'

'Hopefully,' Aria murmured.

The DiLaurentises finally paraded in and sat on the bench right in front of them. Jason settled next to his parents, but he kept fidgeting, first buttoning his jacket, then unbuttoning it, then reaching for his cell phone, checking the screen, turning it off, and turning it on again. Then, suddenly, Jason turned around and stared right at Aria. His blue eyes lingered on her for a good three seconds. He had the same exact eyes as Ali – it was like looking at a ghost.

One corner of Jason's mouth curled into a smile of recognition. He gave Aria – but seemingly *only* Aria – a little wave,

187

as if he remembered her better than he did the other girls. Aria checked to see whether any of her old friends had noticed, but Hanna was reapplying her lipstick, and Spencer and Emily were whispering about how Mrs. DiLaurentis had told them that the family had moved a few towns away from Rosewood for the trial. When Aria looked back at Jason, his back was to her again.

Twenty more minutes slowly passed. Ian's side was still empty. 'Shouldn't he be here by now?' Aria whispered to Spencer.

Spencer's eyebrows knitted together. 'Why are you asking me?' she hissed. 'Why would I know?'

Aria held up her hands and sat back. 'Sorry,' she whispered sharply. 'I wasn't asking you *specifically*.'

Spencer let out a huffing sigh and faced forward. She was clenching her jaw very tightly.

Ian's lawyer stood up and walked to the back of the courtroom, a worried look on his face. Aria looked at the wooden doors to the lobby, expecting Ian and his police escorts to burst through at any second, ready to commence the trial. But the doors remained closed. She ran her hand over the back of her neck, uneasy. The murmurs in the courtroom grew louder.

Aria stared out the side window in an attempt to calm down. The courthouse was on a snowy hill overlooking the Rosewood Valley. In the summer, the thick foliage blocked the view, but now that the trees were bare, all of Rosewood was splayed out below. The Hollis spire looked so small, Aria could squish it between her thumb and pointer finger. The tiny Victorian houses below were like dollhouse toys, and Aria could even make out the star-shaped neon sign outside of Snooker's, where she'd first met Ezra. Beyond that were the vast, untouched fields of the Rosewood Country Club golf course. She, Ali, and the others had spent every day

188

of that first summer they were friends around the country club pool, ogling the older lifeguards. The lifeguard they ogled most was Ian.

She wished she could go back to that summer and revise everything that had happened to Ali – go back to before the workers even started digging that hole for the DiLaurentises' big twenty-person gazebo. The first time Aria had been in Ali's backyard, she'd stood almost precisely where that hole – and Ali's body – would end up being, way at the back of the property near the woods. It was that fateful Saturday at the beginning of sixth grade, when they'd all shown up in Ali's yard to steal the piece of her Time Capsule flag. Aria wished she could go back and change what had happened that day, too.

Judge Baxter emerged from his chamber. He was portly and red-faced, and had a squished-down nose and small, beady eyes. Aria suspected he'd smell like a cigar if she were closer. When Baxter summoned the two lawyers to the bench, Aria sat up straighter. The three of them talked heatedly, pointing every so often at Ian's empty seat.

'This is crazy,' Hanna murmured, glancing over her shoulder. 'Ian's *really* late.'

The courtroom doors burst open, and the girls jumped. A cop Aria recognized from Ian's arraignment strode up the aisle, right through the saloon-style doors and straight to the bench. 'I just reached his family,' he said in a gruff voice. Sunlight glimmered off his silvery badge, bouncing shards of light all over the room. 'They're looking.'

Aria's throat went dry. '*Looking?*' She exchanged a look with the others.

'What do they mean by that?' Emily squeaked.

Spencer bit her thumbnail. 'Oh my God.'

Through the still-open door, Aria could see a black sedan

pulled up to the curb. Ian's father got out of the backseat. He was wearing funeral black and had a solemn, terrified look on his face. Aria assumed his mother wasn't there because she was in the hospital.

A police car pulled up behind the sedan, but only two Rosewood police officers got out.

In seconds, Ian's father walked up the aisle to the bench. 'He was in his bedroom last night,' Mr. Thomas murmured quietly to Baxter – but not quietly enough. 'I don't know how this could happen.'

The judge's face twitched for a moment. 'What do you mean?' he asked.

Ian's father hung his head solemnly. 'He's ... gone.'

Aria's mouth dropped open, her heart ricocheting around in her chest. Emily let out a moan. Hanna clutched her stomach, a gurgling noise escaping from the back of her throat. Spencer stood up halfway. 'I think I should ...,' she started, but trailed off and sat back down.

Judge Baxter banged his gavel. 'I'm calling a recess,' he shouted to the crowd. 'Until further notice. We'll call you back when we're ready.'

He made a motioning signal with his hands. All at once, about twenty Rosewood cops approached the bench, walkie-talkies blaring, guns poised in their holsters, ready to be pulled out and fired. After a few instructions, the cops turned away from the bench and started marching out of the courtroom to their cars.

He's gone. Aria glanced out the window again, into the valley. There was a lot of Rosewood down there. Plenty of places for Ian to hide.

Emily sank onto the bench, raking her hands through her hair. 'How could this happen?'

'Wasn't there a cop watching him at all times?' Hanna

190

echoed. 'I mean, how could he have slipped out of the house without them seeing? It's not possible!'

'Yes, it is.'

They all looked over at Spencer. Her eyes darted back and forth mechanically, and her hands fluttered. She slowly raised her head and gazed at the three of them, her face dripping with guilt. 'There's something I need to tell you,' she whispered. 'About ... Ian. And you're not going to like it.'

24
Et Tu, Kate?

'On your left!' Hanna screamed.

A woman walking a wiener dog jumped and scuttled out of Hanna's way. It was Friday evening after dinner, and Hanna was running the Stockbridge Trail, a three-mile loop that wound behind the old stone mansion that was now owned by the Rosewood Y. It probably wasn't the safest thing, running on a secluded path with Ian Thomas allegedly on the loose. Although if Spencer had just sucked it up and *told* the cops Ian had broken house arrest and visited her the day before, he wouldn't have escaped.

But Ian be damned – Hanna needed a run tonight. She usually came here to purge her stomach after she'd binged on too many Cheez-Its, but tonight, it was Hanna's memory that needed purging instead.

The notes from A had begun to plague her. She didn't want to believe that this new A was real ... but what if what the notes said was true? And if New A *was* Ian and he'd been able to break house arrest, then it made sense that he could know what Kate was up to, right?

Hanna flew past the snow-covered benches and a big

green sign that said, PLEASE CLEAN UP AFTER YOUR DOG! Had she been a fool to so easily befriend Kate? Was this another one of Kate's tricks? What if Kate was as diabolical as Mona was, and this was all a well-laid plan to ruin Hanna's life? Slowly, she let her mind creep over the intricate details of her and Mona's friendship – or maybe enemy-ship. They had become friends in eighth grade, after Ali had been missing for months. Mona had been the one who'd approached Hanna, complimenting her D&G sneakers and the David Yurman bracelet she'd gotten for her birthday. Hanna was weirded out at first – Mona was a dork, after all – but eventually, she'd seen beyond Mona's exterior. Besides, she needed a new BFF.

But maybe Mona was *never* her BFF. Maybe she had just been waiting for the precise moment to take Hanna down, to get revenge for all the horrible things Hanna and her friends had said to her. It was Mona who cut Hanna off from her old friends, and it was Mona who had further perpetuated the animosity with Naomi and Riley. Hanna had considered trying to make amends with them after Ali was presumed dead, but Mona had said absolutely not. Naomi and Riley were strictly B-listers, and they should have nothing to do with them.

It was Mona, too, who first suggested that they shoplift, telling Hanna that it would give her *such* a high. And then there were the things Mona had pulled off as A. Mona had had it so easy with Hanna – she was witness to so many of Hanna's blunders. Who'd been sitting next to Hanna the night she'd totaled Sean Ackard's father's BMW? Who'd been with Hanna when she'd gotten busted for shoplifting from Tiffany?

Her feet sank into random pockets of slush, but she kept running. Everything else Mona had done gushed into her

193

mind, as sloppy and uncontrollable as champagne fizzing out of an uncorked bottle. Mona-as-A had sent her that child-size court dress, knowing that Hanna would wear it to Mona's birthday party and the dress's seams would burst. Mona-as-A had gleefully sent Hanna that note that Sean was at Foxy with Aria, knowing for sure that Hanna would rush back to Rosewood and chew Sean out, ruining her dinner with her dad and making Kate look like the perfect, obedient little daughter yet again.

Wait a minute. Hanna stopped short under a copse of trees. Something about that didn't fit. Hanna had told Mona that she was back in touch with her dad, but she hadn't told her she was ditching Foxy to hang out with him in Philly. Even if Mona somehow found out about it some other way, she couldn't have known that Kate and Isabel would be there too. Hanna remembered how Isabel and Kate had knocked on the door of her father's suite in the Four Seasons. 'Surprise!' they'd called. Mona couldn't have known *that* was going to happen.

Unless ...

Hanna breathed in sharply. The sky seemed to darken a few shades. There was only one way Mona could have known Kate and Isabel were going to show up in Philly: if Mona and Kate had secretly corresponded beforehand.

It made sense. Mona knew about Kate, obviously. An early A note had been a newspaper clipping about Kate receiving yet another school award. Maybe Mona had called Kate and told her the whole evil scheme. And since Kate hated Hanna so much, she'd gone along with it. That could explain how Kate knew to press Hanna to tell her what was wrong in Le Bec-Fin's bathroom. Or how Kate knew to glance in Hanna's purse – maybe Kate already knew Hanna had a Percocet stash. 'She bragged that she had some,' Mona might have whispered to Kate over the phone, prepping her. 'And she'll totally trust that you won't tell on her if you ask if you can have one. But after she's gone for about an hour or so, when her dad's starting to freak, bust it out. Tell him Hanna *forced* you to take it.'

'Oh my God,' Hanna whispered, looking around. The sweat on her neck began to drip icily down her back. Kate and Hanna bonding together as the school's queen bees, Naomi and Riley becoming their BFFs – what if it was all part of Mona's grand scheme? And what if Kate was doing Mona's bidding … and really *was* planning to bring Hanna down?

Hanna's knees buckled. She lowered herself to the ground, dropping awkwardly on her right arm.

What if it never ended?

Her stomach turned over. She lunged to the edge of the trail and threw up into the grass. Tears came to her eyes, and her throat burned. She felt so lost. And lonely. She had no idea anymore what in her life was true and what wasn't.

After a few minutes, she wiped her mouth and turned around. The paved trail was empty in both directions. It was so quiet, Hanna could hear her stomach loudly gurgling. The bushes across the path started to shake. It seemed like there was someone caught between them, trying to get out. Hanna tried to move, but all her limbs felt the way her arm had after her accident – useless. The thrashing in the bushes grew more and more frantic.

It's Mona's ghost, a voice inside Hanna's head screamed. *Or Ali's ghost. Or Ian.*

The trees parted. Hanna let out a strangled yell and squeezed her eyes shut. But when she opened them a few seconds later, the path was still empty. Hanna blinked, looking around. And then she saw what had been making all that fuss – a little gray bunny, twitching near a patch of dried-up clover.

'You scared me,' Hanna scolded the bunny. She creakily stood back up, her pulse slowing down. Her nose burned with the smell of her own vomit. A woman in a pink Windbreaker jogged by, still smelling like the Marc Jacobs Daisy perfume she'd probably worn to work. Then a guy with a big black-and-white Great Dane passed. The world was full of people again.

As the bunny disappeared into the bushes, Hanna's head started to clear. She took a few deep, cleansing breaths, her perspective restored. This was all just a ruse to mess with her head – by Ian, or whatever dumb kid was pretending to be the new A. Mona couldn't control the universe from beyond the grave. Besides, Kate had hinted at her devastating relationship with Herpes Boy. Kate wouldn't have admitted something like that if she was plotting to destroy Hanna forever.

Hanna jogged the half mile back to the Y's parking lot, suddenly feeling much better. Her BlackBerry was nestled on the Prius's passenger seat, and there were no new messages in her inbox. As she drove home, Hanna wanted to open up a reply text to A's last note and write, *Nice try, faux A. You almost got me.* She felt guilty, too, for icily ignoring all Kate's texts today and avoiding her in the halls. Maybe there was a way she could make it up to her. Maybe tomorrow they could drop by Jamba Juice before prepping for the benefit, and Hanna could treat Kate to a sugar-free Mango Mantra.

When she got home, the house was dark and quiet. 'Hello?' Hanna called out, dropping her wet running shoes in the laundry room and unwinding the elastic from her hair. She wondered where everyone was. 'Kate?'

As Hanna made her way upstairs, she heard a small, muffled voice. Kate's bedroom door was closed, and music Hanna didn't recognize filtered out. 'Kate?' Hanna called quietly.

No answer. Hanna raised her fist to knock, when Kate let out a screechy cackle. 'It'll work,' Kate said. 'I promise.'

Hanna frowned. It sounded like Kate was talking on the phone. She pressed her ear to Kate's door, curious. 'No, I promise,' Kate urged in a low voice. '*Trust me*. And it's almost time – I can't wait!'

Then Kate let out a low, nasty snicker. Hanna shot away from the door like it was on fire, covering her mouth. Kate's snicker evolved into a full-on laugh.

Hanna backed down the hall, horrified. It was the kind of laugh she couldn't help but recognize – she and Mona used to snicker like that when they were in the midst of planning something huge. They'd made that snickering noise when Hanna plotted to fake-friend Naomi because she'd stolen Mona's date to the Sweetheart Dance. And they'd snickered like that when Mona created a fake MySpace page for Aiden Stewart, a cute guy from the Quaker school, and used it to torment Rebecca Lowry because Rebecca had nominated herself for Snow Queen, an honor that was rightfully supposed to go to Hanna. *This isn't going to be pretty*, the snicker always implied, *but this is what the bitch deserves. And we're sure as hell going to find it fucking hilarious.*

All of Hanna's worries rushed back in as thunderously as a mudslide cascading down a mountain. It sounded like Kate was planning something huge too, and Hanna had a pretty good idea what it might be.

25

Into The Bathroom . . .
But Out Of The Closet

As soon as Emily and Isaac pulled into the Hastings family's round driveway Saturday evening, a valet rushed to the car door and asked for their IDs. 'We want to get a record of everyone who's here,' the guy said. Emily noticed there was a gun on his belt.

Isaac glanced at the gun, then at Emily. He touched her hand. 'Don't worry. Ian's probably halfway around the world today.'

Emily tried to hide her wince. Ian had been missing for a full day now. Emily had told Isaac she was one of Ali's best friends and had attended the trial yesterday, leaving out, of course, that she had been receiving threatening notes from New A – who Emily was convinced was Ian. Unfortunately, Emily had a pretty good idea that Ian *wasn't* halfway around the world by now, but still here in Rosewood, digging for some big secret he thought the cops were hiding.

Part of Emily was furious at Spencer for not telling them

198

about Ian's eerie visit sooner. At the same time, Emily understood why Spencer hadn't told. Spencer had shown them the note that Ian had sent after his visit, the one that said Spencer would suffer if she said a word about it to anyone. Besides, it wasn't like Emily had said much about her *own* A note, the one that threatened to tell Isaac if Emily told about A. It seemed Ian was as cunning as Mona had been, knowing precisely how to keep all of them quiet.

Still, right after Spencer admitted the truth, the girls had tried to grab a cop to tell him what had happened, but the entire Rosewood PD was already off on an Ian manhunt. Spencer's parents had debated whether holding tonight's fund-raiser was even appropriate, but they'd decided to just be very, very cautious. Spencer had called Emily and her old friends last night and begged them to please come so they could all be together for moral support.

Emily tugged at the bottom hem of the dress she'd borrowed from Carolyn and stepped out of the Volvo. Spencer's house was all lit up like a birthday cake. Wilden's police car was parked front and center, and a few more valets were directing traffic. As Isaac took her hand, Emily noticed Seth Cardiff, her ex-boyfriend Ben's best friend, getting out of a car behind them. She tensed her shoulders and grabbed Isaac's arm.

'This way,' she said urgently, pushing Isaac roughly up the front walk. Then she saw Eric Kahn standing on the porch. If Eric was there, Noel was undoubtedly close by.

'Er, wait.' She pulled Isaac into a shadowy spot next to a large, snow-laden shrub and pretended like she was searching through her silver clutch. The wind shook the branches on the big evergreen next to them. Emily suddenly wondered if what she was doing was nuts. Here she was, standing in the dark, when a crazy murderer was on the lam.

Isaac laughed uncomfortably. 'Is anything wrong? Are you hiding from someone?'

'Of course not,' Emily lied. Eric Kahn finally went back inside. Emily straightened and started up the path again. She took a deep breath and opened the front door. Bright light accosted them from inside. *Here goes.*

A string quartet was set up in the corner, playing a dainty minuet. Women in silk and sequined party dresses laughed with men in sleek, dark suits. A waitress glided by Emily and Isaac, carrying a large tray of full glasses of champagne. Isaac plucked two glasses off the tray and handed one to her. Emily took a sip, trying not to gulp.

'Emily.' Spencer stood in front of her, wearing a short black dress with feather detail around the hem and incredibly high sling-backs. Her eyes fell to Isaac's hand, which was curled around Emily's. A wrinkle formed over her brow.

'Uh, Isaac, this is Spencer. Her parents are throwing this,' Emily explained quickly, slowly unwinding her hand from Isaac's. 'Spencer, this is Isaac.' She wanted to add, *my boyfriend,* but there were way too many people around.

'Rick Colbert, the caterer tonight, is my dad,' Isaac explained, holding his hand out for Spencer to shake. 'Have you met him?'

'I didn't handle any of the arrangements,' Spencer said sourly. She turned back to Emily. 'So did Wilden tell you the rules? We're not allowed to go outside. If someone needs to go to their car, tell Wilden and he'll go for you. And then when you're ready to leave, he'll escort you.'

'Wow.' Isaac rubbed his hair. 'You guys are really taking this seriously.'

'It *is* serious,' Spencer snapped.

When she started to turn away, Emily grabbed her arm. She wanted to ask Spencer if she'd told Wilden about Ian's

200

visit, like she promised she would. But Spencer shrugged her off. 'I can't talk right now,' she said abruptly, and disappeared into the crowd.

Isaac rocked on his heels. 'Well, *she's* friendly.' He looked around the room, at the priceless Oriental rug in the enormous foyer, the stonework on the wall, and the portraits of old Hastings ancestors all over the gallery. 'So this is how kids from your school live, huh?'

'Not all of us,' Emily corrected him.

Isaac walked over to a console table and ran his hands over an ornate Sèvres tea set. Emily wanted to steer him away from it – Spencer always told Emily and the others that it had once belonged to Napoleon – but she also didn't want Isaac to think she was scolding him. 'I bet you live somewhere even bigger than this,' Isaac teased. 'Like a nineteen-bedroom compound with an indoor lap pool.'

'Wrong.' Emily punched him lightly. 'There are *two* indoor lap pools – one for me, and one for my sister. I don't like sharing.'

'So when am I going to see this magnificent house of yours?' Isaac took Emily's hands and swung them back and forth. 'I let you into my house, after all. With my *mom*. Sorry about that, by the way.'

'*Please.*' When Emily had picked up Isaac at his house tonight, his mother had fawned over them, taking pictures and offering Emily homemade cookies. Mrs. Colbert reminded Emily of her own mom. They both collected Hummel figurines and wore the same pale blue Crocs. They could probably be BFFs. 'I thought she was sweet,' Emily said. 'Just like you.'

Isaac blushed and pulled her close. Emily giggled, thrilled to be pressed up against him in his fancy suit, even if he *had* borrowed it from his dad. He smelled like sandalwood and cinnamon gum, and she had the sudden urge to kiss him in front of everyone.

Then she heard a snicker behind them. Noel Kahn and James Freed loitered in the arched doorway to the living room. Both wore expensive black suits, and their red-and-blue striped Rosewood Day ties were knotted loosely around their necks.

'Emily Fields!' James crowed. His eyes swept up and down Isaac, a perplexed look settling over his face. He'd probably first thought Isaac was a butch girl in a tux.

'Hi, Emily,' Noel said in his lazy, half-surfer, half-rich-boy voice, his eyes on Isaac too. 'I see you brought a friend. Or is it a date?'

Emily took a small step backward. Noel and James licked their lips like predatory wolves. Both were no doubt flipping through their list of snarky things they could say next – *Slumming it with the boys tonight? Watch it, dude, Emily Fields is kinky! She might drag you to some lesbian strip club!* The longer they remained quiet, the more horrifying whatever they said was sure to be.

'I have to ...,' Emily sputtered. She whirled around, nearly bumping into Principal Appleton and Mrs. Hastings, who were both sipping cocktails. She blindly stumbled through the foyer, wanting to be as far away from Noel and James as she could.

'Emily?' Isaac called behind her. She kept running. The heavy library doors were just ahead. Emily wrenched the door open fast and ducked inside, breathing hard.

It was warm inside the library, and smelled like a mix of old books and expensive leather shoes. Emily's eyes blurred, then readjusted. Her stomach lurched in horror. The room was packed full of kids from Rosewood Day. Naomi Zeigler's long legs dangled over an arm of one of the leather chairs, and Hanna's stepsister-to-be, Kate, perched queenlike on the chaise. Mason Byers and some of the other lacrosse boys were loitering near a bookcase, no doubt ogling Spencer's dad's books of obscure French photography, which consisted largely of soft-porn shots of naked women. Mike Montgomery and a pretty brunette were sharing a glass of wine, and Jenny Kestler and Kirsten Cullen were nibbling on crusty bread and cheese.

They all turned to look at Emily. And when Isaac burst into the room behind her and placed his arm on Emily's bare shoulder, their eyes feasted on him, too.

It was as if an evil magic spell had stunned Emily into suspended animation. She'd thought she could handle her peers, but with everyone together like this ... everyone who knew her secrets, everyone who had *been there* the day A circulated that picture of Emily and Maya kissing. It was just too much to take.

She couldn't even look at Isaac when she turned around and shoved her way back out the library door. Noel and James were still leaning against the wall, passing a bottle of Patrón back and forth. 'You're back!' Noel cried gleefully. 'Who's that dude you're with? If you're playing for our team again, why didn't you ask me out first?'

Emily bit her lip and kept her head down. She had to get out of here. She had to escape. But she couldn't find Wilden, who could escort her back to her car, and she didn't want to go outside alone. Then she saw the Hastingses' powder room right off the kitchen. The door was slightly open, and the light was off. Emily scampered inside, but when she went to shut the door, someone's foot was in the way.

Isaac pushed his way in. 'Hey.' He sounded annoyed. 'What is going on?'

Emily let out a small squeak and shot to the very corner of

the room, her arms tightly around her chest. The powder room was bigger than most master baths, with a little seating area, an ornate mirror, and a separate room for the toilet. Underneath the heavy, cloying smell of the jasmine candle on the vanity was a slight tinge of vomit.

Isaac didn't follow her to the corner. He remained by the door, his posture very straight and guarded. 'You're acting kind of ... crazy,' he said.

Emily settled down on the peach-colored chaise and picked at a tiny run in her stockings, too nervous to answer. Her secrets throbbed painfully inside of her.

'Are you embarrassed to be seen with me?' Isaac went on. 'Is it because I told that Spencer girl my dad was the caterer? Should I not have said that?'

Emily pressed her palms to her eyes. She couldn't believe Isaac thought her weird behavior was his fault. Again. A feeling of dread slowly settled down around her shoulders like a sheet. Even if she managed to divert this disaster, there would be another one, and another one. And finally, at the end of all that, there would be A ... Ian. And now that Ian had escaped, he was capable of anything. *Let this be a warning*, he'd written after Maya had shown up at the Chinese restaurant. Ian had Emily right where he wanted her.

Unless she made things right.

Emily looked up at Isaac, her throat tight. She just had to get this over with quick, like pulling off a Band-Aid. 'Do you remember that girl in China Rose?' she blurted out. Isaac looked at her blankly, shrugging. Emily took a deep breath. 'She and I used to be ... a couple.'

Everything else tumbled out at lightning speed. She talked about how she'd kissed Ali in her tree house in seventh grade. And how she'd fallen for Maya instantly, intoxicated by her banana gum. Emily explained the A notes, how she'd tried to date Toby Cavanaugh to prove to herself that she liked guys, how a picture of her and Maya kissing had been passed around at a swim meet, and how the whole school knew. She told Isaac about Tree Tops, the gay-away program her parents had forced her into, and that the real reason she'd gone to Iowa was because her parents couldn't accept her sexuality. She also said she'd met a girl named Trista in Iowa and had kissed her, too.

When she finished, she glanced up at Isaac. He looked green and was tapping one foot steadily and nervously ... or maybe angrily.

Emily lowered her head. 'I understand if you don't ever want to speak to me again. I didn't want to hurt you, though – I just thought you'd hate me if you knew. But even though I didn't tell you all this, everything I told you about how I felt about you, that I wanted you to be my boyfriend, that I really liked you, all of that – it's all true. I thought it wasn't possible for me to like a guy, but I guess it is.'

The little room was silent. Even the party seemed to have quieted down. Isaac ran his hands along the edge of his tie. 'So, does this mean you're ... bi? Or what?'

Emily dug her nails into the chaise's plushy silk cushions. It would be so much easier if she just said she was straight, and that the stuff that had happened with Maya and Ali and Trista had been confused mistakes. But she knew that wasn't true.

'I don't know what I am,' Emily answered quietly. 'I wish I did, but I don't. Maybe I just like ... people. Maybe it's the person, not necessarily their gender.'

Isaac's eyes lowered. He let out a small, deflated sigh. When Emily heard him turn, her chest throbbed with despair. In seconds, Isaac would turn the knob, walk out the door, and be gone forever. Emily pictured Isaac's mother standing in the front doorway, eagerly wanting to know how their fairy-tale date had gone. Her face would fall when Isaac told her the truth. *Emily's a what?* she'd gasp.

'Hey.' Hot breath tickled the top of her head. Isaac loomed above her, an unreadable expression on his face. Without saying a word, he wrapped his arms around her. 'It's okay.'

'W-what?' Emily gasped.

'It's okay,' he repeated quietly. 'And I accept it. I accept *you.*'

Emily blinked in disbelief. 'You ... do?'

Isaac shook his head. 'Honestly? It's kind of a relief. I thought you were acting crazy because of me. Or because you already had a boyfriend.'

Thankful tears came to Emily's eyes. 'Not much of a chance of that,' she blurted.

Isaac snorted. 'I guess not, huh?' He took Emily into his arms, kissing the side of her head.

As they were hugging, Lanie Iler, one of Emily's swimming teammates, stuck her head into the bathroom, thinking it was unoccupied. 'Oops,' she said. When Lanie saw Emily in the bathroom, hugging a *guy*, her eyes grew wide. But Emily no longer cared. *Let them see*, she thought. Let Lanie go back and tell everyone. Her days of hiding things were officially over.

26
Spencer Meets Her Match

The Hastingses' doorbell rang for the umpteenth time, and Spencer watched from the corner as her parents welcomed the Pembrokes, one of the oldest families in the area. Mr. and Mrs. Pembroke were notorious for always bringing their animals everywhere with them, and it looked as if they'd brought *two* of their pets tonight: Mimsy, their yapping Pomeranian, and the stole around Hester Pembroke's neck, which still had the fox's head attached. As the couple stampeded hungrily for the bar, Spencer's mother whispered something to Melissa and then drifted away. Melissa caught Spencer looking. Her hand fluttered against her dark red satin dress; then she lowered her eyes and turned away. Spencer hadn't been able to ask Melissa how she felt about Ian's disappearance – Melissa had made herself scarce all day.

Spencer was still unsure why they were even *having* the benefit, although everyone seemed to be having a fantastic time. Heavy drinking, apparently, was Rosewood's salve for a scandal. Wilden had already had to escort Mason Byers's parents out to their Bentley because Binky Byers had downed too many Metropolitan cocktails. Spencer had walked in on Olivia Zeigler, Naomi's mom, throwing up in the powder room, her tanned arms clutching the sides of the sink. If only vodka could numb Spencer, too, but no matter how many Lemon Drops she covertly shot back, she remained clear-eyed and aware. It was as if some karmic force was punishing her, making her suffer through this whole ordeal sober.

She'd made a dreadful mistake, keeping the secret about Ian private. But how was she supposed to know Ian was planning to escape? She thought of the dream she'd had yesterday morning – *it's almost too late*. Well, now it was.

She'd promised her friends that she would tell the cops about Ian's visit, but as soon as Wilden had turned up on the doorstep, ready to guard the party, Spencer just ... couldn't. She couldn't bear to hear someone else give her yet another scathing lecture about how terribly she'd screwed up – again. What good would telling Wilden do, anyway? It wasn't as if Ian had tipped Spencer off to where he was planning to hide. The only interesting hint Ian had given was that he was on the verge of a secret that would blow her mind.

'Spencer, dear,' said a voice to the right. It was Mrs. Kahn, looking gaunt in her emerald green sequined gown. Spencer had heard her tell the society photographers that it was a vintage Balenciaga. Everything about Mrs. Kahn sparkled, from her ears to her neck to her wrists to her fingers. It was common knowledge that last year, when Noel's father had gone to L.A. to finance yet another golf course, he'd bought out half of Harry Winston for his wife. The bill had been posted on a local gossip blog.

'Do you know if there are any more of those delicious mini petit fours?' Mrs. Kahn asked. 'Why the hell not, right?' She patted her flat stomach and shrugged, as if to say, *There's a killer on the loose, so let us eat cake.*

'Uh ...' Spencer spied her parents across the room, next to the string quartet. 'I'll be back.'

She wove around the partygoers until she was a few feet away from her parents. Her father wore a dark Armani suit, but her mom had on a short black number with bat-wing sleeves and a ruched waist. Maybe it was all over the Milan runways, but in Spencer's opinion, it looked like something Dracula's wife would wear when she cleaned the house.

She tapped her mom on her shoulder. Mrs. Hastings turned, a big, rehearsed smile on her face, but when she saw it was Spencer, her eyes narrowed. 'Uh, we're running low on petit fours,' Spencer reported dutifully. 'Should I go check in the kitchen? I noticed the bar is out of champagne, too.'

Mrs. Hastings wiped her hand over her brow, obviously flustered. 'I'll do it.'

'It's no trouble,' Spencer offered. 'I can just –'

'I'm *handling it*,' her mother whispered icily, spitting as she spoke. Her eyebrows arched down, and the little lines around her mouth stood out prominently. 'Would you please just go to the library with the rest of the kids?'

Spencer stepped back, her heel twisting on the highly pol-ished wood floor. It felt like her mother had just slapped her. 'I know you're thrilled I've been disinherited,' Spencer blurted loudly, before she was quite aware of what she was saying. 'But you don't have to make it so *obvious*.'

Her mother stopped, her mouth dropping open in shock. Someone close by gasped. Mrs. Hastings eyed Mr. Hastings, who had gone as pale as the eggshell-white walls. 'Spencer...,' her father rasped.

'Forget it,' Spencer growled, wheeling around and head-ing down the back hall toward the media room. Her eyes burned with frustrated tears. It should've felt delicious, spouting out exactly what her parents deserved, but Spencer felt the same way she always did when her parents dissed her – like a Christmas tree after New Year's, tossed to the curb for the trash truck to haul away. Spencer used to beg for her parents to rescue all the abandoned Christmas trees and plant them in their backyard, but they always said she was being silly.

'Spencer?' Andrew Campbell stepped out of the shadows, a glass of wine in his hand. Snappy little shivers danced up and down Spencer's back. All day, she'd considered texting Andrew to see if he was coming tonight. Not that she was covertly pining for him or anything.

Andrew noticed Spencer's flushed face and his eyebrows knitted together. 'What's wrong?'

Spencer's chin trembled as she glanced back toward the main ballroom. Her parents were gone. She couldn't find Melissa, either. 'My whole family hates me,' Spencer blurted out.

'Come on,' Andrew said, taking her arm. He led her into the media room, flipped on the little Tiffany lamp on the end table, and pointed to the couch. 'Sit. Breathe.'

Spencer plopped down. Andrew sat too. She hadn't been in this room since Tuesday afternoon, when she and her friends had watched Ian's bail hearing on TV. To the right of the TV was a line of Spencer's and Melissa's school pictures, from their very first year in Rosewood Day pre-K up to Melissa's formal senior portrait. Spencer stared at her picture from this year. It had been taken right before school started, before the Ali and A mess started. Her hair was combed perfectly off her face, and her navy blazer had been ironed to perfection. The self-satisfied gloat on her face said, *I'm Spencer Hastings, and I'm the best.*

210

Ha, Spencer thought bitterly. How quickly things could change.

Next to the school pictures was the big Eiffel Tower statue. The old photo they'd found the other day, the one of Ali the day Time Capsule was announced, was still propped up against it. Spencer narrowed her eyes at Ali. The Time Capsule flyer dangled from Ali's fingers, and her mouth was open so wide that Spencer could see her small, square, white molars. At what moment had this photo been taken? Had Ali just announced that Jason was going to tell her where one of the pieces was? Had the idea to steal Ali's piece crept yet into Spencer's mind? Had Ian already approached Ali and told her that he was going to kill her? Ali's wide blue eyes seemed to be staring straight at Spencer, and Spencer could almost hear Ali's clear, chirpy little voice now. *Boo-hoo*, Ali would tease, if she were still alive. *Your parents hate you!*

Spencer shuddered and turned away. It was eerie having Ali in here, gawking at her.

'What's going on?' Andrew asked, chewing concernedly on his bottom lip. 'What did your parents do?'

Spencer flicked the fringe detail on the hem of her dress. 'They won't even look at me,' she said, feeling numb. 'It's like I'm dead to them.'

'I'm sure that's not true,' Andrew said. He took a sip of his wine and then put it down on the end table. 'How could your parents hate you? I'm sure they're really proud of you.'

Spencer quickly slid a coaster under the glass, not caring if she seemed OCD. 'They're not. I'm an embarrassment to them, an out-of-fashion *decoration*. Like one of my mom's oil paintings in the basement. That's it.'

Andrew cocked his head. 'Are you talking about the ... the Golden Orchid thing? I mean, maybe your parents are upset about that, but I'm sure they're upset for *you*.'

Spencer bit back a sob, and something hard and sharp pressed down on her chest. 'They knew I plagiarized the paper for the Golden Orchid,' she burst out, before she could control herself. 'But they told me not to say anything. It would have been easier if I'd just lied and accepted it and lived with the guilt for the rest of my life, than for them to look like idiots.'

The leather couch groaned as Andrew sat back, aghast. He stared at Spencer for five long rotations of the overhead ceiling fan. 'You're kidding.'

Spencer shook her head. It felt like a betrayal to say it out loud. Her parents hadn't exactly told her *not* to tell anyone that they'd known about the Golden Orchid mess, but she was pretty sure they thought she never would.

'And *you* were the one who admitted you plagiarized the paper, even though they told you not to?' Andrew sounded out. Spencer nodded. 'Wow.' Andrew ran his hand through his hair. 'You did the right thing, Spencer. I hope you know that.'

Spencer started crying, hard – like a hand inside her head had just turned on a faucet. 'I was just so stressed,' she blubbered. 'I didn't understand econ at all. I thought it wouldn't matter, taking that one little paper from Melissa. I thought no one would know. I just wanted to get an A.' Her throat caught, and she buried her face in her hands.

'It's okay.' Andrew tentatively patted Spencer's back. 'I totally get it.'

But Spencer couldn't stop sobbing. She bent over, the tears running into her nose, her eyes puffing shut, her throat closing and her chest heaving. Everything seemed so bleak. Her academic life was ruined. It was her fault that Ali's murderer had slipped away. Her family had disowned her. Ian was right – she *did* have a pathetic little life.

212

'Shhh,' Andrew whispered, making small circles on her back. 'You didn't do anything wrong. It's okay.'

Suddenly, a noise came from the inside of Spencer's silver clutch bag, which was sitting on the coffee table. Spencer raised her head. It was her phone.

She blinked through her tears. *Ian?*

Her eyes flickered toward the window. There was a single, yellow spotlight on their backyard, illuminating the big deck. Beyond that, everything was pitch-black. She strained to listen for anyone scuttling around in the bushes by the window, but there was nothing.

The phone rang once more. Andrew took his hand off her back. 'Are you going to see who that is?'

Spencer licked her lips, considering. Slowly, she reached for her purse. Her hands shook so much she could hardly undo the small metal clasp.

She didn't have a new text, but a new e-mail. The sender's name swam into view. *I Love U.* And then the subject line: *You might have a match!*

'Oh my God.' Spencer shoved her Sidekick under Andrew's nose. In the chaos of the last week, she'd almost forgotten about the Web site. '*Look!*'

Andrew breathed in sharply. They opened the e-mail and squinted at the message. *We are pleased to inform you that someone in our database matches your personal birth information*, it said. *We are contacting her now, and she should be in touch in a few days. Thank you, The I Love U Team.*

Spencer scrolled down frantically, skimming the rest of the note, but it didn't offer much more information. I Love U hadn't disclosed what this woman's name was, or what she did, or where she lived.

Spencer let her Sidekick fall to her lap, her head spinning. 'So ... this is real?'

Andrew grabbed her hands. 'Maybe.'

Spencer gradually smiled, tears still streaming down her face. 'Oh my God,' she cried. 'Oh my God!' She threw her arms around Andrew and gave him a huge hug. 'Thank you!'

'For what?' Andrew sounded baffled.

'I don't know!' Spencer answered giddily. 'Everything!'

They pulled away, grinning at each other. And then, slowly and carefully, Andrew's hand moved down and circled her wrist. Spencer froze. The party noises outside fell away, and everything in the room felt cozy and close. A few long, slow seconds ticked by, marked only by the flashing dots on the DVD player's digital clock.

Andrew leaned forward and touched his lips to hers. His mouth tasted like cinnamon Altoids, and his lips were soft. Everything felt … right. He kissed her deeper, slowly pulling her closer to him. Where on earth had *Andrew Campbell* learned to kiss like this?

The whole thing took five seconds at the most. When Andrew pulled back, Spencer was too shocked to speak. She wondered if she'd tasted like salty tears. And her face probably looked hideous, all puffy and red from crying. 'I'm sorry,' Andrew said quickly, his face paling. 'I shouldn't have done that. You just look so pretty tonight, and I'm so excited for you, and …'

Spencer blinked hard, hoping that the blood would soon return to her head. 'Don't apologize,' she finally said. 'But … but I'm not sure I deserve this.' She let out a loud sniff. 'I've been so nasty to you. Like … at Foxy. And in every class we've been in together. I've been nothing but a bitch.' She shook her head, a tear trickling down her cheek. 'You should hate me.'

Andrew wound his pinkie around hers. 'I was mad at you

about Foxy, but that was just because I liked you. And everything else ... we were just being competitive.' He poked Spencer's bare knee. 'I *like* that you're competitive ... and determined ... and smart. I wouldn't want you to change any of that.'

Spencer started to laugh, but her mouth contorted into a new batch of sobs. Why was she crying when someone was being so *nice* to her? She looked at her phone again and tapped the screen. 'So you would like me even if I'm *not* a real Hastings?'

Andrew snorted. 'I don't care what your last name is. Besides, even Coco Chanel came from nothing. She was an orphan. And look what happened to her.'

One corner of Spencer's mouth curled up in a smile. 'Liar.' How did bookish Andrew know anything about haute fashion designers?

'It's true!' Andrew nodded fervidly. 'Look it up!'

Spencer drank in Andrew's thin, angular face, how his longish, wheat-colored hair curled sweetly over his ears. All this time, Andrew had been right in front of her, sitting next to her in classes, rushing to finish math problems at the board before she did, campaigning against her for class president and leader of Model UN – and she'd never noticed how damn cute he was. Spencer melted into his arms again, wishing they could stay like this all night.

As she nestled her chin into Andrew's shoulder, her eyes drifted back to the picture of Ali propped up against the Eiffel Tower. All of a sudden, the photo looked completely different. Although Ali's mouth was still open in mid-laugh, there was a worried, urgent look behind her eyes. It was almost like she was crying out to the photographer, trying to send an unspoken message. *Help me*, a glimmer in her eyes said. *Please.*

215

Spencer thought of her Ali dream again. She'd been standing right next to Ali by those very same bike racks. Younger Ali had turned to her, this same fragile expression on her face. Both Alis wanted Spencer to uncover something. Maybe something that was very close.

You shouldn't have thrown it away, Spencer, both of them chanted. *It was all there. Everything you need. It's up to you, Spencer. You have to fix this.*

But what had she recently thrown away? How could she fix it?

Suddenly, Spencer pulled away from Andrew. 'The trash bag.'

'Wha –?' Andrew seemed disoriented.

Spencer looked out the back window. The grief counselor had made them bury all that Ali crap last Saturday – essentially *throwing it away.* Was that what the two Alis in her dream had meant? Could there be something in there that would solve everything?

'Oh my God,' Spencer whispered, jerkily standing.

'What?' Andrew asked again, standing up too. 'What is it?'

Spencer glanced at Andrew, then out the window toward the barn, where they'd buried the Ali trash bag. It was a long shot, but she had to make sure. 'Tell Officer Wilden to come look for me if I'm not back in ten minutes,' she said hurriedly as she tore out of the room, leaving a very bewildered Andrew behind.

27
Hanna Marin, Queen Bee

By the time Hanna and Lucas got to the Hastingses' house, the grand living room was packed with people. A string quartet had just finished playing, and a jazz band was setting up. Waitresses offered appetizers, and bartenders poured Scotches, G&Ts, and big glasses of red wine. Hanna could smell alcohol on almost everyone's breath. They were all probably horrified that this Ian thing was even happening. Before Ali had disappeared, the most crime anyone in Rosewood ever saw was when one of their neighbors quietly got audited by the IRS.

Lucas undid the lens cap on his Olympus SLR camera – he was covering the event for the Rosewood Day newspaper. 'Do you want me to get you a drink?'

'Not yet,' Hanna said, thinking about all the empty calories in alcohol. She ran her fingers nervously over her lipstick-red, chiffon-and-silk Catherine Malandrino party dress. Last week, the silk band around her waist had fit perfectly, but now it was the teensiest bit snug. She'd made herself scarce all day, trying to ignore Kate, Naomi, and Riley's constant calls and texts, all invitations to the pre-party primping session at Naomi's house. Finally, Hanna had answered, saying she was too upset about Ian skipping town to pre-party.

'Oh, kids, hi.' Mrs. Hastings rushed over to them, looking irritated that they were here. 'The young people are in the library. This way.'

She began steering them toward the library, as if they were pesky clutter that needed to be stuffed into a closet. Hanna shot Lucas a helpless look. She wasn't ready to face Kate. 'Don't you need to take photos of the adults?' she squeaked desperately.

'We have a society photographer for that,' Mrs. Hastings snapped. 'You just take pictures of your friends.'

As soon as Mrs. Hastings threw open the library's big double doors, someone cried, 'Oh, shit.' There were whispers and a flurry of activity, and then the entire room looked up at Spencer's mom with big *I'm not drinking* smiles on their faces. A Quaker school girl quickly slid off Noel Kahn's lap. Mike Montgomery tried to hide his wineglass behind his back. Sean Ackard – who probably *wasn't* drinking – was talking to Gemma Curran. Kate, Naomi, and Riley were holding court in the corner. Kate was in a white strapless gown; Naomi wore a multicolored, knee-length halter dress; and Riley wore the green Foley + Corinna Hanna had picked out for her in *Teen Vogue*.

Mrs. Hastings closed the door again, and everyone brought out their bottles, glasses, and champagne flutes. Kate, Naomi, and Riley hadn't seen her yet, but in seconds, they would.

It's almost time! Kate had cackled. *I can't wait!*

Lucas noticed Kate and the others across the room. 'Should we go say hi?'

Kate's head was now bent toward Naomi's ear. Then they

both broke away and laughed raucously. Hanna made no effort to move.

'Aren't you going to go talk to them?' Lucas asked.

Hanna stared at her Dior sling-backs. 'I've changed my mind about Kate.'

Lucas's eyebrows raised so high, they practically merged with his hairline.

'I don't think she's what she seems,' Hanna added.

She could feel Lucas's eyes on her, waiting for an explanation. 'She tried to *destroy* my relationship with my dad back in the fall,' she whispered, pulling him into the far corner. 'This whole *let's be friends* thing ... I think I jumped into it way too soon. It's all been too easy. I've been enemies with Naomi and Riley for *years*, and suddenly everything's perfect between us, just because Kate's here?' She shook her head forcefully. 'Uh-uh. This is not how it works.'

Lucas narrowed his eyes. 'That's not how *what* works?'

'I think Kate's up to something,' Hanna explained, gritting her teeth as Noel Kahn shouted at James Freed to chug the rest of a bottle of vodka. 'And I think she, Naomi, and Riley are banding together to ruin me for good. But I have to figure out a way to call Kate out on it first. I have to figure out a way to get her before she gets me.'

Lucas stared at her. The jazz band in the living room was a few measures into their next number before he spoke again. 'This is because of Mona, right?' Lucas's voice softened. 'I understand that you might think every person you become friends with after her is going to ruin you. But they're not, Hanna. No one wants to hurt you. Seriously.'

Hanna fought the urge to stomp her pointy heel. How *dare* he patronize her! She'd been considering telling him about Maybe-Not-So-Faux A, too – but not now. He'd

219

probably patronize her about that as well. 'This isn't some paranoid little thing in my head,' she said angrily. 'It has nothing to do with Mona and everything to do with *Kate*. What about that don't you get?'

Lucas blinked rapidly. A disappointed feeling washed over Hanna. He didn't get it because this wasn't his world. Suddenly, Hanna realized how different she and Lucas really were.

She sighed. 'This is popularity we're talking about, Lucas,' she said in an overly simplistic voice. 'It's very … calculated. It's not something you'd understand.'

Lucas's eyes widened. He pressed himself against the French doors. 'I wouldn't understand because I'm not popular, right? Well, sorry, Hanna. Sorry I'm not cool enough for you.'

He waved his hand dismissively and stalked to the window. A sour, oily taste filled Hanna's mouth. She'd just made things worse.

Kate's thin arm shot up through the crowd. 'Omigod, *Hanna*! You're here!'

Hanna whipped her head around. Naomi and Riley were waving her over too, their smiles wide. It would look ridiculous if she just turned around and walked away, after she'd so obviously seen them. At least she was in her own dress tonight, and not some seam-popping thing Mona had sent her.

Steeling herself, Hanna slowly walked toward them. Naomi moved over, clearing a space for Hanna on the big leather couch. 'Where have you been?' she asked, giving Hanna an enormous hug.

'Oh, around,' Hanna said vaguely. Across the room, Lucas was watching her. She looked away fast.

'I've been worried about you,' Kate said, her eyes solemn

and serious. 'This whole Ian thing is scary. I totally don't blame you for going MIA.'

'Well, we're so glad you're here now,' Naomi said. 'You missed an awesome pre-party.' She bent down and whispered into Hanna's ear. 'Both Eric Kahn *and* Mason Byers came. They're both totally into Kate.'

Hanna licked her lips, shrugging, not really wanting to get into an actual conversation. But Kate was now fluffing the chiffon hem of Hanna's dress. 'Naomi took me to the best boutique called Otter yesterday, which is where I got this.' She pointed to the bold Swarovski crystal pendant around her neck. 'We wanted you to come too, but you weren't picking up your phone.' She stuck out her lip in a pout. '*But* we'll have to go next week, right? They have these super-dark William Rast jeans there that would look *so* cute on you.'

'Uh-huh,' Hanna mumbled. 'Sure.' She reached for a wine bottle that was tucked behind one of the chairs. Unfortunately, it was empty.

'Here, have the rest of my glass,' Kate said quickly, handing over her half-filled goblet. 'I'm buzzed from the pre-party anyway.'

Hanna stared dizzily into Kate's glass, the dark red wine reminding her of blood. *It'll work*, Kate had whispered. *It's almost time! I can't wait!* So what the hell was all this friendliness? Was it possible Hanna had made a mistake?

And then it hit her. *Of course.* Kate was fake-friending her. Hanna felt silly for not realizing it before.

The rules of fake-friending were simple. If Hanna wanted to get revenge on someone for something she had done to Mona, she acted as if she and Mona were fighting, infiltrated the other girl's group, and bided her time until she could stab the girl in the back. Maybe Mona had told Kate about fake-friending back when she'd become A.

221

Eric Kahn walked over and plopped down on a big paisley cushion on the floor next to the couch. He was taller and lankier than Noel, but had the same big, brown eyes and toothy smile. 'Hey, Hanna,' he said. 'Where have you been hiding this pretty stepsister of yours?'

'You make it sound like she had me stuffed in a closet,' Kate giggled, her eyes sparkling.

'Did you?' Eric asked Hanna, which made Kate giggle even harder.

Noel and Mason sat down, too, and Mike Montgomery and his date crowded in next to Riley and Naomi. There were so many people around them, Hanna couldn't get up if she tried. She searched the room for Lucas, but he had vanished.

Eric leaned forward, stroking Kate's wrist. 'So, how long have you girls known each other?'

Kate looked at Hanna, thinking. 'I guess ... four years ago, was it? We were in seventh grade. But we didn't speak for a long time. Hanna only came to my house in Annapolis once. I think she was too cool for me – she brought Alison DiLaurentis. Remember that *huge* lunch we had, Hanna?'

Kate gave Hanna a wide, smirking smile, Hanna's binging secret probably on the tip of her tongue. Hanna felt like she was on a roller coaster that was slowly climbing to the top of a hill. Any minute now, it would spill down the other side, and she'd lose her stomach ... and her reputation.

Fake-friending is simple, Mona probably said to Kate, as if she already knew that one day, Kate and Hanna would be forced to live under the same roof. *Just get one little secret from Hanna. That's all it'll take to ruin her for good.*

She thought of A's note, too. *Ruin her before she ruins you.*

'Did you guys know Kate has herpes?' Hanna blurted out. It didn't even sound like her voice, but the voice of someone who was far meaner.

Everyone looked up sharply. Wine spewed out of Mike Montgomery's mouth onto the carpet. Eric Kahn quickly dropped Kate's hand.

'She told me earlier this week,' Hanna went on, a toxic, black feeling metastasizing through her body. 'Some guy gave it to her in Annapolis. You should probably know that, Eric, before you try and get in her pants.'

'Hanna,' Kate whispered desperately. Her face had turned as white as her gown. 'What are you doing?'

Hanna smiled smugly. *You were going to do the same thing to me, bitch.* Noel Kahn took another big swig of wine, shuddering. Naomi and Riley glanced at each other uneasily and stood up. 'Is that true?' Mike Montgomery wrinkled his nose. '*Nasty.*'

'It's not true,' Kate squealed, looking around at everyone. 'Really, guys, Hanna just made that up!'

But the damage was already done. '*Ugh,*' someone whispered behind them.

'Valtrex,' James Freed coughed into his hand. Kate stood up. Everyone took another big step away from her, as if the herpes virus could jump off her body and onto theirs.

Kate shot Hanna a horrified look. 'Why did you just do that?'

'"*It's almost time,*"' Hanna recited in a monotone voice. '"*I can't wait.*"'

Kate gawked at her, confused. Then she took a few steps back, fumbling for the library door. When she slammed it shut, the crystals on the chandelier tinkled together melodically.

Someone gradually turned the music back up. 'Wow,' Naomi murmured, sidling up to Hanna. 'No wonder you haven't wanted to spend time with her the past couple days.'

'So who's the guy who gave it to her?' Riley whispered, instantly at Naomi's side.

'I *knew* there was something skanky about her,' Naomi sneered.

Hanna brushed a piece of hair out of her eyes. She'd expected to feel amazing and powerful, but instead she felt kind of shitty. Something about what had just happened seemed a little ... off. She set Kate's wineglass down on the floor and started for the door, just wanting to get out of there. Only, someone was blocking her way.

Lucas glowered at her, his lips small and pursed. It was obvious he'd seen everything. 'Oh,' Hanna said in a meek voice. 'Hi.'

Lucas crossed his arms over his chest. There was a sour look on his face. 'Bravo, Hanna. I guess you got her before she got you, huh?'

'You don't understand,' Hanna protested. She took a step toward him to put her arm around his shoulders, but Lucas held up his hand to stop her.

'I understand completely,' he said icily. 'And I think I liked you better when you weren't popular. When you were just ... normal.' He slung his camera back around his neck and walked toward the door.

'Lucas, wait!' Hanna cried, stunned.

Lucas stopped in the middle of the enormous Oriental rug. There were a few strands of dog hair on his dark suit jacket – he'd probably snuggled with his Saint Bernard, Clarissa, after he got dressed. All of a sudden, Hanna loved him for not caring about looking perfect. She loved him for not caring about popularity. She loved him for every dorky thing he did.

'I'm sorry.' Hanna's eyes filled with tears, not caring that everyone was watching.

Lucas's face was stony and impassive. 'We're done, Hanna.' He turned the doorknob that led to the foyer.

'Lucas!' Hanna beseeched, her heart lurching. But he was gone.

28

Socially Awkward Artist No More

Aria stood in front of an enormous oil portrait of Spencer's great-great-great-grandfather Duncan Hastings, a debonair man awkwardly clutching a floppy-eared, sad-eyed beagle in his lap. Duncan had the same exact ski-slope nose Spencer did, and it looked like he was wearing women's rings on his fingers. Rich people were so weird.

Aria supposed she should be in the library with the rest of her peers – Mrs. Hastings had all but shoved her in there when she'd arrived. But what did she really have to say to a bunch of prissy Typical Rosewood Girls in designer gowns and Cartier jewels they'd stolen out of their mothers' trousseaus? Did she really want them judging the long, black, backless silk dress she was wearing? And did she really want to put up with drunken Noel and all his touchy-feely cronies? She'd rather hang out here with good old grumpy Duncan, getting drunk on top-shelf gin.

Aria wasn't quite sure why she'd come to the benefit at all. Spencer had urged them all to be here for moral support now that Ian was on the loose, but Aria hadn't seen Spencer or any of her other old friends since she'd arrived twenty minutes ago. And it wasn't like she wanted to discuss Ian's scary and mysterious disappearance with anyone else, as the rest of the guests were doing. She would rather crawl into her walk-in closet, curl up into a ball with Pigtunia, her stuffed pig puppet, and wait for all this to blow over, like she did when there were thunderstorms.

The library door opened and a familiar figure strode out. Mike was dressed in a dark gray suit, an untucked purple-and-black striped button-down, and shiny, square-toed shoes. A small, pale girl followed behind him. They walked right up to Aria and stopped. 'There you are,' Mike said. 'I wanted to introduce you to Savannah.'

'Uh, hi.' Aria offered Savannah her hand, shocked Mike was actually letting her meet his girlfriend. 'I'm Aria. Mike's sister.'

'Nice to meet you.' Savannah's smile was wide and sweet. Her long, curly, dark chocolate-colored hair rippled down her back, and she had pinchable pink cheeks. A pretty black silk dress hugged her curves but didn't cut off her circulation, and the small red clutch she was carrying didn't have a logo plastered all over it.

She seemed ... *normal*. Aria couldn't have been more astounded if Mike had shown up with a seal from the Philadelphia Zoo as his date. Or, for that matter, an Icelandic horse.

Savannah touched Mike's shoulder. 'I'm going to grab us some apps, okay? The shrimp looks amazing.'

'Sure,' Mike said, smiling at her like an actual human. As Savannah skipped away, Aria let out a low whistle, crossing her arms over her chest.

'Look at you, Mikey!' she crowed. 'She seems really nice!'

Mike shrugged. 'I just have her around until my stripper honey from Turbulence gets back into town.' He chuckled lewdly, but Aria could tell his heart wasn't in it. His eyes were still on Savannah as she plucked a few bruschetta squares off a passing tray.

Then Mike noticed someone across the room. He nudged Aria. 'Hey, Xavier's here!'

Nerves rippled through Aria's stomach. She stood on her tiptoes to look over the crowd. Sure enough, Xavier was standing in line at the bar, dressed in a dapper black suit. 'Ella's working tonight,' she murmured suspiciously. 'What's he doing here?'

Mike scoffed. 'Because it's a benefit for our *school*, maybe? Because he really likes Mom and wants to support us? Because I mentioned it to him and he seemed really into coming?' He put his hands on his hips and glared at Aria for three long beats. 'What is your deal? Why do you hate that dude?'

Aria swallowed hard. 'I don't *hate* him.'

'Then go talk to him,' Mike insisted through his teeth. 'Go apologize for whatever it was you did.' He pushed his fist gently into Aria's back. She glared at him, irritated – why did Mike automatically assume *she* had done something? – but it was too late. Xavier saw them. He stepped out of his place at the bar and made his way over. Aria pressed her nails into her palm.

'I'll leave you two alone so you can kiss and make up,' Mike said, scuttling over to Savannah. Aria felt stuck – and uncomfortable with Mike's choice of words. She watched as Xavier moved closer and closer until he was right next to her. His brown eyes looked almost black against the dark gray of his suit. There was an awkward, embarrassed look on his face.

'Hey,' Xavier said to her, fiddling with his pearl cuff links. 'You look nice.'

'Thanks,' Aria answered, picking at an invisible thread on the strap of her dress. She suddenly felt so formal and ridiculous with her blue-black hair in a dumb French braid and her mother's faux-fur angora stole around her shoulders. She tilted away from Xavier, not wanting to expose her bare back.

All at once, she couldn't be standing here, being all polite to him. Not now. 'I have to ...,' she blurted out, then swirled around and ran up the stairs to the second level. Spencer's bedroom was the first door on the left. The door was open, and thankfully no one was inside.

Aria stumbled in, taking deep breaths. It had been at least three years since she'd been inside Spencer's bedroom, but it didn't seem like Spencer had changed a thing. The room smelled like fresh-cut flowers, which were arranged in vases all over the room. The antique mahogany vanity was still pushed against the wall, and the four oversize chairs – which folded out into twin beds, perfect for when they all used to sleep over – made a small, intimate circle around a teak coffee table. Dramatic red velvet drapes framed the big bay window that offered a full view into Ali's old bedroom. Spencer used to gloat about how she and Ali secretly communicated by flashlight at night.

Aria continued to look around. The same tasteful framed photographs and paintings hung on Spencer's walls, and the same snapshot of the five of them was still wedged into the corner of her vanity mirror. Aria walked up to it, her chest filling with longing. The photo was of Aria, Ali, Spencer, Emily, and Hanna, sitting on Ali's uncle's yacht in Newport, Rhode Island. They all wore matching white J. Crew bikinis and wide-brimmed straw hats. Ali's smile looked confident and relaxed, while Spencer, Hanna, and Emily looked deliriously euphoric. This had been just a few weeks after they'd become friends – the high of being part of Ali's exclusive clique hadn't worn off yet.

Aria, on the other hand, looked freaked, as if she were certain that Ali was going to push her into the Newport Harbor any minute. In fact, Aria *had* been worried that day. She was still certain Ali knew the truth about what had happened to her stolen piece of the Time Capsule flag.

But Ali had never confronted Aria about it. And Aria had never admitted what she had done. It was obvious what would happen if Aria told Ali the truth – Ali's face would crinkle in confusion, then slowly morph to rage. She'd drop Aria for good, just when Aria was getting used to having friends. As October faded into November, Aria's secret withered away. Time Capsule was a stupid game, nothing more.

Xavier coughed in the hallway. 'Hey,' he said, poking his head into the room. 'Can we talk?'

Aria sucked in her stomach. 'Um ... okay.'

Xavier slowly walked up to Spencer's bed and sat down Aria settled into the paisley-covered chair at Spencer's vanity, staring at her lap. A few long, awkward seconds went by. The sounds of the party throbbed below, everyone's voices muddled together. A glass shattered to the wood floor. A little dog yapped viciously.

Finally, Xavier let out a guttural sigh and looked up, 'You're killing me, Aria.'

Aria cocked her head, confused. 'I'm sorry?'

'A guy can only take so many mixed signals.'

'Mixed ... signals?' Aria repeated. Maybe this was some weird-artist way to break the ice. She waited for the punch line.

Xavier stood up and slowly padded across the room until he was right next to her. He curled his hands over the edge of the top of the vanity chair, and his hot, pungent breath brushed against Aria's neck. It smelled like he'd had a lot to drink. Suddenly, Aria wondered if this wasn't an icebreaker at all. Her head started to ache.

'You flirt with me at my opening, but then you get all weird when I draw a picture of you at the restaurant,' Xavier explained in a low voice. 'You walk around at breakfast in a see-through shirt and shorts, you spill your guts, you initiate a *pillow fight* . . . but when I kiss you, you get all freaked out. And now, you run up to a bedroom. I'm sure you knew I was going to follow you.'

Aria shot up and leaned against Spencer's vanity. The old wood made a creaking noise under her weight. Was he implying what she *thought* he was implying? 'I didn't want you to follow me!' she cried. 'And I haven't been sending *any* signals!'

Xavier raised his eyebrows. 'I don't believe that.'

'It's true!' Aria whimpered. 'I *didn't* want you to kiss me. You're going out with my *mom*. I thought you were coming up here to apologize!'

The room was suddenly so quiet that Aria could hear the ticking of his watch. There was something about Xavier that seemed so much bigger tonight, raw and powerful.

Xavier sighed, his eyes intense. 'Don't try to turn it around and act like this is *my* fault. And anyway, if you were truly freaked out about the kiss, why haven't you told anyone about it yet? Why is your mother still taking my calls? Why is your brother still inviting me over to play more Wii with him and his new girlfriend?'

Aria blinked helplessly. 'I . . . I didn't want to cause problems. I didn't want anyone to get mad at me.'

Xavier touched her arm, his face looming closer. 'Or maybe you didn't want your mom to kick me out quite yet.'

He leaned closer, his lips starting to pucker. Aria shot

231

away from the bureau and across the room to Spencer's half-open closet, nearly tripping over her long dress. 'Just ... stay away from me,' she said in the strongest tone of voice she could find. 'And stay away from my mom, too.'

Xavier made a few clucking noises with his tongue. 'Okay. If that's how you're going to be. But know this – I'm not going anywhere. And if you know what's best for you, you won't say anything to Mom about what happened.' He stepped back, snapping his fingers. 'You know how easily things can be twisted around, and you're just as guilty as I am.'

Aria blinked in disbelief. Xavier kept smiling, like this was funny. The room swirled dizzily, but Aria tried to remain calm. 'Fine,' she blurted out. 'If you're not going to leave, then I will.'

Xavier looked unimpressed. 'Where are you going to go?'

Aria bit her lip, turning away. It was, of course, a valid question – where *could* she go? But there was only one place. She shut her eyes and pictured Meredith's swollen belly. The small of her back began to ache, anticipating the cramped bed in Meredith's studio/spare bedroom.

It would be painful watching Meredith start to nest and Byron get all new-parent giddy. But Xavier had made things crystal clear. Things could get so easily twisted around, and he seemed more than happy to twist them if need be. Aria would do everything she could not to wreck her family ever again.

29
The Whole, Pathetic Truth

Spencer had an advantage over everyone else at the benefit who might have wanted to leave without Wilden noticing – it was her house, and she knew all the secret exits. Wilden probably didn't even know that there was a door at the back of the garage that led straight into the backyard. She paused only to grab a small flashlight by her mom's gardening supplies, put on a forest green rain slicker that was hanging on a peg on the wall, and stuff her feet into a pair of extra riding boots, which were flung haphazardly on the garage floor next to her dad's old Jaguar XKE. The boots weren't lined, but they'd do a better job keeping her feet warm than her strappy Miu Miu heels.

The sky was purplish black. Spencer ran along the perimeter of the yard, grazing the frozen blueberry bushes that separated her property from Ali's old house. The flashlight's tiny beam danced against the uneven ground. Luckily, most of the snow had melted, so it would be easy to see where they'd buried the trash bag.

Halfway across her yard, Spencer heard a twig snap and froze. She turned around slowly. 'Hello?' she whispered.

There was no moon tonight, and the sky was eerily clear, filled with stars. Muffled noises from the party drifted across the lawn. Somewhere very far away, a car door slammed.

Spencer bit down hard on her lip and kept going. Her boots sloshed through the half-slush, half-mud. The barn was just ahead. Melissa had turned on the porch light, but the rest of the barn was dark. Spencer walked right up to the edge of the porch and stood very still. She was breathing hard, as if she'd just run six miles with her old field hockey team. From back here, her house seemed so small and far away. The windows glowed yellow, and she could see the vague shapes of people inside. Andrew was in there, as were her old friends. Wilden too. Maybe she should have left this to him. But it was too late now.

A little breeze curled around her neck and down her bare back. The hole they'd dug for the trash bag was easy to find, a few paces to the left of the barn near the winding bluestone path. Spencer shuddered, overcome by a fore-boding sense of déjà vu. Their seventh-grade sleepover had been on a moonless night a lot like this. After their argument, Spencer had followed Ali out here, demanding that she come back inside. And then they'd had that stupid fight about Ian. Spencer had suppressed the memory for so long, but now that it was out in the open again, she was sure she'd never forget Ali's twisted face as long as she lived. Ali had laughed at Spencer, taunting her for taking Ian's kiss seriously.

Spencer had been so hurt, she'd shoved Ali hard. Ali had gone flying, her head making a horrible *crack* against the rocks. It was a wonder the cops had never found the rock Ali hit – it must have had a trace of blood on it, or at least a hair. In fact, the cops barely investigated *anything* back here besides the inside of the barn those first crucial weeks after

Ali went missing. They'd been pretty convinced Ali had run away. Had that just been a sloppy oversight? Or was there some reason they didn't want to look more carefully?

There's something you don't know, Ian had said. *The cops know it, but they're ignoring it.* Spencer gritted her teeth, chasing the words from her head. Ian was crazy. There wasn't some secret the world was hiding. Just the truth: Ian had killed Ali because she was going to reveal that they were a couple.

Spencer hiked up her dress, knelt down, and plunged her hands into the soft, dug-up dirt. Finally, her hands touched the edge of the plastic garbage bag. Condensed water from the melted snow dripped off the ends as she pulled it out. She set the bag on a dry patch of dirt and undid the ties. Everything inside was still dry. The first thing she pulled out was the string bracelet Ali had made for them after The Jenna Thing. Next was Emily's pink quilted purse. Spencer forced it open, feeling around the interior. The faux-patent leather squeaked. It was empty.

Spencer found the piece of paper Hanna had dropped in and shined the flashlight on it as best she could. It wasn't a note from Ali, as she'd originally thought, but a student evaluation form Ali had filled out, ranking Hanna's oral report on *Tom Sawyer*. All the Rosewood Day sixth-grade English classes had to rate their peers' reports, sort of as a school-wide experiment.

Ali's assessment of Hanna's report was fairly mild – nothing too nice, nothing too mean. It seemed like she'd dashed it off quickly, busy with something else. Spencer pushed it aside. She pulled out the last thing at the bottom of the bag, Aria's drawing. Even back then, Aria had drawn people remarkably well. There was Ali, standing in front of Rosewood Day, a smirk on her face, as if she was laughing about someone behind their back. A few of her underlings stood in the background, snickering.

Spencer let it flutter to her lap, disappointed. There didn't seem to be anything unusual about this, either. Had she really expected a miracle answer? Was she really that big an idiot?

But she shined the flashlight over the drawing once more. Ali was holding something in her hands. It looked like ... *a piece of paper.* Spencer pressed the flashlight right against the paper. Aria had sketched the headline. *Time Capsule Starts Tomorrow.*

This drawing and the photo propped up against the Eiffel Tower had both been from the same day. Just like the photo, Aria had captured the precise moment when Ali ripped down the flyer and announced that she was going to find a piece of the Time Capsule flag. Aria had sketched someone behind Ali, too. Spencer pressed her flashlight against the paper. *Ian.*

A chilly gust of wind danced across Spencer's face. Her eyes kept tearing up from the cold, but she struggled to keep them open. Aria's sketch of Ian wasn't as diabolical or conniving as Spencer had thought it would be. Instead, Aria had made him look kind of ... pathetic. He was gazing at Ali, his eyes wide, a dopey smile on his face. Ali, on the other hand, was turned away from him. Her expression was cocky, as if she was thinking, *Aren't I the shit? Even gorgeous upperclassmen are wrapped around my little finger.*

The paper crinkled in Spencer's hands. Aria had drawn this right as it was happening. She certainly hadn't known anything about Ali or Ian back then, but had merely sketched what she saw – Ian looking lovesick and vulnerable. And Ali looking ... like Ali. Like a bitch.

Ali and I flirted a lot, but that was all. She never seemed interested in taking it further than that, Ian had said. *But then ... suddenly ... she changed her mind.*

The trees around the pool made black, spidery shadows. The wooden wind chimes that hung from the eave of the barn knocked together, sounding like bones rattling. A shiver ran from the base of Spencer's neck all the way to her coccyx. Could it be true? *Had* Ian and Ali harmlessly flirted with each other, merely having a little fun? What, then, had made Ali change her mind and decide to like him?

But that was so hard to accept. If Ian was telling the truth about Ali, then everything else he'd said to Spencer two days ago on her porch could possibly be true, too. That there was a secret he was on the verge of finding out. That there was something *more* to all this that they didn't understand. And that Ian hadn't killed her – someone else had.

Spencer pressed her hand to her chest, afraid her heart was about to stop. *What notes?* Ian had asked. But if Ian wasn't sending A notes ... who *was*?

The cold slush seeped right through Spencer's riding boots, straight to her toes. Spencer stared at the bluestone path at the back of her yard, the very spot where she and Ali had fought. After Spencer shoved Ali to the ground, her memory had gone spotty. She'd only recently remembered that Ali had gotten up and continued down the path. What Spencer saw next flickered in front of her mind, blurring and sharpening. Ali's thin legs poking out the bottom of her JV field hockey kilt, her long hair dripping down her back, the bottoms of her rubber flip-flops worn at the insteps. There was another person with her too, and they were arguing. A few months ago, Spencer had been positive that person was Ian. But now when she tried to access the memory, she couldn't see the person's face. Had she latched onto Ian because Mona had fed her that information?

Because she just wanted it to be *someone*, so this would be over?

The stars twinkled peacefully. An owl hooted in one of the big oaks behind the barn. Spencer's nose itched, and she thought she smelled a cigarette smoldering somewhere close. And then her Sidekick began to ring.

It echoed loudly across the vast, empty yard. Spencer plunged her hand into her bag, hitting Mute. She felt numb as she pulled it out. Her screen announced that she had a new e-mail from someone called Ian_T.

Her stomach swooped.

Spencer. Meet me in the woods, where she died. I have something to show you.

Spencer sucked in her teeth. *The woods where she died.* That was just on the other side of the barn. She stuffed the drawing into her purse and hesitated for a moment. Then she took a deep breath and started to run.

30

Frailty, Thy Name Is Woman!

Hanna was finishing her third thorough round of the Hastings house, looking for Lucas. She'd passed and re-passed the jazz band, the drunks at the bar, and the snooty Main Liners talking smack about the priceless artwork that lined the walls. She saw Melissa Hastings slip upstairs, talking on her cell phone. When she pushed into Spencer's father's office, she interrupted what looked like an argument between Mr. Hastings and Principal Appleton. But no Lucas, anywhere.

Finally, she wandered into the kitchen, which was thick with steam and smelled like shrimp, duck, and heavy glaze. The caterers were busy unpacking appetizers and mini desserts from foil-lined carriers. Hanna half-expected to see Lucas helping them out, feeling bad that they were so over-worked – that would be just like him. But he wasn't there, either.

She tried Lucas's phone again, but it went straight to voice mail. 'It's me,' Hanna said quickly at the beep. 'There was a good reason I did what I did. Please let me explain.'

When she hit End, the phone's screen went dark. Why

hadn't she just told Lucas about the notes from A when she'd had the chance? But she knew why: She wasn't sure they were real. When she'd begun to think they *were* real, Hanna had worried that if she said anything to anyone, something horrible might happen.

And so she'd kept her mouth shut. But now it seemed like horrible things were happening anyway.

Hanna reached for the door to the media room and poked her head inside, but the room was disappointingly empty. The red afghan that was usually lying neatly on top of the couch was flung across the cushions, and there were a few empty cocktail glasses and crumpled-up napkins on the coffee table. Beyond it, that big, weird wire Eiffel Tower teetered on the credenza, so tall it almost grazed the ceiling. The old photo of Ali from sixth grade was still propped up against it.

Hanna stared at it warily. Ali held the Time Capsule flyer in her hand, her mouth open in mid-laugh. Noel Kahn stood behind her, laughing too. A shadowy figure loomed in the background, mostly out of focus. Hanna leaned forward, her stomach dropping like it was weighted down with lead. It was *Mona*. She was leaning on the handlebars of her pink Razor scooter, her eyes on Ali's back. It was like seeing a ghost.

Hanna sank into the couch, staring hard at Mona's blurry shape. *Why did you do this to me?* she wanted to scream. Hanna had never gotten to ask Mona that question – by the time she'd realized that Mona was A, Mona and Spencer had already been on their way to Falling Man Gorge. There were so many things Hanna wanted to ask Mona, things that would forever go unanswered. *How could you have secretly hated me all that time? Was anything we did together real? Were we ever really friends? How could I have been so wrong about you?*

Her eyes focused again on Ali's wide, open mouth. When

240

Hanna and Mona had become friends in eighth grade, Hanna had poked fun at Ali and the others to show Mona that they weren't really that great. She told Mona the story about how she'd shown up in Ali's backyard the Saturday after Time Capsule was announced, determined to steal Ali's piece of the flag. 'And Spencer, Emily, and Aria were there, too,' Hanna remembered saying, rolling her eyes. 'It was so weird. And even weirder, Ali came storming out of her back door, all the way across the yard to us. "You guys are too late," she said.' Hanna had even squeakily imitated Ali's voice, ignoring the shameful twinge inside her. 'And then she said some asshole already stole her piece, even though she'd already decorated it and everything.'

'Who took it?' Mona asked, hanging on every word.

Hanna shrugged. 'Probably some freak who built a shrine to Ali in his bedroom. I bet that's why he never turned the piece in to be buried with the Time Capsule – he probably still sleeps with it every night. And maybe he tucks it in his underwear every day.'

'*Ewww*,' Mona squealed, writhing.

That conversation with Mona had taken place at the beginning of eighth grade, right as that year's Time Capsule game started. Three days later, Hanna and Mona jointly found a piece of the Time Capsule flag stuffed into the W volume of an encyclopedia set in the Rosewood library. It was like finding a golden ticket in *Charlie and the Chocolate Factory* – a sure omen that their lives were going to change. They'd decorated the piece together, putting *Mona and Hanna 4-EVAH* in big, bold letters all over the fabric. Their names were buried now, a metaphor for their farce of a best-friendship.

Hanna wilted against the couch, tears pricking her eyes. If only she could run out to the practice fields behind Rosewood Day, dig up that year's capsule, and burn her and Mona's piece.

If only she could burn every other memory they'd created as friends, too.

The recessed lights above Hanna's head reflected off the picture. When she looked at the photo again, she frowned. Ali's eyes seemed so almond-shaped, and her cheeks were awfully puffy. All at once, the girl in the photo looked like a knockoff Ali instead, an Ali turned a few degrees to the left. But when Hanna blinked, it was Ali again who was staring back at her. Hanna ran her hands over her face, feeling like her skin was crawling with worms.

'There you are.'

Hanna cried out and turned around. Her father stepped through the door. He wasn't in a suit like the rest of the men here, but a pair of khaki pants and a navy blue V-neck sweater.

'Oh,' she gasped. 'I-I didn't know you were coming.'

'I wasn't planning on it,' he said. 'I'm only here for a moment.'

There was a shadowed figure behind him. She wore a strapless white gown, a brand-new Swarovski crystal pendant, and satin Prada peep-toes. When she stepped into the light, Hanna's heart sank. *Kate.*

Hanna bit down hard on the inside of her cheek. *Of course* Kate would run to Stepdaddy and tell him everything. She should've seen this coming.

Mr. Marin's eyes blazed. 'Did you or did you not tell your friends that Kate has ... *herpes*?' He mumbled the last word.

Hanna shrank back. 'I did, but –'

'What on earth is *wrong* with you?' Mr. Marin demanded.

'She was about to do the same thing to me!' Hanna protested.

'No, I wasn't!' Kate squealed passionately. A bit of her French twist had come undone, and a few tendrils spilled over her shoulders.

Hanna's mouth dropped open. 'I heard you on the phone on Friday! "It's almost time. It'll work. I can't wait." And then you ... cackled! I know what you meant, so don't even pretend like you're all perfect and innocent.'

A helpless squeak escaped from Kate's throat. 'I don't know what she's talking about, Tom.'

Hanna stood up and faced her father. 'She wants to destroy me. Just like Mona did. They were working together.'

'Are you cracked? What are you *talking* about?' Kate threw up her hands in despair.

Mr. Marin raised a bushy eyebrow. Hanna crossed her arms over her chest, glancing once more at the photo of Ali. Ali seemed to be staring right out at Hanna, smirking and rolling her eyes. Hanna wished she could turn it upside down – or even better, tear it to shreds.

Kate made a loud gasp. 'Wait a minute, Hanna. When you heard me yesterday, was I in my bedroom? Were there long pauses between things I was saying?'

Hanna sniffed. 'Uh, *yeah*. That's what happens when you're on the phone.'

'I wasn't on the phone,' Kate said coolly. 'I was practicing lines for the school play. I got a part – if you would've *talked* to me, I would have told you that!' She shook her head, amazed. 'I was waiting for *you* to come home so we could hang out. Why would I be plotting to get you? I thought we were friends!'

Down the long hall, the jazz band stopped playing, and everyone applauded. A strong scent of blue cheese wafted from the kitchen, making Hanna's stomach turn. Kate had been practicing *lines*?

Mr. Marin's eyes grew blacker and darker than Hanna had ever seen them. 'So let me get this straight, Hanna. You ruined Kate's reputation because of something you heard

243

through a *door*. You didn't even bother to *ask* Kate what she meant or what she was doing, you just went ahead and told everyone a blatant lie about her.'

'I thought …,' Hanna stuttered, but then trailed off. Was that what she'd done?

'You've gone too far this time.' Mr. Marin shook his head sadly. 'I've tried to be lenient with you, especially after everything that happened this fall. I've tried to give you the benefit of the doubt. But you can't get away with this, Hanna. I don't know what it was like, living with your mother, but I don't allow this kind of stuff in my house. You're grounded.'

From this angle, Hanna could see every new little wrinkle by her dad's eyes and all the new flecks of gray in his hair. Before her dad had moved out, he'd never punished her once. Whenever she messed up, he simply *talked* to her about it until she understood why it was wrong. But it looked like those days were gone.

An enormous lump formed in Hanna's throat. She wanted to ask her father if he remembered all their talks. Or how much fun the two of them used to have. For that matter, Hanna wanted to ask why he'd called her a little piggy in Annapolis all those years ago. It wasn't remotely funny – her dad must have known that. But maybe he didn't care. As long as it amused Kate, he was happy. He'd taken Kate's side ever since she and Isabel came into his life.

'From now on, you'll associate with Kate and only Kate,' Mr. Marin said, straightening his sweater. He began listing things on his fingers. 'No boys. No friends over. No Lucas.'

Hanna gaped. '*What?*'

Mr. Marin gave Hanna his *don't talk until I'm finished* look. 'No sitting with other people at lunch,' he went on. 'No loitering with other girls before or after school. If you want to go to the mall, Kate has to go with you. If you want to go to the gym, Kate has to go with you. Or I start taking more things away. First your car. Then your handbags and clothes. Until you actually understand that you can't treat people like this.'

The roof of Hanna's mouth began to itch. She was pretty sure she was about to faint. 'You can't do that!' she whispered.

'I can.' Mr. Marin's eyes narrowed. 'And I *am*. And you know how I'll know if you're breaking the rules?' He paused and looked at Kate, who nodded. They'd probably discussed all this beforehand. Kate had probably *suggested* it.

Hanna gripped the arm of the couch, stunned. Everyone at school was skeeved out about Kate now – all because of what Hanna had told them. If Hanna came into school all BFFs with Kate and only Kate, people would … *talk*. They might even think Hanna had herpes too! She could already imagine the names everyone would call them: *The Valtrex Vixens. The Blister Sisters.*

'Oh my God,' she whispered.

'Your punishment will start tomorrow,' Mr. Marin said. 'You can use the rest of tonight to tell your friends that you'll no longer be associating with them. I expect to see you at home in an hour.' Without another word, he turned and stalked out of the room, Kate following behind.

Hanna listed woozily to the left. This didn't make any sense. How could she have been so wrong about what she'd overheard outside Kate's bedroom? The things Kate had said had sounded so sinister. So *obvious*! And Kate's hideous little snicker … It was hard to believe she was just rehearsing for a lame-ass high school production of *Hamlet*.

Hamlet. A light went on in Hanna's brain. 'Wait a minute,' she shouted.

Kate turned abruptly, almost bumping into the ornate

Tiffany lamp on the table by the door. She raised an eyebrow, waiting.

Hanna licked her lips slowly. 'Um, what part are you playing in *Hamlet*, anyway?'

'Ophelia.' Kate haughtily sniffed, probably figuring Hanna didn't know who Ophelia was.

But Hanna *did* know. She'd read *Hamlet* over the winter break, mostly to understand the Hamlet-wants-his-mother jokes everyone in her AP English classes was always making. Nowhere in the play's five acts did fragile, pathetic, get-thee-to-a-nunnery Ophelia have lines that even remotely resembled anything like, *It's almost time, I can't wait.* Nor did Ophelia snicker. Kate insisting she was rehearsing for the play was a lame crock of shit, but her dad had bought it hook, line, and sinker.

Hanna's mouth gaped open. Kate met her look with a cool, self-assured shrug. If she realized she'd been caught in the lie, she didn't seem to care. Hanna already had her punishment, after all.

Before Hanna could say another word, Kate smiled and started out the door again. 'Oh, and Hanna?' She curled her fingers around the doorjamb, giving Hanna a coy little wink. 'It's not herpes. I just thought you should know.'

31

Everyone's A Suspect

The line to the downstairs powder room was five people deep by the time Emily and Isaac emerged. Emily ducked her head, even though she had nothing to be embarrassed about – all they'd done was cuddle. A pin-thin woman shoved past them into the bathroom, slamming the door.

As they walked into the middle of the ballroom, Isaac draped his arm around Emily's shoulders and kissed her cheek. An ancient woman in a Chanel suit clucked her tongue at them, smiling. 'What a cute couple,' she cooed. Emily had to agree.

Isaac's cell phone, which was tucked into his jacket pocket, began to ring. Emily's hands immediately turned into fists – *it could be A* – but then she remembered. Isaac knew all her secrets. It didn't matter.

Isaac looked at the little lit-up window on his phone. 'It's my drummer,' he said. 'I'll be back in a sec.'

Emily nodded, squeezing his hand. She drifted over to the bar for a Coke. A few girls in matching black shifts were standing in line in front of her. Emily recognized them as former Rosewood Day students.

'Remember how Ian used to watch us practice?' a pretty Asian girl with long, chandelier earrings was saying. 'All that time, I thought he was watching because Melissa was playing, but maybe it was because of *Ali*.'

Emily's ears pricked up. She stood very still, pretending she wasn't listening.

'He was in my science class,' whispered the other girl, a brunette with ultra-short hair and an upturned nose. 'When we were dissecting the fetal pig, he stabbed that thing like he was really enjoying it.'

'Yeah, but all the guys got super violent with those pigs,' the other girl reminded her, opening up her silver clutch and pulling out a stick of Trident. 'Remember Darren? He pulled out the intestines like they were spaghetti!'

They both shuddered. Emily wrinkled her nose. Why was everyone suddenly talking about how creepy Ian used to be? It seemed like revisionist history. And she couldn't believe the stuff Ian had told Spencer – that he'd liked Ali far more than she liked him, that he wouldn't have hurt her, ever. Why couldn't he just admit it? Nothing said *guilty* like an accused criminal fleeing his own trial, after all.

'Emily?'

Officer Wilden stood behind her, a worried but stern look on his face. Tonight he wore a crisp black suit and tie instead of his Rosewood PD uniform, though Emily guessed he had a gun hidden in his jacket. Emily shuddered, feeling uneasy. The last time she'd seen Wilden had been in the parking lot on the edge of town, telling someone on the phone to *just stay away*. She couldn't even recall seeing him at Ian's trial yesterday, but he must have been there.

There was a nervous little tremor under Wilden's left eyelid. 'Have you seen Spencer?'

'About a half hour ago.' Emily quickly adjusted the strap

of her dress, hoping it wasn't painfully obvious that she'd just spent the last few minutes lying on the floor, making out with a boy. She glanced behind her, looking for the older Rosewood girls, but they'd slunk away. 'Why?'

Wilden rubbed his clean-shaven chin. 'I'm supposed to do head counts every thirty minutes or so, just to make sure no one leaves. And I can't find her anywhere.'

'She's probably up in her bedroom,' Emily suggested. It wasn't as if any of them were in a partying mood tonight.

'I checked already.' Wilden tapped his fingers against his tumbler of water. 'You're sure she didn't mention anything about going outside?'

Emily stared at him, suddenly recalling Wilden's first name. *Darren.* Those Rosewood Day girls had just been talking about someone named Darren who had brutally removed a pig's intestines. It must've been him.

She often forgot that Wilden wasn't much older than she was – he'd graduated from Rosewood Day the same year as Spencer's sister and Ian. Wilden hadn't been a model student like Ian, though, but his antithesis, the type who was sent to detention every other week. It was amazing how they'd turned out: Ian the murderer, Wilden the good cop.

'She knows we're not supposed to go outside,' Emily said firmly, snapping back to the present. 'I'll go upstairs and check myself. I'm sure she's up there somewhere.' She lifted up her dress and put one foot on the first step, trying to quell her shaking hands.

'Wait,' Wilden called.

Emily turned. An ornate, elaborate crystal chandelier hung right over Wilden's head, making his eyes look almost chartreuse. 'Did Aria and Spencer tell you they've received more notes?'

Emily's stomach flipped. 'Yeah ...'

'How about you?' Wilden asked. 'Have you gotten any others?'

Emily nodded faintly. 'I've gotten two, but none since Ian disappeared.'

Something fluttered over Wilden's face, but it quickly passed. 'Emily, I don't think it was Ian. The guys guarding Ian's house searched the place. There weren't any cell phones, and all the computers and fax machines were removed from his house before he was released. So I really don't see how he could have sent you any messages. We're still trying to track down where the messages are coming from, but we haven't found anything yet.'

The room started to spin. The notes *weren't* from Ian? That didn't make sense. And anyway, if Ian had so easily gotten out of the house to visit Spencer, then he could've found a way to text them from a secret phone. Maybe he'd planted a disposable somewhere, like in a dead tree or an unused mailbox. Or maybe someone had planted it for him.

Emily stared at Wilden, wondering why he hadn't considered this. And then it hit her – Spencer hadn't told him about Ian's visit. 'Well, actually, there *is* a way it could be Ian,' Emily started, trembling.

The phone inside Wilden's jacket started to ring, interrupting her. 'Hang on.' He held up a finger. 'I need to get this.'

He tilted away from her, one hand curled over the edge of the side table. Emily gritted her teeth, annoyed. She looked around the room and saw Hanna and Aria standing next to an enormous abstract painting of a bunch of intersecting circles. Aria was fidgeting nervously with a white stole around her shoulders, and Hanna was running her hands through her hair again and again like she had lice. Emily strode up to them as fast as she could. 'Have you seen Spencer?'

Aria shook her head, seeming distracted. Hanna looked just as dazed. 'Nope,' she answered in a monotone.

'Wilden can't find her,' Emily urged. 'He checked the house a bunch of times, but she's gone. And Spencer never told him about Ian, either.'

Hanna wrinkled her nose, her eyes beginning to get wide. 'That's weird.'

'Spencer's got to be in the house somewhere. She wouldn't just leave.' Aria stood on her tiptoes, looking around.

Emily glanced back at Wilden. He paused from his phone call, taking a big sip from his water glass. Then he laid the glass on the table and spoke into the mouthpiece again. 'No,' he barked, rather forcefully.

She faced the others again, wringing her sweaty palms together. 'You guys ... do you think there's any possibility that this new A could be someone else? Like ... *not* Ian?' she sounded out.

Hanna stiffened. '*No.*'

'It has to be Ian,' Aria said. 'It makes perfect sense.'

Emily stared at Wilden's rigid back. 'Wilden just told me they searched Ian's house but couldn't find a cell phone or a computer or anything. He doesn't think Ian's behind it.'

'But who else could it possibly be?' Aria squeaked. 'Who else would want to do this to us? Who else knows where we are and what we're doing?'

'Yeah, A is apparently *from* Rosewood,' Hanna blurted out.

Emily shifted her weight, rocking back and forth on the plushy woven rug. 'How do you know that?'

Hanna ran her hands along her bare collarbone, staring blankly toward the big picture window in the Hastingses' living room. 'So I got a note or two. I didn't know they were *real* at the time. One of them said A grew up in Rosewood, just like we did.'

Emily's heart thrummed fast. 'Did your notes say anything *else*?'

Hanna squirmed, as if Emily were plunging a needle into her arm. 'Just this dumb stuff about my stepsister. Nothing important.'

Emily fiddled with the silver fish-shaped pendant around her neck, her forehead prickling with sweat. What if A wasn't Ian ... but not a copycat, either? When Emily had found out that Mona was the first A, she'd been completely caught off guard. Sure, Ali and the others had been nasty to Mona, but they'd been nasty to a lot of people. People Emily couldn't even *remember*. What if someone else – someone close – was just as mad at them as Mona had been? What if it was some-one in this very room?

She swept her eyes around the grand living room. Naomi Zeigler and Riley Wolfe emerged from the library, glaring at them. Melissa Hastings cut her eyes away, the corners of her mouth turning down. Scott Chin silently aimed his camera right at Emily, Aria, and Hanna. And Phi Templeton, Mona's old, yo-yo-obsessed best friend, paused on her way to the library to glance over her shoulder, coolly meeting Emily's eye.

And then a memory from Ian's arraignment struck Emily forcefully. They'd been coming out of the courthouse after Ian had been sent to prison without bail, so happy because they thought everything was over. But then Emily had seen a figure in one of the limos parked at the courthouse curb. The eyes in the window had seemed so familiar ... but Emily had forced herself to believe they were just a figment of her imag-ination.

Just thinking about it made a chill run up her spine. *What if we have no idea who A is? What if nothing is what it seems?*

Emily's phone began to ring. Then Aria's. And then Hanna's.

'Oh my God,' Hanna breathed.

Emily canvassed the room. No one was looking in their direction anymore. And no one was holding a phone.

There was nothing she could do but pull out her Nokia. Her friends watched nervously. 'One new text,' Emily whispered.

Hanna and Aria crowded around her. Emily pressed Read.

You all told, and now one of you has to pay the price. Wanna know where your old BFF is? Look out the back window. It might just be the last time you see her . . . – A

The room began to spin. A horrible, cloying smell of a sickly, floral perfume filled the air. Emily gazed around at her friends, her mouth bone-dry.

'The last time we see her ... *ever*?' Hanna repeated, blinking rapidly.

'It can't ...' Emily's head felt stuffed with cotton balls. 'Spencer can't ...'

They ran into the kitchen and peered out the back window, toward the Hastingses' barn. The yard was empty.

'We need Wilden,' Hanna demanded. She ran back to where he'd last been standing, but there was no one there. Only Wilden's drained water glass remained, abandoned on the highly polished side table.

Emily's cell phone lit up again. Another text had come in. They all gathered around to look.

Go now. Alone. Or I make good on my promise. – A

32

Be Quiet … And No One Gets Hurt

Hanna, Aria, and Emily slipped out the back door into the cold, wet backyard. The porch was bathed in warm, orangish light, but once Hanna stepped beyond it, she couldn't see a few feet in front of her face. Off in the distance, she heard a small, muffled noise. The hair on Hanna's arms stood on end. Emily let out a whimper.

'This way,' Hanna whispered, pointing in the direction of the barn. She and the others started to run. Hopefully they weren't too late.

The ground was slippery and a bit soft, and Hanna's strappy, high-heeled shoes kept sinking into the dirt. Her friends breathed hard beside her. 'I don't understand how this could have happened,' Emily whispered, her voice thick with tears. 'How could Spencer have let Ian – or whoever A is – lure her out here alone? Why would she be so stupid?'

'*Shhhh*. Whoever it is will hear us,' Aria hissed.

It took mere seconds to cross the vast yard to the barn. The hole where Ian had dumped Ali's body was to their right, the reflective police tape glowing in the blackness. The woods were beyond, a small opening between two trees like an ominous gateway. Hanna shivered.

Aria rolled back her shoulders and plunged into the woods first, her hands out in front of her for guidance. Emily followed, and Hanna brought up the rear. Damp leaves rubbed against their bare ankles. Sharp, jagged branches brushed against the girls' arms, instantly drawing blood. Emily stumbled over the uneven ground, crying out. When Hanna looked up, she couldn't see the sky. The leaves had made a canopy over their heads, trapping them.

They heard another whimper. Aria stopped and cocked her head to the right. 'That way,' she whispered, pointing. Her pale arm glowed in the darkness. She pulled up the hem of her dress and started to run. Hanna followed, her body throbbing with terror. Branches continued to assault her bare skin. A giant, spiny bush pressed against her side. She didn't even realize she'd tripped over something until her knees hit the ground hard. Her head smacked against the dirt. Something in her right arm snapped. White-hot pain shot through her. She tried not to cry out, clenching her teeth together and wincing in agony.

'Hanna.' Aria's footsteps stopped. 'Are you okay?'

'I'm ... fine.' Hanna's eyes were still squeezed closed, but the pain had begun to subside. She tried moving her arm. It felt okay, just stiff.

They heard the whimper again. It sounded closer. 'Just go find her,' Hanna said. 'I'll catch up in a second.'

For a moment, neither Aria nor Emily moved. The whimper turned into a sound more like a cry. 'Go!' Hanna urged more forcefully.

Hanna rolled onto her back, slowly moving her arms and legs. Her head spun, and the ground smelled like dog poop. The back of her neck began to tingle, numbed from the cold slush. Aria and Emily's footsteps grew fainter and fainter until she couldn't hear them at all. The trees shifted back and forth, as if they were alive.

'Guys?' Hanna called out weakly. No answer. The whimper had sounded close – where had they gone?

An airplane soared high overhead, its little blinking light barely visible. An owl hooted, low and angry. There was no moon in the sky. Suddenly, Hanna wondered if this was an incredibly stupid idea. They were out here, alone in the woods, because of a note that surely Ian sent them. They'd been lured out here as easily as Spencer had been. Who was to say Ian wasn't hiding in the shadows, somewhere close, ready to pounce and kill them all? Why hadn't they waited for Wilden to come out here with them?

The bushes across the clearing started to shake. Heavy footsteps crunched through the leaves. Hanna's heart began to thump. 'Aria?' No answer.

A twig snapped. Then another. Hanna stared in the direction of the noise. Something was looming in the bushes. Hanna held her breath. What if Ian was hiding right *here*?

Hanna pushed herself up to her elbows. A figure burst out from between the trees, shaking off branches. A scream lingered in Hanna's throat. It wasn't Aria or Emily ... but it wasn't Ian, either. Hanna couldn't tell if it was a guy or a girl, but whoever it was seemed thinner, maybe a little shorter. The figure paused in the middle of the clearing, staring straight at Hanna, as if startled by her presence. With its hood pulled tightly over its head and its face completely in shadow, the person reminded Hanna of the Grim Reaper.

Hanna tried to scuttle backward on her butt, but her body sank uselessly into the mud. *I'm going to die*, she thought. *This is it.*

Finally, a hand moved to the person's lips. '*Shhhhh.*'

Hanna dug her nails into the cold, half-frozen ground, her teeth chattering with terror. But the figure took three big steps away from her. Then, just like that, whoever it was turned and vanished, without the slightest sound of footsteps. It was as if Hanna had dreamed the whole thing.

33

Someone Knew Too Much

The whimper kept growing closer and then farther away, as if it were being bounced around by a mirror. Aria ran through the woods without looking where she was going or checking to see how far she had gone. When she turned around, she realized that the Hastingses' house was far in the distance, just a minuscule glowing yellow light through the thick, tangled branches.

When she came to a small ravine, she froze. So many of the trees were twisted and knotted, growing improperly. One tree right in front of her split into two, forming a seat between the two trunks. Even when Aria, Ali, and the others had been friends, they'd rarely come back here to hang out. One of the few times Aria had been back here was when she'd staked out Ali's house to steal her Time Capsule flag.

After Ali had marched to the back of her yard and told the four of them that someone else had already stolen her piece of the flag, the girls had gone their separate ways, disappointed. Aria cut through these woods back to her house. As she was passing a clump of particularly eerie-looking trees – maybe these very trees exactly – she'd seen someone running right for her from the other direction. Her insides had crackled with excitement when she realized it was Jason.

Jason had stopped, a guilty look washing over his face. His eyes immediately dropped to something dangling out of his hoodie's front pocket. Aria looked too. It was a piece of blue cloth, the same bold cerulean as the Rosewood Day flag that hung in every classroom. There were drawings all over the cloth, too, and words in familiar, bubbly handwriting.

Aria thought about where she'd just been, what Ali had just told all of them. *You're too late*, she said. *Someone already stole my piece. I'd decorated it and everything.* She pointed at Jason's pocket, her hand shaking. 'That's not ...?'

Jason looked from Aria to the flag, disarmed. And then, wordlessly, he thrust it into Aria's hands. He disappeared through the trees, back toward the DiLaurentis house.

Aria sprinted home, Ali's piece of the flag burning in her pocket. She didn't know what Jason wanted her to do with it – give it back? Redecorate it for herself? Was it somehow tied to the weird fight Jason and Ian had had on the Rosewood Day common just days before? Over the next few days, she'd waited to see if he'd tell her what he'd been thinking and what she should do. Maybe Jason *had* realized they were soul mates, and had given it to Aria specifically because he thought she deserved it. But no instructions ever came. Even when the Rosewood Day administration made an announcement over the PA that one piece of the Time Capsule flag hadn't been accounted for and that whoever had it should please come forward. Was it some kind of test? Was Aria just supposed to *know*? If she passed, would she and Jason be together forever?

After Aria became friends with Ali, she felt too embarrassed and ashamed to explain the whole debacle, so she'd hidden the piece of the flag in her closet, never looking at it again. If she opened the shoe box at the back of her closet marked *Old Book Reports*, there Ali's piece of the flag would still be, completely decorated and ready to go.

Footsteps crunched behind her. Aria jumped and swiveled around. Hanna's eyes glowed in the darkness. 'You guys,' she breathed heavily. 'I just saw the weirdest –'

'*Shhh*,' Aria interrupted. A dark shadow on the other side of the ravine caught her eye. She clamped down hard on Emily's arm, trying not to scream. A flashlight clicked on, sliding across the ground. Aria put her hand to her mouth, letting out a relieved, shuddering sigh.

'Spencer?' she called, taking a tentative step through the slush.

Spencer was wearing a rain slicker that came to her knees and big riding boots that flapped around her skinny calves. She beamed her flashlight up at them, looking like an animal caught in the headlights of an oncoming truck. The whole front of her black dress was covered in mud and slush, as was her face. 'Thank God you're okay.' Aria took a few steps forward.

'What the hell were you doing out here?' Emily cried. 'Are you crazy?'

Spencer's jaw trembled. Her eyes lowered toward whatever it was on the ground. 'It doesn't make any sense,' she said tonelessly, as if she were hypnotized. 'I just got a *note* from him.'

'From who?' Aria whispered.

Spencer pointed her flashlight at a massive object next to her. At first, Aria thought it was just a fallen tree, or maybe a dead animal. But then the light danced over something that looked like ... skin. It was a large, pale, human hand, curled into a fist. There was what looked like a Rosewood Day class ring on one of the fingers.

Aria took a huge step back, clapping her hand to her mouth. 'Oh my God.'

Then Spencer shined the light on the person's face. Even in the darkness, Aria could tell that Ian's skin was a ghostly, oxygenless blue. One eye was closed and the other was open, as if he were winking. Dried blood pooled at his ear and his lips, and his hair was matted with dirt. There were big purple welts around his neck, as if someone had grabbed him hard and squeezed. There was something about him that seemed very cold and stiff, as if he'd been like this for quite some time.

Aria blinked rapidly, unable to comprehend what she was looking at. She thought about how Ian hadn't shown up at his trial yesterday. The cops had run out of the room, vowing to find him. Ian could have been here all along.

Emily dry-heaved. Hanna took a huge step back, crying out. It was so quiet out in the woods, it was easy to hear Spencer's shaky swallow. She shook her head. 'He was like this when I got here,' she whimpered. 'I swear.'

Aria was afraid to move any closer to Ian, and kept her eyes fixed on his immobile hand, almost certain he was going to spring up and grab her. The air around him was absolutely dead and still. Far off in the distance, she swore she heard someone giggle.

And then Aria's cell phone, tucked inside her small, clam-shaped clutch, started to ring. She let out a small 'eep,' surprised. Then Spencer's buzzed, and Emily's chimed. Hanna's cell phone, which was nestled inside her now-muddy clutch, let out a bleat.

The girls stared at one another in the darkness. 'There's no way,' Spencer whispered.

'It can't ...' Hanna held her phone by the very tips of her fingers, as if afraid to really touch it.

Aria stared at her Treo's screen in disbelief. *One new text message.*

She glanced back at Ian, his stiff limbs twisted, his beautiful face vacant and lifeless. With a shudder, she looked down at the screen again and forced herself to read the text.

He had to go. – A

What Happens Next...

Yup, Ian's dead. And our favorite foursome probably wish they were. Hanna's daddy hates her. Spencer's broke. Aria's a hot mess. And Emily's switched teams so many times I'm getting whiplash. I'd feel bad for them, but y'know, that's life. Or, um, death, in Ian's case.

I suppose I could let bygones be bygones, forgive and forget, yadda yadda. But where's the fun in that? These pretty little bitches got everything I ever wanted, and now I'm going to make sure they get exactly what they deserve. Does that make me sound awful? Sorry, but as every pretty little liar knows, sometimes the truth's ugly – and it always hurts.

I'll be watching . . .

Mwah!

– A

Acknowledgments

I am overjoyed to be writing yet another acknowledgment letter for the next Pretty Little Liars adventure. Thanks, as usual, to those at Alloy who help flesh out the creepy, thrilling world of Rosewood: Josh Bank and Les Morgenstein, whose ideas are beyond compare, Sara Shandler, who is thoughtful and incredibly smart, Kristin Marang, who brought PLL to online fans, and Lanie Davis, who nurtured *Wicked* from start to finish with such clever, poignant insights and suggestions. Thank you all for caring so much about this series! Words cannot properly express my gratitude. Thanks too to Jennifer Rudolph Walsh at William Morris, and to the lovely team at HarperCollins: Farrin Jacobs, Elise Howard, and Gretchen Hirsch. All of you give these books that extra-special sparkle. Love to my parents, Shep and Mindy, to my sister, Ali, and her killer cat, Polo, and to my husband, Joel, for yet again reading various drafts of this book – and providing me with a few factual tidbits woven through the pages. And last but not least, a huge shout out to my fabulous cousins: Greg Jones, Ryan Jones, Colleen Lorence, Brian Lorence, and Kristin Murdy. Here's to plenty more human pyramids and feats of strength in the very near future!

The mystery continues in . . .

Pretty Little Liars

KILLER

1
The Girl Who Cried 'Dead Body'

Spencer Hastings shivered in the frigid, late-evening air, ducking to avoid a thorny briar branch. 'This way,' she called over her shoulder, pushing into the woods behind her family's large, converted farmhouse. 'This was where we saw him.'

Her old best friends Aria Montgomery, Emily Fields, and Hanna Marin followed quickly behind. All of the girls teetered haphazardly in their high heels, holding the hems of their party dresses – it was Saturday night, and before this, they'd been at a Rosewood Day benefit at Spencer's house. Emily was whimpering, her face streaked with tears. Aria's teeth were chattering, the way they always did when she was afraid. Hanna wasn't making any sounds, but her eyes were huge and she was brandishing a large silver candlestick she'd grabbed from the Hastingses' dining room. Officer Darren Wilden, the town's youngest cop, trailed after them, beaming a flashlight at the wrought-iron fence that separated Spencer's yard from the one that had once belonged to Alison DiLaurentis.

'He's in this clearing, right down this trail,' Spencer called.

It had started to snow, first wispy flurries, but harder now – fat, wet flakes. To Spencer's left was her family's barn, the very last place Spencer and her friends had seen Ali alive three and a half years ago. To her right was the half-dug hole where Ali's body had been found in September. Straight ahead was the clearing where she'd just discovered the dead body of Ian Thomas, her sister's old boyfriend, Ali's secret love, and Ali's killer.

Well, *maybe* Ali's killer.

Spencer had been so relieved when the cops arrested Ian for Ali's murder. It all made sense: the last day of seventh grade, Ali had given him an ultimatum that either he break up with Melissa, Spencer's sister, or Ali was going to tell the world they were together. Fed up with her games, Ian had met up with Ali that night. His fury and frustration had gotten the best of him ... and he'd killed her. Spencer had even seen Ali and Ian in the woods the night she died, a traumatic memory she had suppressed for three and a half long years.

But the day before Ian's trial was set to start, Ian had broken his house arrest and sneaked onto Spencer's patio, begging her not to testify against him. Someone *else* had killed Ali, he insisted, and he was on the verge of uncovering a disturbing, mind-blowing secret that would prove his innocence.

The problem was, Ian never got to tell Spencer what the big secret was – he vanished before the opening statements of his trial last Friday. As the entire Rosewood Police Department sprang into action, combing the county to find out where he might have gone, everything Spencer thought was true was thrown into question. Had Ian done it ... or hadn't he? *Had* Spencer seen him out there with Ali ... or had she seen someone else? Then, just minutes ago at the party, someone by the name of Ian_T had sent Spencer a text. *Meet me in the woods where she died*, it said. *I have something to show you.*

Spencer had run through the woods, anxious to figure it all out. When she came to a clearing, she looked down and screamed. Ian was lying there, bloated and blue, his eyes glassy and lifeless. Aria, Hanna, and Emily had shown up just then, and moments later they'd all received the same exact text message from the new A. *He had to go.*

They'd run back into Spencer's to find Wilden, but he hadn't been anywhere in the house. When Spencer went out to the circular driveway to check one more time, Wilden was suddenly *there*, standing near the valet-parked cars. When he saw her, he gave her a startled look, as if she'd caught him doing something illicit. Before Spencer could demand where Wilden had been, the others ran up in hysterics, breathlessly urging him to follow them into the woods. And now, here they were.

Spencer stopped, recognizing a familiar gnarled tree. There was the old stump. There was the tamped-down grass. The air had an eerie static, oxygenless quality. 'This is it,' she called over her shoulder. She looked down at the ground, bracing herself for what she was about to see.

'Oh my God,' Spencer whispered.

Ian's body was ... gone.

She took a dizzy step back, clutching her hand to her head. She blinked hard and looked again. Ian's body had been here a half hour ago, but now the spot was bare except for a fine layer of snow. But ... how was that *possible*?

Emily clapped her hands over her mouth and made a gurgling sound. 'Spencer,' she whispered urgently.

Aria let out a cross between a moan and a shriek. 'Where is he?' she cried, looking around the woods frantically. 'He was just *here*.'

Hanna's face was pale. She didn't say a word.

Behind them was an eerie, high-pitched squawking sound. Everyone jumped, and Hanna gripped the candlestick tightly. It was only Wilden's walkie-talkie, which was attached to his belt. He gazed at the girls' expressions, and then at the empty spot on the ground.

'Maybe you have the wrong place,' Wilden said.

Spencer shook her head, feeling pressure rising up into her chest. 'No. He was *here*.' She staggered crookedly down the shallow slope and knelt on the half-thawed grass. Some of it seemed flattened, as if something weighty had recently been lying there. She reached out her fingers to touch the ground, but then pulled back, afraid. She couldn't bring herself to touch a place where a dead body had just been.

'Maybe Ian was hurt, not dead.' Wilden fidgeted with one of the metal snaps on his jacket. 'Maybe he ran away after you left.'

Spencer widened her eyes, daring to consider the possibility.

Emily shook her head fast. 'There was no way he was just *hurt*.'

'He was definitely dead,' Hanna agreed shakily. 'He was ... blue.'

'Maybe someone moved the body,' Aria piped up. 'We've been gone from the woods for over a half hour. That would've given someone time.'

'There *was* someone else out here,' Hanna whispered. 'They stood over me when I fell.'

Spencer whirled around and stared at her. 'What?' Sure, the last half hour had been crazed, but Hanna should have said something.

Emily gaped at Hanna too. 'Did you see who it was?'

Hanna gulped loudly. 'Whoever it was had a hood on. I

think it was a guy, but I guess I don't know. Maybe he dragged Ian's body somewhere else.'

'Maybe it was A,' Spencer said, her heart thudding in her chest. She reached into her jacket pocket, pulled out her Sidekick, and showed A's menacing text to Wilden. *He had to go.*

Wilden glanced at Spencer's phone, then handed it back to her. His mouth was taut. 'I don't know how many ways I have to say this. Mona is dead. This A is a copycat. Ian escaping is hardly a secret – the whole country knows about it.'

Spencer exchanged an uneasy glance with the others. This past fall, Mona Vanderwaal, a classmate and Hanna's best friend, had sent the girls twisted, torturous messages signed A. Mona had ruined their lives in countless ways, and she'd even plotted to kill them, hitting Hanna with her SUV and almost pushing Spencer off the cliff at Floating Man Quarry. After Mona slipped off the cliff herself, they thought they were safe ... but last week they began receiving sinister messages from a *new* A. Originally, they thought the A notes were from Ian, as they'd started getting them only after he'd been released from prison on temporary bail. But Wilden was skeptical. He kept telling them that was impossible – Ian didn't have access to a cell phone, nor could he have freely skulked around while under house arrest, watching the girls' every move.

'A is real,' Emily protested, shaking her head desperately. 'What if A is Ian's killer? And what if A dragged Ian away?'

'Maybe A is Ali's killer too,' Hanna added, still holding the candlestick tightly.

Wilden licked his lips, looking unsettled. Big flakes of snow were landing on the top of his head, but he didn't wipe them away. 'Girls, you're getting hysterical. *Ian* is Ali's killer.

You of all people should know that. We arrested him on the evidence *you* gave us.'

'What if Ian was framed?' Spencer pressed. 'What if A killed Ali and Ian found out?' *And what if that's something the cops are covering up?* she almost added. It was a theory Ian had suggested.

Wilden traced his fingers around the Rosewood PD badge embroidered on his coat. 'Did Ian feed you that load of crap during his visit to your porch on Thursday, Spencer?'

Spencer's stomach dropped. 'How did you know?'

Wilden glared at her. 'I just got a phone call from the station. We got a tip. Someone saw you two talking.'

'*Who?*'

'It was anonymous.'

Spencer felt dizzy. She looked at her friends – she'd told them and only them that she and Ian had secretly met – but they looked clueless and shocked. There was only one other person who knew she and Ian had met. *A.*

'Why didn't you come to us as soon as it happened?' Wilden leaned closer to Spencer. His breath smelled like coffee. 'We would've dragged Ian back to jail. He never would've escaped.'

'A threatened me,' Spencer protested. She searched through her phone's inbox and showed Wilden that note from A, too. *If poor little Miss Not-So-Perfect suddenly vanished, would anyone even care?*

Wilden rocked back and forth on his heels. He stared hard at the ground where Ian had been not an hour ago and sighed. 'Look, I'll go back to the house and get a team together. But you can't blame everything on A.'

Spencer glanced at the walkie on his hip. 'Why don't you radio them from here?' she pressured. 'You can have them meet you in the woods and start looking right now.'

An uncomfortable look came over Wilden's face, as if he hadn't anticipated this question. 'Just let me do my job, girls. We have to follow ... procedure.'

'Procedure?' Emily echoed.

'Oh my God,' Aria breathed. 'He doesn't believe us.'

'I believe you, I believe you.' Wilden ducked around a few low-hanging branches. 'But the best thing you girls can do is go home and get some rest. I'll handle this from here.'

The wind gusted, fluttering the ends of the gray wool scarf Spencer had looped around her neck before running out here. A sliver of moon peeked out from the fog. In seconds, none of them could see Wilden's flashlight anymore. Was it just Spencer's imagination, or had he seemed eager to get away from them? Was he just worried about Ian's body being somewhere in the woods ... or was it because of something else?

She turned and stared hard at the empty ravine, willing Ian's body to return from wherever it had gone. She'd never forget how one eye bugged open, and the other seemed glued shut. His neck was twisted at an unnatural angle. And he'd still been wearing his platinum Rosewood Day class ring on his right hand, its blue stone glinting in the moonlight.

The other girls were looking at the empty space too. Then, there was a *crack*, far off in the woods. Hanna grabbed Spencer's arm. Emily let out an *eep*. They all froze, waiting. Spencer could hear her heart thudding in her ears.

'I want to go home,' Emily cried.

Everyone immediately nodded – they'd all been thinking the same thing. Until the Rosewood police started searching, they weren't safe out here alone.

They followed their footsteps back to Spencer's house. Once they were out of the ravine, Spencer spotted the thin golden beam of Wilden's flashlight far ahead, bouncing off the tree trunks. She stopped, her heart jumping to her throat all over again. 'Guys,' she whispered, pointing.

Wilden's flashlight snapped off fast, as if he sensed they had seen him. His footsteps grew more and more muffled and distant, until the sound vanished altogether. He wasn't heading back toward Spencer's house to get a search team, like he'd said he was going to do. No, he was quickly creeping deeper into the woods ... in exactly the opposite direction.

Sara Shepard graduated from New York University and has an MFA from Brooklyn College. She currently lives in Tuscon, Arizona, with her husband. Sara's Pretty Little Liar novels were inspired by her upbringing in Philadelphia's Main Line.